Leave Before I Love You

max monroe

New York Times & USA Today Bestselling Author

Author Note

Dear Reader,

Buckle up, because you're about to embark on a journey filled with *the best* banter, smokin' hot chemistry, and just the right amount of chaos. This book is hilarious (you will snort in public), spicy (you might need a fan), and downright addictive (cancel your plans now).

Now, let's address the elephant in the room—or rather, the two larger-than-life, stubborn-as-hell, wildly-attracted-to-each-other-but-fighting-it main characters at the heart of this story.

How do two people like that ever come together?

In a way you won't see coming at all. (No, seriously. You'll never guess. But let's just say… When life hands you breadfruit, you make a love story.)

Oh, and one more thing—this is a brother's best friend romance. Which means rules will be broken, sparks will fly, and someone is finding themselves in the best kind of trouble.

Enjoy the ride.
XOXO,
Max & Monroe

Dedication

To people who aren't afraid to be themselves—flaws, quirks,
questionable life choices,
and all.

To the people who love them anyway—even when they steal the
covers, talk through movies, and have an alarming number of
unread emails—you're the real MVPs.

And to the people who think they're superior or better-than
somehow—nobody cares. Get a life. LOL.

Chapter 1

January 1st
Avery

WHEN PEOPLE SAY *"NEW YEAR, NEW ME,"* MY FIRST instinct is to choke dramatically on my own saliva.

I mean, I have *questions.*

Why don't you like the you that you are now?

And if you don't, why wait for some magical ball drop to change it? *Time is a construct, Tiffany.*

Me? I happen to like myself—some might say too much. But I disagree. The one person you can always count on is yourself, so you might as well be your own favorite bitch. And I, Avery Banks, know *exactly* what I'm bringing to the table. *You're welcome, world.*

What I'm not as in control of is what the world gives me or just how vulnerable I am going to be to yet another New Year's cliché.

Six months ago, my best friend June, my brother Beau (who also happens to be her husband), and his best friends—Henry Callahan, Ronnie Damon, and Maverick Catalano—planned the ultimate New Year's trip to a private island in the Exumas. We all chipped in to make it as obnoxiously extravagant as possible, and that resulted in the mansion having two pools, a sauna, three water slides into the Caribbean, and a chef-staffed kitchen to cater to our every whim.

According to eternal optimist June, it was the *perfect* way to kick off the new year—a fresh start with our favorite people. For me, that meant one favorite person—*my bestie June*—and a bunch of losers—*my older brother and his friends.*

Unfortunately, a few things have shifted since we originally scheduled this adventure, and as a result, I can*not* believe I'm still going.

"Go and start the new year off with a bang," Beau said when I tried to back out. Easy for him to say—*he* gets to stay home. When June bailed due to morning sickness—and general buzzkill status— my brother immediately pulled the plug too, leaving *me* alone with the three amigos.

To cheer myself up, I plan to drink my body weight in cocktails and bake in the sun every day—and if June hadn't let my brother knock her up for the *second time* at such an inopportune interval, I wouldn't have to do it alone.

Ughhhhh. Love that I'm getting a new baby nephew this summer. Hate that June didn't plan this pregnancy better.

I sigh heavily and pull my G-Wagon into the parking lot outside the small private airport hangar, located on the north end of Miami Beach, looking for other cars I recognize. I'm normally last to arrive to group ventures, but for a change of pace, I'm on time today, and as a result, some of the morning fog is still burning off over the ocean.

Running a hand over my slicked-back ponytail while Billie Eilish sings "Birds of a Feather," I glance in the rearview mirror to fix my lip gloss briefly before paying attention to the twenty-spot blacktop lot and its white-lined spaces. Several are open, so I pull my Mercedes into one on a small screech of tires and scope the area.

My brother Beau's best friend Henry Callahan's Mustang is three spaces down, at the end of the line—a sign that I'm in the right place—so I unbuckle, shut off the engine, and climb out to adjust my outfit. I'm dressed casually—something I'm told by my mother, Diane Banks, is appropriate when your plans include jumping out of a plane—settling for Golden Goose sneakers, Nili Lotan

Bolero jeans, and a Ravella cashmere sweater instead of my usual Louboutin heels and a cultivated variation of Dior and Saint Laurent and Versace.

Those outfits are, of course, in my suitcase, but I'll save them for the safety of the Bahamian island we're planning to vacation on for the next few days instead of the wind of the stratosphere or whatever the hell you have to deal with at several thousand feet with a parachute strapped to your back.

You think I'm kidding, but I'm not. We're *literally* parachuting into the island.

Opening the hatch at the back of my SUV, I pull the small roller bag out from its spot in the trunk and shut it again, beeping the locks as I stroll toward the arched hangar. My suitcase follows dutifully, and I settle a pair of Chanel sunnies onto the bridge of my nose to shield the bright sun.

A heavy sigh fills my lungs with air and then exits in one big huff. *Ugh. I can't believe I'm going to be stuck with Henry, Ronnie, and Maverick all by myself.*

And to make matters worse, I have to freaking *skydive* to get there.

Which is ridiculous.

Henry's company Adrenaline Junkie is the foremost extreme sports equipment company in the country, but that doesn't mean we have to include it in our every move. I mean, sane people take yachts to expensive, exclusive island getaways—not some bullshit airdrop-express-backwoods plane delivery service. The plane doesn't even *land* on a runway, mind you. We're just supposed to jump out midair like we're Amazon Prime packages being delivered by drone to a deserted island.

"Hey, Ave," Henry greets as soon as I step inside the dark hangar. My eyes haven't adjusted yet, so I can't see him, but I've known him nearly all my life at this point, so the voice is a dead giveaway. He and my brother have been friends since grammar school and, for all intents and purposes, have continued to be stuck together like glue well into adulthood.

The two of us have a little history too, but that's neither here nor there right now. I've kissed plenty of hot guys in my life—that doesn't mean they don't irritate me.

"Hi," I say a little snottily, aggravated with this whole dog and pony show. I never liked the idea of spending my vacation time parachuting out of planes with people I barely tolerate anyway, but with June backing out because she's preggo and Beau doing the same to "take care of her," I'm questioning more and more by the minute why I didn't do the same. *My brother's three ridiculous bros and me for three whole days?* What the hell was I thinking?

"Where should I put my suitcase?"

"Suitcase?" Henry questions, his little laugh grating my nerves since it's clearly aimed at me. "You can't bring a suitcase. Just a small pack."

I roll my eyes and state the obvious. "This *is* a small pack. I didn't even bring my full skincare regimen. What the hell do you mean?"

"I mean," he says slowly, his hard jaw and stupid plump lips flexing with tried patience. I *hate* that now that my eyes have adjusted, I'm able to see just how *fine as hell* he's looking at the moment. "You can't jump with that thing," he blathers on. "You'll fucking kill yourself. I have an extra waterproof waist pouch that fits below your buddy harness you can use. Whatever you can fit, you can take, but nothing more."

He reaches over to the table behind him and hands me a small pouch with a high-tech-looking strap and buckle system. It's no bigger than a Lululemon crossbody bag and in no way big enough for all the stuff I have in my suitcase. Not even close.

"You can't be freaking serious." I glare at him. "We're staying for three days! How the hell am I supposed to fit what I need in a…a…a fanny pack!"

"What do you need other than a bathing suit and some

deodorant?" he questions like a total idiot. "Everything else in the house is supposed to be pre-stocked, and we're only going for a couple of days."

"Listen, Henry, until you grow a vagina and have to deal with all the complexities that come with one, don't ask me things like *what could you possibly need*, okay?"

Good-natured as usual, Henry smiles at my mocking of his voice rather than getting offended, and I flip him the bird as a rebuttal. I don't need him being all sexy and cute and smoldery while I'm trying to have a tantrum.

Hand to my hip, I direct a raised eyebrow at him. "So, what am I supposed to do now?"

Henry shrugs. "Well, you could take the suitcase with you…"

"Yeah?" I ask, hopeful.

"But then we'd basically have to chuck it out of the plane ahead of us, and who knows where it'll land or if it'll be in one piece when *and if* we find it."

I groan and stomp my foot. "You're really fucking irritating me right now."

"I know." He nods. *And smiles.* The hot bastard. "But look at it this way…at least you'll have three days of relaxation to get over your aversion to me."

"Are you kidding?" I scoff. "Three days of you and two of the three stooges, and I'm going to be ready to jump out of a plane without a parachute."

"The three stooges?"

"Beau, Mav, and Ronnie. Two out of three is still too many."

Henry's eyebrows draw together. "Ron and Mav aren't coming either. They're both uproariously hungover from last night's New Year's Eve bash at that new club Ransom and hugging the porcelain throne. It's just you and me."

"What?" I shriek. "*Everyone* backed out? Why the hell are we still going, then?"

Henry barely reacts. His obscenely attractive face remains

infuriatingly calm, his ocean-blue eyes steady as he says, "We already paid for the house." His tone is a little too condescending for my liking, even if his jawline is cut from stone. "Nonrefundable. Maybe *you* care fuck all about money, but I'd like to at least enjoy what I paid for."

"I *care* about money," I snap.

Henry laughs. "Right."

"I do!"

"You're right. You do care about money—you care about making sure Neil gives it to you so you can spend it on expensive shit."

"I'll have you know, when I turn thirty, Daddy plans to cut down my allowance. He just told me a couple days ago."

Henry grins, all wolfish amusement. "Ohhh nooo," he mocks. "So, you have three years left of bullshit spending. Though, if you were smart, you'd start saving instead of blowing it all, so by the time he *cuts you off,* you'd have a nice little nest egg."

I huff. *God, he's annoying.* Not because he's wrong—he's actually alarmingly right—but because I refuse to admit it. So, I choose to ignore him completely and bend down to unzip my suitcase and try to figure out what I can transfer into the ridiculously small fanny pack.

But my mind starts to spiral.

Just me and Henry freaking Callahan for three whole days?

That sounds crazy—and dangerous in ways I'm not sure I'm comfortable with. My whole body pulses with a mix of repressed arousal and adrenaline. Suddenly, I'm not feeling so well. And technically, this is money *already* spent, so it wouldn't change anything if I didn't go on this trip...

"I don't think I should go," I blurt, grasping for a way out. "Look at us. We're already fighting. Three days alone? We'll end up on some true crime podcast."

Henry shrugs, completely unbothered. "Suit yourself."

Then, because the universe is cruel, he casually grabs his parachute backpack, strapping it over his black utility pants and long-sleeved shirt.

I blink. Um…*Excuse me?* Why does he look like a goddamn action hero?

He is giving off gritty, *Mission: Impossible* stuntman, or an assassin who also models on the side, vibes. If I didn't know it was Henry Callahan, I'd think a young Tom Cruise had arrived at this fucking hangar to film an action flick. Hell, even the yellow prop plane out in front of him looks like a Hollywood backdrop.

My brain misfires.

And his back. *Holy shit, his back.* The broad, muscular ridges flex as he tightens his straps, the whole "badass against a golden sun" aesthetic making my knees weak in protest.

Five-years-ago Avery would have already been sprinting toward him. Hell, three-years-ago Avery would have probably thrown herself at his feet and asked him to sweep her into some ridiculous adrenaline-fueled adventure.

And then there's current Avery.

Avery, whose best friend is laid up puking her guts out. Whose parents are in Key West. Whose second-tier friends are all conveniently unavailable on New Years' trips of their own.

Avery, who would be sitting alone in her apartment for days, doing absolutely nothing except regretting her ten-grand investment in this trip. *And probably spending her late nights stalking Henry's adrenaline-junkie thirst traps on Instagram like an idiot.*

Ugh.

"Wait!" I yell impulsively, shoving two bikinis, my toothbrush, deodorant, and a hairbrush into the stupid fanny pack and abandoning my suitcase like it's a corpse I no longer wish to claim.

Henry stops at the opening of the big garage-style door, the light of the sun backing him like he's a freaking Marvel character.

"I'm coming," I say begrudgingly. "Just let me go throw this bag back in my car."

"Hell yeah, Ave." Henry smiles, and I can just barely make it out among his features in the shadows.

I ditch my bag, run to leave my keys with the airport office so I don't do something stupid like lose them while I'm gone, and rush after my brother's superhero-looking best friend like a fool.

By the time I get back inside the hangar, Henry is smiling at me like only an insane person would do when they're about to board a plane to jump out of said plane to get to their destination. "You ready to have the time of your life?" he questions and I snort.

"Trust me, Ave," he adds with the kind of sexy wink I feel all the way to my toes. "You won't regret it."

Famous last words. Fucking *famous*. Last. Words.

Chapter 2

Henry

A RUSH OF SOUND SURROUNDS US AS THE BLADES OF THE single prop engine get going at the front of the banana-colored plane that reads *Hot Drop Buns* on the side, and I slam the door hatch and lock it into place once Avery and I settle inside.

Mario, our pilot, a grizzled, no-nonsense guy with an unlit cigar clenched between his teeth, waves a finger at the side of his head in a tight circle, signaling that we're about to get moving. I nod, lifting a hand in acknowledgment.

Mario isn't my usual pilot, but what he's communicating isn't exactly rocket science either. I've only used this aviation company a couple of times—my regular drop service doesn't fly as far off the coast as we needed for this trip.

The flight to our private island is just over two hours, meaning a four-hour round trip after we bail. This company runs bigger planes with the fuel capacity and space we needed when we booked for our original group, and at the end of the day, it all functions the same.

The whole point, after all, is that you're leaving the plane behind.

Avery scurries into the back corner of the mostly bare cargo interior, her movements jittery, her breathing a little shallow. Her fanny pack bounces against her hip as she adjusts the chest buckle of our tandem harness, yanking at it like it's trying to strangle her.

She lets out a deep, heaving breath—one of those first-jump, holy-shit-I'm-really-doing-this breaths—and I can't help but glance over at her. For someone so clearly on edge, she looks infuriatingly beautiful. Her dark hair is pulled back into a sleek ponytail, cheekbones high, lips full, eyes sharp even as they dart around the cabin.

I pretend to focus on the window instead.

The engine climbs to a roar as Mario floors it down the runway, and I hold on to the handle at the side of the door to steady myself as our wheels leave the ground and we ascend into the air. Clouds trail by and fog rolls water beads over the glass of the windows as we make our way into the sky, and I climb forward on my knees to watch out the windshield as we float out over the ocean.

Boats make white lines of wake in the water below us, and colored flags fly in the wind of the beach as umbrellas and chairs take shape in the sand.

I take a seat behind Mario and watch with avid interest as he flips switches on and off and messes with the whole panel of controls. In the center, I notice the radar screen that marks where other planes are around us, but beyond that, the whole instrumentation panel is pretty much beyond my comprehension.

Back in my early twenties, I considered going to flight school and getting my pilot's license a couple of times, but in the end, it seemed counterintuitive to my ultimate desire to be the one doing the skydiving. I still find it interesting, but watching Mario now, I'd be lying if I didn't admit how complicated and stressful it all looks.

He tries to talk to me a little, but with English being his second language and my only having four years of Spanish in high school, I still struggle to keep up. I have a feeling a lot of it has to do with the Spanish translation of airplane terminology not being at the top of my classes' priority list.

In the end, we settle for companionable silence and, occasionally, pantomiming with our hands.

I glance back at Avery a couple of times during the first thirty minutes of airtime and then again about fifteen minutes later. She's fidgeting even more now, and I smirk lightly at the way she mumbles to herself and fusses with her pretty hair.

It's been over a decade since I made my first jump out of a plane, but I can still remember the tingle in my chest and the flapping in my stomach. Hell, I can even remember the taste of bile as it teased the back of my throat and feel the pinch of my nerves firing in the tips of my fingers.

It goes against nearly all basic human instinct to hurl yourself out of a perfectly good aircraft, but a millisecond into the free fall when you first hit the air, you understand why you did. It's cathartic and cosmic and out-of-body in a way I've made my living selling to people all over the world.

To be untouchable, if even for just a moment, is a feeling that changes you.

Avery isn't exactly my target audience, but with her relatively narrow worldview and silver-spoon upbringing at the forefront of her every action, I can't wait to see how the experience changes her when it's over. It's an intrinsic lesson in just how small we are in the scale of the world.

Still, I understand completely why she's nervous, so I move toward her to try to help her settle.

"You doing okay?" I ask, squatting down in front of her and checking the fit of her harness straps myself. They're tight, but I give another yank on both sides for good measure. Her body jerks, and her already-big hazel eyes widen.

"I cannot freaking believe I'm doing this," Avery admits, the wild wind and noise of the prop making her voice sound corrugated. "All those injectables in my face, and for what? Plunging toward the earth is going to ruin my structure completely! And the wrinkles! My God."

I laugh. "Your face will look funny during the free fall, but it's hardly permanent." I wink, posing in something akin to Zoolander's expression. "Look at me. Fresh as a fucking newborn, and I've jumped thousands of times."

She rolls her eyes, worrying her full bottom lip with her teeth. She's panicking, not that she'd ever admit it.

"You're going to be okay. I promise. I'll take care of you." I squeeze her knee. "We'll strap in together, and you won't even have to do anything but hold on. I'll handle everything."

"That's a hell of a lot of trust to put in you. You know that, right?"

"Of course." I nod, locking my eyes with hers. "Belief in your jump partner is absolutely crucial. Now, I believe in you, but do you believe in me?"

She snorts. "Do I have a choice?"

"You always have a choice while you're still planeside. We can fly right back where we came from if you want to."

She sighs heavily before shaking her head. "No. That won't be necessary. I…" Her lip nearly curls. "*Trust* you."

I laugh. "Good. I'm looking forward—"

A violent jolt sends the plane plummeting, the sudden drop like an elevator free-falling with no brakes. Avery and I slam into the cabin floor, the impact rattling my bones. Her scream is sharp, panicked, a perfect match for the piercing whine of the wind as the plane tilts sharply downward.

"Shit," I mutter, trying to make sense of what's happening. The sound of the wind increases to a loud, high-pitched shriek as the plane takes on an increasingly scary angle, forcing both Avery and me to grab on to any available surface for purchase.

Turning quickly to address the pilot or ask for guidance, I find the reason for the change in altitude and pitch, and a pit of panic takes root in my abdomen, gnawing at the lining of my stomach.

Mario isn't moving. He's just slumped over in his seat, and I fight against the g-force to get to my feet.

"Oh my God! What is happening?" Avery screams, scratching the wall behind her as she starts to slide forward. She finally finds the handle above her head at the backside of the jump door, and I scramble to the front to check on Mario, all control of my movement getting harder and harder with every small step.

He's folded over, and his now-gray face is lifeless. I shake his shoulder brusquely, but he doesn't stir, and all I can see out the windshield now is the sputter of the propeller and the ocean down below. *Fuck.*

Rubbing vigorously at his chest with my knuckles, I try to get a response, but he slumps even farther forward and onto the controls, sending the plane careening at an ear-piercing descent.

Avery's breathing turns to panicked sobs. "Henry—*fix it!*"

I check for Mario's pulse—*nothing*. I rub at his sternum again with vigorous knuckles—*nothing*.

"I think Mario's gone," I say, the words tasting like lead in my mouth.

"What?!" Avery shakes her head frantically, tears streaking down her face. "No, no, no—*do something!*"

I check Mario's pulse one last time. Nothing. No second chances. No miracles. Just a dead man at the controls and a plane in free fall.

"Avery, get ready to jump!" I yell harshly, pulling Mario to the side to try to get control of the plane, but the lift is totally gone, and with my very limited—*nonexistent*—experience operating an aircraft, I'm afraid this fall is unrecoverable.

The world narrows to one brutal, terrifying fact—I have seconds to get us out or we die here too.

I move as quickly and efficiently as possible to get back to Avery. It's not easy, given the angle of the plane and the smooth surface I have to climb, but somehow, I do it.

Avery is the definition of terrified, her eyes as wide as her face and her chest heaving with each shaky pant of air. She's in shock, clearly, and when her gaze refuses to meet mine, I grab her face between my hands and force her to look at me.

"Avery," I bark. "We have to jump. Right now."

She shakes her head wildly, gripping my wrists like they're her only lifeline. "I *can't!* Henry, I can't! What if—what if—"

I cut her off, my voice steady and firm. "You *can*. I'm going to get you out of this, but you have to listen to me. Right now."

She nods frantically, tears dripping off her chin. "O-okay. Okay."

I yank us toward the jump door, fighting the sharp incline of the plane. Avery's body is shaking so hard it's making it harder, but I don't let go.

She's wide-eyed and scared, and I don't blame her, but with the rate we're headed for the ocean, I don't have time to coddle her about it. I'm rough and jerky as I maneuver her body in front of mine and secure us together, and she cries audibly while I'm doing it.

Compartmentalizing, I ignore the fact that we're very much leaving Mario to a certain death—though I'm pretty sure he's well and truly gone already—and turn a blind eye to how understandably upset Avery is as she screams and cries into the noise around us.

I wrench the door open with a roar, adrenaline giving me the strength I need. The wind rips through the cabin and makes Avery scream louder.

I pull her flush against me, my arm like iron around her waist. One last squeeze to her thigh, and we're gone.

The free fall is immediate and brutal, and the jagged edge of rapidly approaching air steals the breath from Avery's screams for a short moment in time.

The yellow plane plummets from the sky just a short distance to our south, and I use our aerodynamics to gain as much space between us and it as possible. The quickly approaching ground below is a frighteningly vast view of ocean and desolation, as I know for a fact that we haven't been flying long enough to be anywhere near our jump point, but I focus on taking on one problem before considering another, and I time the opening of our chute to when I know we're completely clear of getting hung up with the plane or anything else.

Our bodies jerk to a hard stop in the air, our momentum cut

off by the beautiful security of our parachute opening like it's supposed to, and I take the first deep breath I have in a full five minutes.

My heart races, and my mind mirrors it as I try to figure out a plan for how to land us somewhere survivable in the next five or so minutes of our canopy ride.

There's no way we're making it all the way to the only land in sight—a lone island what I'd guess is a mile east of us—but I think if I concentrate, I can get us close enough to land in the water current that's headed that way just shy of it. It'll be another fucking nightmare to disengage us in the water while Avery's panicking, but it's the safest, best option, knowing we can float our way there somewhere in the neighborhood of ten minutes.

If I try to hold off our landing until we get closer, we'll end up on the side of the island where the current is leaving, and I don't think either of us is a strong enough swimmer to fight our way upstream for the amount of time it would take to reach land.

"Avery," I call, realizing only at the weird mix of our voices that she's screaming again, and try to get her attention. Explaining the plan ahead of time is going to be my best bet at keeping her from panicking when we hit the water. "Avery, listen!" I snap. It's meant to be a slap, a shock—a catalyst to make the screaming stop, if only briefly. "I need you to listen to me."

"Oh my God, oh my God, oh my God," she repeats over and over and over, the trauma of the nose dive, the pilot's unresponsive body, and the sudden and very necessary jump making her manic. Changing tactics, I try to calm my voice while still being loud enough to be heard in the open-air environment, knowing I need to do everything I can to soothe her so she's ready to fight when I need her to.

"Avery. Honey. Take a breath. I need you to breathe for me, and then I need you to listen because the next ninety seconds are extremely important, okay? Can you do that for me?"

"I…I…I can't believe I'm going to die a virgin!" she sputters, the words harsher than normal as she tries to catch her breath.

"Aver—what?" My comprehension is slowed by the impending events and by the sudden switch to complete, cohesive sentences rather than screeches. She keeps going, though, which allows my brain to catch up.

"All these years of slutting it up, and I could never find it in me to take it all the way, and now I'm doing to *die*. Perish. *Expire!* Be eaten alive by sharks instead of a muscular, suave hero with a dimpled cheek and freakishly large thighs! I can't believe it! I can't!"

It's big news. Cataclysmic, even. *Avery Banks is a virgin?*

Maybe if we weren't plummeting toward the surface of the earth without an ideal location for landing, it'd be at the forefront of my mind. But we are, and I really, *really* need Avery to focus right now like she's never focused before.

"Avery, I need you to concentrate!" I yell, returning to my initial discourse since the soothing tones clearly haven't worked. "We can talk about all this baggage later because I *promise*, I'm going to keep us alive. Do you hear me?"

She nods quickly, the sound of sobs racking her chest taking over again. I have a feeling it's the calmest version of my best friend's flagrantly spoiled, fashionista little sister I'm going to get, given the circumstances, so I start into my spiel.

"We're going to land in the water, and because of that, I need you to be ready," I instruct as swiftly and concisely as possible. "As soon as we hit, I'm going to pull the quick release on your harness and free you from my chest. While I'm detaching the chute from my back, I need you to tread water and wait for me. Can you do that?"

She nods. "I…I think so."

"Good. The water's warm, so you won't have to worry about it being a shock that way, but our clothes are going to make us feel much heavier than we'd like to, very quickly. Do *not* panic."

Her head moves up and down again jerkily, so I continue.

"If it gets to be too much, just float on your back, okay? Once I'm free, I'll work on making sure we're in the right spot to ride the current into the island down there to the right. Do you see it?"

"Yes," she manages, her voice much steadier than before. Immediate pride swells my chest over her composure. It takes character to find a way to fight the instinct for raw panic, especially if the only normal day-to-day stressors on your nervous system are making sure the barista at Starbucks gets your order right.

"Good girl. Fifteen seconds until we land, now, okay? Remember. Tread water, don't panic."

"Tread water, don't panic," she repeats, making me smile.

"Good. Good job, Avery. We'll be on land soon, okay? You're doing great."

I just have to get us to land, and then, I can make a new plan from there, I tell myself.

I knew this experience would change Avery, but it's become really fucking obvious in the last ten minutes or so that it's going to change me too.

Quite possibly—*most probably*—in ways I can't even imagine.

I grit my teeth, tightening my hold.

Three, two, one—impact.

Chapter 3

HENRY STARES OUT AT THE STUNNING, UNFORGIVING azure of the Caribbean, waves pounding against the shore like a cruel joke. His hands are laced together behind his head, and his chest rises and falls in deep, unsteady breaths.

I lie in the sand, panting, disoriented, my limbs trembling from the final fight with the surf. Inside my chest, my heart hammers violently, each beat so forceful I half expect it to crack through my rib cage. My clothes cling to me like dead weight, my skin is sticky with salt, and my lips are coated in the briny taste of survival.

Above me, the sky is endlessly blue, peaceful—a sick joke of a contrast to the absolute chaos churning inside me.

My mind stutters, everything sluggish, like my brain refuses to process the sheer insanity of what just happened.

One hour ago, I was admiring Henry's muscles from the safety of a bright-yellow plane. Now, I'm washed up on a deserted island like some Wish-version of Tom Hanks in *Cast Away*—minus Wilson but plus a single, soaked designer shoe.

Heaviness clogs my throat, and I can't immediately tell if it's seawater or unshed tears. Maybe, I guess, it's a combination of both.

I sit up slowly, testing the trustworthiness of my exhausted limbs before climbing to my feet. The toes of one sock-covered foot curl into the sand. My sweater scallops at the bottom with the weight of the water, so I wring it out with a twist of my hands and stare mindlessly at the fabric. It's warped and misshapen, and I fear, without a dry cleaner on this little slice of serene hell, it'll never be the same.

And just like that, the last fragile thread holding me together snaps.

A wretched sob tears from my throat as I yank the cashmere over my head and hurl it to the ground, completely ignoring the fact that my bra is the only thing covering my tits now.

"It's ruined!" I scream, my obnoxious volume echoing in the otherwise soothing atmosphere of lapping waves. "That was an eight-hundred-freaking-dollar sweater, and it's garbage!"

Henry's head snaps toward me, his expression shifting from exhaustion to outright disbelief. Hands planted on his soaked hips, shoulders stiff, gaze burning.

"And my shoes! My brand-new freaking Golden Gooses June got me for Christmas!" I gesture wildly at my feet. "One's missing, and the other might as well be! It's destroyed!"

"Your shirt?" Henry asks quietly, walking toward me with a noticeable edge to his movements. "Your fucking shirt and your fucking shoes?" Every word escalates in volume until he's screaming too, louder than me by at least several decibels. "You've got to be fucking kidding me with that shit!" He turns away and back again quickly, pointing an agitated finger in my face. "Of all the spoiled-brat-ass things to think about in a situation like this, you're worried about your fucking *clothes*?" His tone is seething. "A man is fucking dead, Ave, and you and I? We don't have a fucking clue where we are."

Tears blur my vision, but I don't back down. I get right up in his face, fists clenched, voice shaking with fury.

"You think I don't know that?" I shout back, rising up on my toes to get even more in his space. Tears stream down my cheeks unchecked. "You think I don't *know* that none of this shit matters? I'm standing here topless, on a beach in the literal middle of nowhere, Henry, in One. Fucking. Shoe! I know a man is dead. I *know*." My voice shakes. "But I am coping the only way I know how! I am *try-ing* to cope!"

He runs an angry hand through his hair and spins in a circle, his movements jerky and agitated, as I struggle to get my violent breaths under control.

Oh my God. Oh my *God*. Our plane *crashed*. Our pilot *died*. And we don't know where we fucking are. *No one* does.

Henry squats briefly before jumping to standing, an ungodly scream of the mightiest proportions breaking the sound barrier around us and rending the air.

His chest heaves as he stares at the ocean again for a singular long moment, and then he turns back to me, his eyes a mask of calm I wish desperately I felt myself.

"Come here." He steps forward quickly and pulls me into a bone-mending hug, his tight grip on my head pushing it deep into his wet chest. It's shocking and nearly breakdown-inducing, and I hold on as tight as my tired arms will let me, a sob bucking my entire body.

"Shh," he comforts, the soft warmth of his breath on the shell of my ear. "It's okay. We're safe. We're together. And I'm going to figure out what we need to do, okay? I promise, I'm going to figure out what we need to do."

I don't know why, but I believe him. Maybe it's the way he handled it all when it started to go wrong, or how he took control in the water when I started to get tired, or how he pulled himself together just now in the face of everything saying he shouldn't, but I *believe* that Henry will figure out what we need to do.

Flashbacks of only a couple of short hours ago in the hangar in Miami taunt me as I try to make sense of how in the hell I've found myself in this situation. I almost didn't come. I almost stayed home, and the only reason I didn't is because I thought I might be *bored*.

Fucking bored. How naïve of me to think that was the *worst possible outcome* for the first few days of this brand-new year.

I startle myself with a laugh as Henry releases me slowly,

working through the stupidity with which I packed my dumb waist pack.

Bikinis? I should have brought a survival knife.

Oh, but I have my hairbrush! I snort. I'm sure it'll be super important that I look good while we're trapped here for God only knows how long.

Clean teeth? I'll have them. Oh, and fresh-smelling pits too—

"Holy shit!" I shriek as realization dawns on me, pulling free of Henry's arms and frantically scraping at the buckle on my waist pack until I can get it open.

"What? What is it?"

"My phone! I put my phone in here before we left!"

Henry pats wildly at the cargo pockets of his pants before frowning. "I forgot mine. Or lost it in the water or something, I guess. Doesn't fucking matter. Bottom line, I don't have it."

"I have mine!" I shout again, finding it quickly and pulling it free from my bikinis as they spill out onto the sand at my feet. "I have it!"

Henry reaches out and grabs it from me when I tuck it to my chest, and I yank it back. We repeat the motion two more times before I narrow my eyes at him. "Hey! That's mine."

"Avery, for fuck's sake, just look at the screen, please." Henry sighs, letting go of my phone. "Do you have service?"

Properly chastised, I click anxiously at the screen until it comes to life, and I watch as the bars in the top right of the display dance, trying to find a signal. I shield my phone from the sun to make sure I'm seeing it right and then take off at a run with it held out in front of me. I go down the beach and then back to the other side and then up into the palm-tree-lined brush. I jump in the air and spin in circles, and Henry watches silently from the spot I left him the whole time, a stoic expression on his handsome face.

The bars dance and dance and dance…

And then, they stop dancing altogether.

No service. No connection. *Nothing.*

Panic crashes over me, and I sink to the sand, phone limp in my hands. My breath shudders, and a sob racks my chest.

"It's okay, Ave." Henry's voice is soft, closer than before. His hand settles on my back, warm and steady in a way I wish I felt. "We'll figure out another way."

I believe him.

But God, I wish I didn't have to.

I wish I were at home, in my dry bed, dreaming about designer clothes and Starbucks and nail appointments and the girl I used to be.

The girl I fear, with great disappointment, is about to be evicted, making way for a bootleg GI Jane, survivalist-in-training, starring in my own unwanted episode of *Naked and Afraid: Deluxe Disaster Edition.*

Chapter 4

Henry

A FIRE CRACKLES ON THE BEACH AS AVERY SITS STIFFLY beside it, her clothes laid out like expensive roadkill on the sand to dry. She's in one of the bikinis from her miraculously useful waist pack—a state of undress I've seen her in more times than I can count—but safe to say, this is as far from a choreographed champagne spray at one of her parents' famous pool parties as it gets.

Avery and Beau grew up with the world as their oyster, and there's nothing their parents, Neil and Diane, wouldn't do for them. They've been to private school, the University of Miami, and even now, at twenty-seven, Avery still lives off Neil's money.

Beau works hard for his dad at his marketing firm, Banks & McKenzie—though the McKenzie half sold out to Neil about three years ago after a huge scandal broke out about Chris McKenzie at Beau and Juniper's wedding and forced him to lose half his net worth in his subsequent divorce—but Avery flies by the seat of her pants, the life of her own little party.

She's never met a responsibility she couldn't charm her way out of. Technically, she works at Banks & McKenzie, but according to Beau, if she actually shows up to the office, they might as well call it a holiday and give everyone the day off.

Tonight, though, in the aftermath of arriving on this tiny,

uninhabited island, she's different. Her demeanor is much more closed off than usual, and her shoulders, normally proud and cocky, are curled forward in duress. She looks small. She looks *fragile*. Things I never thought would ever be associated with the larger-than-life party girl Avery Banks.

After her hysterical breakdown about her phone, and a brief scream-fest a couple hours ago, she's been largely silent as I work to get us set up for the night. Some people might be upset at her lack of help, but honestly, I don't mind. I know none of this is in her wheelhouse, and beyond that, I have a persistent feeling that she's a millisecond away from a full-on breakdown at any moment.

Avery Banks is beautiful, smart, and incredibly, painfully sheltered. She doesn't know the worth of earning your own dime, she works only when she deigns to, and she takes little to no personal responsibility for her life at any given time. She breezes from one moment to the next, collecting men like accessories—though, evidently, she's not actually sleeping with them, which is a whole other bombshell for another time—and she literally parties her way through life, never missing a club opening or VIP night supplied by one of her friends.

At thirty-two, and five years older than her, I'm no straight arrow myself, but as a self-certified adrenaline junkie with a sordid family structure that dwindled to zero when my dad died a few months ago, I'm *far* more prepared for turmoil.

Avery needs time. And that's okay. I don't mind giving it to her.

I've been plenty occupied with my own stuff and the very real need to figure out how the fuck we're going to, you know, *survive*.

After a quick survey of what tools I had in my pack, I got to work scouting the island.

From the air, it looked like a vacation postcard. From the ground? It's a deserted hellscape. And from what I've covered on foot so far, it's a desolate, rough terrain, with beaches on both the south and north sides. There's a pretty steep hill in the center, and a ridgetop with what I'm sure will be an advantageous viewpoint eventually, but there's very little edible vegetation or things of obvious use.

Fire? Handled it. Thank God I always carry a flint.

Shelter? Slapped together a temporary hut with palm fronds, loose sea grape leaves, and sheer willpower.

Water? That's the real problem. I'll have to reconfigure the sea grape leaves to collect rain, but for now, I've got what's left in my hydration pack. Normally, I carry one when I jump. After today, I'll *always* carry two.

I finish tying down the last section of the shelter and head back to the fire, dropping into the sand catty-corner from Avery. Close enough to read her mood, but still far enough to give her space.

"We're all set for tonight," I declare, leaning back into the sand with my hands and letting the heat from the flames lick my grimy skin. "It's not exactly the Four Seasons, but it'll keep us out of the weather if we get any."

Avery nods, tucking her knees to her chest, her voice so small it almost gets swallowed by the crackling fire. "Thank you."

I nod. "Of course."

Then, *silence.* The kind that crawls under your skin. The kind that is thick and suffocating and makes you feel desperate to end it with something…*anything.*

Fuck, we need a distraction—*badly.* And since Avery still appears as if she's in the middle of an existential crisis, it looks like I'm up.

"Did I ever tell you about the time Beau pissed his pants in a McDonald's parking lot?"

"What?" Her gaze jerks to mine, her pretty hazel eyes a haze of warring emotion and her cheeks pink with stress.

"Yep. He did." I laugh, remembering what is probably Beau's worst nightmare and one of my favorite memories. "We were there one night, getting a bite to eat after the club, fresh out of U of M at this point, and a cop came to the window just as Beau was getting ready to go inside and break the seal from the entire night." I grin at her and keep going. "The cop had questions because I guess some kids had been seen littering and breaking shit in the parking lot the last couple nights, and he wanted to make sure it wasn't us. Ron was driving and DD, so there was no danger of DUI or anything crazy like that, but the more we answered, the more questions the cop had, and every time Beau tried to make a move to go to the bathroom, the cop panicked and started yelling at him. This went on for like fifteen minutes, and eventually, Beau couldn't hold it anymore and ended up fucking pissing his Bottega Veneta slacks for all, including the cop, to see."

"Oh my God!" Avery squeals, her face relaxing into its normal state for the briefest of moments as she slaps her hands into the sand beside her thighs. "I can't believe I've never heard that before!"

"Yeah. Well." I snort. "We were sworn to secrecy under the threat of certain death, but given the circumstances…" I shrug. "It feels like we deserve to tell a few secrets."

Her eyes dance as she nods, her teeth gnawing at her lip in concentration. "Okay. I definitely have some Beau secrets."

Maybe I should feel bad for making my best friend the target of all these *fun memories*, but knowing he's probably curled up in a dry, warm bed with his pregnant wife while we're damp and half damaged on some beach in the middle of fucking nowhere has run my well of sympathy dry. Plus, he wouldn't mind. Beau Banks is as fucking stand-up, self-sacrificing, team-player as it gets.

I smile, curling my fingers into the sand mindlessly. "Let her rip, then. Let's hear one."

Avery's face is noticeably lighter as she transports herself into her memories.

"When we were little, I used to like to play dress-up tea party. My mom used to make Beau play with me. At first, he hated it. But then? He got into it. Like, *aggressively* into it." Her eyes brighten with amusement, and she fights the urge to laugh. "And when I grew out of it? He made me keep playing. He called himself 'Pretty

Little Princess,' held out his pinkie when he drank imaginary tea and everything."

"Holy shit!" I say in a burst, my face aching from the size of my smile. "And how long did this go on?"

"He was in eighth grade the last time he made me play!" she screams, and I fall back into the sand with a thud, hysterical and howling.

"Oh my God! More! I need more!"

Avery laughs, turning to face me and getting up on her knees for this one, her whole body vibrating. "Okay. High school graduation. Beau got drunk on my dad's vodka and puked in our bushes out front. You could smell the vomit for days until the landscapers found it, and to this day, my parents think it was Ronnie."

I guffaw. "Ronnie always holds his vodka! It's whiskey that's his problem."

"I know! What about you? You have to have another one!"

I smile lazily. "Oh, Ave, I've got secrets for days."

"Do one about Beau again," she insists. "It's distracting me."

I nod, thinking through my Rolodex of twenty-five years of memories, settling on another night Beau would kill to have expunged from God's official record. "Oh yeah. This one's gold."

"What? What?" Avery presses, shuffling closer on her knees, eyes bright with anticipation.

"One night, we were out at a club…Poison, I think, right after it opened. Beau and Bethany had just broken up, and she was very obviously with Seth. Tension? Off the goddamn charts." I grimace. "This girl in a tight black dress was all over Beau the whole night, and because he was mad and mixed up and all fucked in the head from that stupid dickhead stealing his girl, he was eating it up. Feeding her shit out of his teeth and letting her grind all over him and everything. He gets three fingers into a good time with the girl in the booth, and this giant lurch of a fucking guy comes over spouting angry threats about rearranging his body for getting with his wife."

"Oh my God!" Avery cracks up, already loving where this is going.

And of course, I keep talking.

"Beau's all bravado and shit, thinking he's an upstanding gentleman like usual, thinking he's got it under control. And he's being all polite, trying to reason with the guy like he's in a goddamn courtroom. But the dude just points to the girl…the one in the black dress… and says, *Oh yeah? This is her. My wife.*"

Avery gasps before bursting into laughter, clutching her stomach.

"We've never gotten out of somewhere so fucking fast," I add through a chuckle, running a hand through my sandy hair. "Mav threw a drink in the dude's face just to buy us some time, and we hightailed it out of there like Usain Bolt. I swear, Beau went to Mass for like three weeks straight, hoping to cleanse his soul or some shit, but the fact that he got shanghaied into helping someone cheat still haunts him."

"He's such a do-gooder, I swear." Avery rolls her eyes. "And that bitch Bethany and the sad excuse you guys had as a friend in Seth McKenzie can go straight to hell."

Crazy to think that, back then, the tragic breakup between Beau and his high school sweetheart—*aka total cheating bitch*—Bethany was such a *big* deal. No doubt, it was a true mindfuck that Beau's girlfriend was down-low fucking Seth McKenzie, a guy that had been in our friend group since we were kids. It had felt like the end of the world back then. But in hindsight? It pales in comparison to what Avery and I are facing now.

Unexpectedly, a sob bubbles up from her chest and startles me. "Beau's stupid and perfect and such a good brother, and I'm never going to see him again," she wails.

"Hey," I comfort, scooting over to her and pulling her under my arm.

I lay us back in the sand and pull her into my side, rubbing at her long brown hair with the hand behind her back. I know the Avery of a day ago would be complaining about the sand in her hair or that the way I'm holding her is twisting her expensive bathing suit, but this one is still too busy grappling with shock. I'm hoping the heat of my body against hers will be grounding—that she'll snap out of the haze and yell at me for hugging her without her permission or tell me she's way out of my league.

It's a weird wish, but at the same time, it'd be confirmation that she's okay.

"Shh. It's going to be all right. I'm sure they're looking for us by now, and they all knew our destination and our flight path and everything. They'll find us in no time."

"Are you sure?"

I have no idea if it's true.

But for her? I'll believe it until my last breath.

"Yeah. I'm sure."

She nods into my chest, and I pull her closer, smelling the remnants of her perfume or shampoo or something that still clings to her hair. It smells like roses.

"Come on. Let's go to bed. Get some rest. Everything will feel better in the morning after we've had a chance to recharge and reset."

"I don't know if I can sleep out here in the open like this."

"I built us a shelter."

"You did?" she asks, her voice going up in unconcealed shock. Obviously, the silent time she spent by the fire while I was working was spent largely disassociating entirely.

"Yeah. Come on."

Slowly and carefully, I help her to her feet, dusting the sand off myself and offering a hand for her to lead the way. She grabs her sweater from its spot beside the fire and shakes it out before slipping it on, and she then walks woodenly toward the palm tent I made. I follow behind, rubbing at my arms to ward off the growing chill since my clothes are still a little damp, and wait for her to climb inside before doing the same.

It's a tight space, but that's a boon as our body heat fills it quickly. We lie down on our backs, our eyes pointed to the fronds above us, and bask in silence. There's the soft lull of the waves lapping at the beach and a keening cry from some kind of bird, but other than that, I can't hear anything—not even Avery's breath.

I chance a look toward her, finding silent tears cascading down her cheeks in rapid repetition. My chest squeezes at the sight of the most confident girl in the world at her literal rock bottom. "Hey. It's okay, Ave."

She nods, but the movement is jerky as she fights herself to find her bravado. "I know. I... Thank you for making this. My mind just won't stop racing."

I hum thoughtfully. "Do you think it would help to cuddle?" I ask, adding, "Respectfully, of course."

Surprisingly, she doesn't even pause for a beat before scooting to my space, burrowing her body into mine just like it was by the fire a few minutes ago. I stroke the strands of her hair, both for her and for me.

For some reason, it reminds me of the way I used to play with my mom's hair as a little boy, and it's soothing—which is fucked up for a whole reason of its own, but not for worrying about right now.

Born of the same memory, the song my mom used to sing to put me to sleep falls from my lips with ease. *"Hush now, little bird with special wings. Rest your head and your mind, for now it's time. Close your eyes, and hush now, little bird with special wings."*

Avery's body feels heavier now, much like my own, and before I know it, I drift off to sleep, just as my mother's song intended.

And isn't irony a bitch? This song, right here, on a beach in the middle of nowhere, is the most comfort my mom's given me in twenty fucking years.

Fuck it. Whatever works, right?

Chapter 5

MY LIMBS ACHE WITH STIFFNESS, AND MY SKIN FEELS stretched tight as I pry my eyes open into the blinding assault of sunlight. A single beam cuts through the small gap in the makeshift tent Henry made us, but somehow, it's aimed with sniper-like precision directly at my face. Wincing, I carefully shift, trying to slip free from the weight of Henry's arm without waking him.

My body feels sore and abused, and I haven't felt this dirty since the Kappa Kappa farewell party at the University of Miami right before Juniper and I graduated. There was foam and neon and a sordid amount of alcohol, and if I stretch my memory to the brink of its boundaries, I can almost remember attending it.

And while the feeling of this morning is similar, the experience is…remarkably less fun.

I thought waking up would come with a haze of confusion—that I'd blink at my surroundings, question how I got here, or wonder why Henry was letting me cling to him like some desperate, heat-seeking vine. But no. Instead, I'm painfully, almost comically aware.

Henry and I are stranded and alone on an indiscriminate island in the middle of seemingly infinite blue waters after self-ejecting from a plane destined for the bottom of them. His phone is MIA, my phone may as well be a potato for all the good it does, and there are no signs of life in sight. Not to mention, I spent last night sleeping on the fucking ground. The only reason I got any rest at all was because of Henry's big, muscular frame cuddling mine, and his deep, raspy voice serenading me away from our terrifying reality until the sweet, numb silence of sleep consumed me.

Whether it's because of the missing comfort of my sleep mask, the scratchy press of leaves beneath me, or the unfamiliar scent of man—something I never, *ever* let invade my bed at home—I can't say. But if I'm anything this morning, it's shockingly, almost painfully clearheaded.

And I'm also criminally lacking in caffeine. There's not much strife in my regular life, but when there is, I handle it with coffee. And this situation *most definitely* deserves coffee.

Carefully climbing over Henry's lax body and out into the sand, I stand and stretch my arms to the sky, looking out at the beauty of the water and white sand in front of me. It's picturesque and serene and so at war with how I feel about it, I should be carrying a rifle or something.

Taking a deep sigh, I pull my poor, destroyed Ravella sweater off my body and walk toward the water, wading in to my knees and scooping up palmfuls to rinse my body. I know it'll leave me feeling crusty later because of the salt, but for right now, it feels both invigorating and refreshing. I brush the water down my arms and scoop it up to rub it over my face, removing any and all remaining makeup from yesterday until my hands look clean.

Raccoon eyes and runny mascara aren't a good look for anyone—even in these hellish conditions.

I consider dunking my hair but, for now, decide not to. I'm afraid it'll only make it rattier, and the gel I used to make sure my slicked-back ponytail was crispy yesterday is bound to get even cakier without my Iles Formula clarifying shampoo and conditioner.

Leaving the water slowly, I make my way back onto the sand

and turn to sit, lying back on my elbows to expose my stomach. I look up to the bright sun and mutter, "Might as well get a tan." Even laughing at the absurdity of it all as I adjust my body into an optimal sunbathing position.

This is all so fucking insane.

I close my eyes and imagine I'm at a five-star resort, laid out on a lounger and waiting on my butler service to arrive with a perfectly curated drink. Unfortunately, the silly little fantasy only reminds me how dry my mouth is, and I huff out a sigh of frustration and squeeze my eyes tighter.

How the hell did I go from having a five-hundred-dollar lunch at Selatare, my favorite Italian fine dining in Miami, two days ago…to this?

Something taps me on the arm, startling me into a frightened jump, but Henry's voice is quick to follow.

"Here. Drink some water."

The thing I felt isn't a giant spider, thank God, but the hydration pack I vaguely remember pressing against last night in the tent. Still half full of clear liquid, it's a large mercy. I snag it quickly and put the straw to my mouth, sucking heartily for several long, deep gulps until I notice Henry watching me. It's only then that I realize this is probably all the water we have for both of us and that there are no quick trips to the store to get more when we run out.

Shit.

"Sorry," I say with a wince, more than three-quarters of the bag already on its way to my stomach. I force myself to focus on the ground, on the trees—anywhere but Henry. Because, *holy hell,* does he look good.

Sun-kissed skin, damp, dark hair, broad shoulders that taper into a sculpted chest and abs—every inch of him looks like he walked straight out of a cologne ad. I can practically hear the dramatic voice-over now, *"Masculine. By Versace."*

"It's fine," he refutes, running a hand through his hair. "I already had some, but I just realized how thirsty you had to be. I'm going to set up a water collection system today, so we'll have more if it rains."

"A water…collection system," I repeat slowly, trying to ignore the way his abs flex as he shifts. Between that and the tent we slept in last night because of him, I'm starting to think he's been waiting for this moment his whole life.

"Yeah," he replies, a smirk lifting one corner of his mouth. "With some sea grape leaves and stuff. Not sure what container will be easiest to funnel it into, but I'll figure it out."

I squint at him. "How do you know so much about being stranded on an island? Seriously. Are you a prepper? Some kind of survivalist freak?"

Henry shrugs, his blue eyes flashing with amusement. "Would you believe I was obsessed with *Gilligan's Island* as a kid?"

Realistically, it's a perfectly viable reason, but I know for a fact after spending so much time growing up around him that his body language is all wrong. He's lying—though, I have no clue why.

"No." I narrow my eyes at him. "Actually, I don't believe that at all."

"Well…" He shifts slightly, rubbing the back of his neck, and for the first time since we crash-landed on this godforsaken island, Henry Callahan *blushes*. His normally hard jaw softens into something much more boyish as red creeps up his cheeks.

"I guess it could also be because I was—*am*—a Boy Scout leader for a troop in Miami."

"Wait…" My eyes widen. "*You're* a Boy Scout?" My voice goes up at least three octaves as a giggle bubbles out of me.

"A *scout leader*," he corrects, pinching the bridge of his nose. "I haven't been a Boy Scout since I was a kid."

"Well, well." I grin, tilting my head. "I guess Beau isn't the only one with secrets, huh? This is fantastic news. I'm stranded with a professional camper."

Henry sighs, rolling his eyes. "It's not like that. My dad signed me up after…" His voice is even, but it trails off for a moment, leaving something unspoken in the space between his words. "He wanted to find something for us to do together. Give us something structured, somewhere to go. And I liked it. I liked learning how to build things, start fires, tie knots. It felt…useful. So, when my old troop leader asked me to come back and help, I did. And I just never stopped." He shrugs. "Feels equal parts obligation and something I actually enjoy. The kids are great. The parents, too."

I blink, caught off guard. I expected something ridiculous—maybe some Henry-style bullshit about preparing for the apocalypse or training for some kind of survivalist reality show. Not…*that*.

Before I can process the full weight of what sits between his words, Henry nods to the water still in my grasp. "Have as much as you want. I'll go work on the collection system, and then we can go for a hike around the island to see if there's anything useful."

"A hike?" I question, shaking my head. "Henry, you must be forgetting my clothing rant from yesterday and the tale of the girl with one shoe." I wiggle my bare feet in the sand for dramatic effect, as the one shoe I do have is still up by the side of the tent with my waist pack.

He smiles. "Your other one just washed up on the beach a minute ago." I turn to follow the point of his finger and see my shoe, my missing Golden Goose, floating and rolling carelessly at the very edge of the lapping water.

It's surely waterlogged and mostly destroyed, but the joy I feel at seeing it is almost overwhelming.

"Oh my God! My shoe!"

"See that?" Henry says victoriously with a pump of his fist and a waggle of his eyebrows. "Things are looking up already."

It's not a rescue boat or a trip to a five-star resort while wearing Valentino, but I have to admit, having two shoes is, at the very least, a start.

Still…my God, how the mighty have fallen.

Chapter 6

AVERY SITS ON THE BEACH BUT IN THE SHADE OF A PALM frond, her normally supple, even-toned skin taking on a reddening aesthetic as she fans herself with a hand.

I'm lucky enough to have the kind of complexion that takes a flamethrower to really burn, and so far, I've done nothing but darken even further, but Avery's already fighting for her life.

Even living in Miami, our day-to-day lives are spent in and out of buildings. All this sun exposure is completely outside of our normal routine, and the two of us will have to be careful not to get sun poisoning without any hope of getting treatment.

Her normally silky, dark hair is frizzy, and her precious shoes are covered in both dirt and debris from our short trek around the island earlier, but she's in much better spirits than yesterday and, frankly, I'm impressed.

This kind of adversity would be too much for anyone, let alone a woman who's spent her literal entire life being catered to. Food, clothes, time, energy—all of it has been at her disposal and whim from the day she was born until yesterday morning.

All thanks to my father's lucrative career in hedge funds, I may be rich and come from money, but everything I have now—every dollar in my bank account, every asset in my name—is because of the company I built on my own back, *Adrenaline Junkie.* My mom left my dad and me when I was a kid, and a few months ago, my dad left too—though it wasn't exactly his choice. *Fuck cancer very much.* For me, this? Being stranded? It's just another chink in the chain in a lifetime of less-than-ideal scenarios.

"Henry, I hope you know you're literally morphing into Tom Hanks before my eyes."

I scoff, sharpening the stick I procured to use for spearfishing while we were out exploring. "Really. Morphing before your eyes, huh?"

"Yep." Avery nods, her face steady. "I expect a full monologue about your beloved volleyball Wilson before bedtime."

"You'll have to find one first. I, unfortunately, didn't have the foresight to go down on a plane full of FedEx packages."

"I'll get started now."

I laugh, shaking my head. "Or—wild idea—you could come help me catch us some dinner instead."

"Yeah, no." She grimaces, her lip curling as she stretches her hands out in front of herself and laces her fingers together, pushing her palms out. "I don't really like fish."

My laughter rings out in the quiet around us like a gunshot. "Yes, you do. Are you forgetting that I've known you nearly all your life, Avery? You ate fish at Christmas, like, a week ago."

"That was salmon dip," she explains, holding her hands out to her sides. "Not some wild-caught island squidward thing! I eat fish, but I only eat *fish*." The final word drips with snobbery, and once again, I can't help but laugh.

"Oh my God. The level of delusion is off the charts." I smirk and mimic her tone. "We have fish. Plain and simple. So, you can either eat it, or you can go hungry."

She scowls, a stubborn streak kicking in. "I'll go hungry, then. I've been meaning to start a diet anyway."

I want to tell her to fucking starve, then—I mean, *fuck, she's a pain in the ass.* But the part of me that knows how different this is from her real life forces me to gentle parent her instead.

"Avery, come on. You have to eat. Both of us staying strong and healthy is our best chance at making it long enough for people to find us."

She makes a mocking face, mouthing my words like a chipmunk, and just like that, all my patience is gone. There's no way we're going to survive this shit if I have to fight her every step of the way.

"Are you a child? What the hell is wrong with you?" I shout, the strain making my neck feel tight. She raises an eyebrow in challenge, so I push it, leaning toward her and raising my voice even more.

"I mean, fuck, Avery. I know you're sheltered, but it doesn't take a genius to realize we're just a couple weeks away from starving to death," I rail, frustration getting the better of me to the point of being mean.

Her face crumples and she shoves to her feet, and immediately, I regret losing my cool. Gone is the headstrong woman I know, and in her place is someone who's scared out of her mind and barely hanging on. Her whole body shakes as she tries to contain herself, but when it's too much, she spins in the sand and takes off.

No volleying insults, no smart retort. Because of me, all the progress she's made toward keeping it together is gone.

"I'm sorry," I call out as she runs toward the shelter, her cries audible even from my spot near the water. "Avery, I'm sorry."

She doesn't turn around and she doesn't look back, and tired from the emotional toll of it all, I don't go after her. I know I should, but I just…can't. Neither of us signed up for this, and despite it being only our second day on the island, it feels like a lifetime.

Instead, I work on the things I can control, like finishing my fishing spear and trying for two solid hours to come up with a single fucking fish.

One. One freaking fish in two long, really fucking hot hours, and I only got him because my spear glanced off his head at just the right angle to stun him.

Tom Hanks, my ass. He made it look a hell of a lot easier than this.

A few hours later, when Avery walks out of the makeshift tent, her face is as contrite as I imagine my own. Both of us feel badly for having lashed out at each other; that much is obvious, even if saying it aloud cuts a little too close to the bone.

The sun is down and the moon is out, and as far as I'm concerned, that may as well mean our fight happened on a different planet.

Timidly, Avery takes a seat in the sand on the other side of the fire, and I offer the remaining half of the fish I saved for her to eat should she change her mind and want it.

Her nose scrunches as she takes it and puts it to her mouth to try a bite, and I smother a smile of both pride and gratitude that we don't have to fight about this anymore. I know the taste is bland, the only appeal the gentle smokiness from the fire, but it's sustenance, and at this point, that's what's important.

Two hours have passed since I sent her running into the tent crying, and things, seemingly, are as back to normal as normal gets when you're stranded in the middle of nowhere with no communication with the outside world.

When she takes a second bite, I clear my throat and test out bringing polite conversation back between us. A lot of topics seem tricky, given our circumstances, but there's one thing Avery loves more than anything in this world—her best friend, Juniper.

"You think June went all Helen Hunt when she found out we didn't make it to our destination yesterday?" I ask, trying to cut some of the lingering tension with humor. "Like, has the Coast Guard been involved and a whole map with search grids and shit?"

Avery nods. "I'm sure. She's probably ready to strap herself inside a helicopter, not that Beau'll let her." A frown creases her forehead. "I just hope she's not stressing herself too much with the baby and all."

"She's strong," I say with reassurance. "I'm sure she's out there rolling heads but taking care of herself at the same time. And if she's not, Beau will do it for her."

"She's the strongest person I've ever met," Avery agrees, glancing at me in a flash of firelight that makes me feel a tingle of vulnerability.

This is probably the most serious I've ever seen her, and in some ways, I don't know what to do with it. We've always had a chemistry between us, but her personality is normally a force field against it. Seeing the exposed raw edges of what's underneath might just make us both a little too defenseless.

"Other than you, actually," she adds quietly. "Both of you are stronger than I'll ever be."

The compliment is both fortifying and uncomfortable, and my fingers tingle with an overwhelming surge of anxiety. She has no idea that being strong is usually happening when you feel your very weakest.

And for good reason.

Resilience, as it were, is best tested under a load, and for better or worse, Avery's never had to carry much of anything on her own.

Until now, that is.

"Are you kidding?" I say, my voice as warm as I can manage, given the subject matter. "Avery, look at us. At where we are and what we're dealing with. It's at complete odds with your normal life, and yet you're rallying. You took my direction on the dive and fought in the water just like I told you. You've adapted to the circumstances and, despite not wanting to, just ate that stupid fish because you know it's the best thing for both of us. I think you're handling everything really well."

Avery smiles, and for the first time, without the perfectly curated makeup, the designer clothes, the endless distractions of her world, I feel like I'm *really* seeing her.

No parties to get to. No stores to shop at. No shiny things to show off.

It's just her. And me. And the wild, wide open.

The moon looks massive out here, hanging over the water like something out of a painting, making me feel incredibly small in the scheme of things. Making *us* feel small. And yet, all I can focus on is her. The way the firelight flickers against her skin, casting shadows over the delicate slope of her nose, the high arch of her cheekbones, the deep golden of her hazel eyes.

Avery has always been my best friend's little sister—the one with the beautiful eyes and gorgeous smile and a personality too big for any one room to contain. But today, on day two of no one but each other to count on, she's turning out to be a hell of a lot more.

Millions of expected things. And even more surprises.

I mean, she's a *virgin*, for fuck's sake. *Avery.* Boy-crazy, kiss-crazy, plain-crazy Avery.

Tonight feels too fragile to push anything further—especially since she was mad at me no less than ten minutes ago—but tomorrow, I'm making it my mission to figure out why.

"Well, thanks," she says, stretching her legs out toward the fire. "But will you change your mind if I complain about how much I miss my warm bed and Starbucks and, *ah God*, Marty, my nail tech…he's going to be wondering where I am!"

Shaking my head, I laugh softly and watch as the fire pops and crackles and sparks into the pitch-black night sky. "Nah. I'd say those are fair complaints. It's all the stuff you're used to."

"And what about you?" she hedges. "What are your complaints—other than being here with me?"

"Complain about being stuck here with a beautiful woman? Are you kidding? I could be having to cuddle with Ronnie at night right now. Or Mav. Trust me, I am not complaining about being here with you."

Avery smiles. "You think I'm beautiful?"

I roll my eyes. "You know you're beautiful."

"Pshh. Duh. But *you* think I'm beautiful."

"Yes," I say simply. "You, Avery Banks, are beautiful."

Avery tucks her face behind her legs, but I can tell by the small creases at the sides of her eyes that she's enjoying this a lot. That's no surprise, though. If there's one thing she's always loved, it's bringing a man to his knees.

Her dad. Her brother. Her many boy toys. *Me.*

We're all at her mercy.

In Miami, I'm able to keep her at a distance, but here…here, everything is different.

And though I don't dare voice it, not feeling in control of my own emotions is my biggest, most pertinent complaint.

Chapter 7

January 3rd

Avery

HENRY SCALES ANOTHER BREADFRUIT TREE IN SEARCH OF something—anything—ripe enough to eat. With zero luck catching another fish this morning and only one measly fish between us last night since we got here, we're toeing the line between *mildly uncomfortable* and *one of us is going to snap and eat the other.*

Even on my strictest diets, I've never fasted for this long, and being that this is the modern era of hot girls, we do shit healthy. No disordered eating bullshit, right? Right.

As such, I'm a proponent of focusing on protein, and one of my fav morning protein options sounds so good, and so unattainable at the moment, I'm feeling violent. In fact, I'm pretty sure I'd freaking *kill* for a turkey bacon, egg, and cheese English muffin from Starbs right now.

I shield my eyes from the sun, wipe some of the sweat from my chin with my now-crusty Ravella sweater I have draped over my shoulders to protect them from burning, and squint up at Henry as he moves from one side of the tree to the other, scouting like he's been a jungle bushcrafter all his life.

His shirtless skin glistens under the sun, every ridge and groove of his muscles slick with sweat. His black cargo pants are tattered at the ankles from hours spent trudging through water and sand, and the whole look is just unfair—like some rugged model who belongs on the cover of *Survivalist Vogue.*

In Miami, my lack of practical skills has never been an issue—nobody's ever needed me to start a fire or fashion a fishing spear at a club opening—but out here? Turns out, being strictly a *book the vacation, not survive it* kind of girl is a slight disadvantage.

Still, my brain buffers as I take in the way his sweat-slicked skin practically glows under the golden light, every subtle movement of his body making his stupid muscles flex like they were designed to taunt me. Immediately, my mind spirals back to the fake cologne campaign I invented for him—Masculine by Versace—and before I can stop myself, I start picturing it in vivid detail.

Black-and-white shots. Slow-motion water droplets sliding down his abs. Him being all broody and intense while he stares into the camera while a deep, raspy voice-over murmurs, *"For the man who conquers."*

I shake my head. *Focus, Avery. You will not be conquered.*

"Hey, Ave!" Henry shouts down to me, chucking one fruit to the ground and then another.

"Yeah?"

"I've been meaning to ask you…"

"Yeah?"

"That whole virgin thing you mentioned on the way down from the sky… What's that all about?"

My whole body locks up so fast my limbs practically forget how to function. "E-excuse me?"

"Yeah. On the canopy down, you said, *'Oh my God! I can't believe I'm going to die a virgin!'*"

"No. No, I didn't."

"Yep," he says, casually perching on a branch to peer down at me. "You did. Said it a couple times, actually. Kept rambling about it. I was slightly preoccupied with, you know, keeping us alive, but it just hit me again… So, what's that about?"

My stomach churns as he smirks down at me, a full-on daring me expression.

"Nope. No way." I shake my head once, twice, and then three more times. "Henry, I'm not doing this right now."

"Why not?" he asks, far more shocked than he should be, given the subject matter. I mean, of course I'm not talking about my sexual history. We're trying to *survive* here.

"Are you serious?" I gesture wildly to the literal survival situation we're currently in. "Look at what we're doing right now, for Pete's sake!"

"Gathering fruit? And what? You have a spa appointment to get back to before the end of the hour? We're on an island, Ave. Just you and me. What else are we going to do to entertain ourselves?"

I huff but, surprisingly, see his point. What the hell else is there to do if not expose ourselves entirely? *But two can play at that game, and I hope his head rolls when he realizes what he's getting himself into.*

"Fine. But if I'm going to talk about this, you're going to talk about something deep and top secret too. No backing out, you hear me?"

"That's fair." Henry laughs, jumping down from the lowest branch of the breadfruit tree and scooping up two of them from the ground.

I bend down to get the other two, and as we walk back toward the other side of the island and what I now think of as our beach, I talk. I don't really have a direction or plan; it's all just a stream of consciousness.

"It wasn't intentional. At least, not at first." I toss my hair over my shoulder, avoiding his gaze. "I just got used to bouncing from guy to guy, and to be honest, none of them would win any bachelor contests if it came down to it. I kind of made a rule for myself that I'd do anything but penetration, and well, however many years later, here we are."

"So, there hasn't been a guy who's pushed you past the point of no return? Someone good with their mouth who led you into sex from there?"

My entire body seizes at the way he says that. At the way his voice drops on *good.*

I shake my head quickly. "I never stick around long enough."

"Wow."

"Wow what? Like it's so hard to believe I'm not this huge slut or something?"

"I never said slut, Avery. You did." Henry laughs, nonplussed by my accusation. "And you know exactly how you've depicted yourself over the years, so don't even try acting like it wouldn't be news to me or anyone else that you haven't had sex. I respect it, but I didn't *expect* it. Okay?"

"Yeah, whatever," I agree. I mean, he's not wrong. I go through men quicker than I go through Louboutins, and that's saying a lot because I purchase a new pair of red bottoms more than I get bi-weekly facials.

But still.

Henry hit the nail on the head—no one in my life knows I'm a virgin. Not even my best friend June. Somewhere along the way, I just took on this persona of the girl who hooked up with whoever she wanted, whenever she wanted, without a second thought. I don't even know when it started or why I let people believe it.

I've never been the type of girl who needed to fit into other people's standards, but maybe, in this case, that's exactly what I was doing. Or maybe I just wanted to keep that truth to myself, like a secret I wasn't willing to share.

Or maybe—deep down—I've just never found a man I wanted to give myself to.

The thought lingers longer than I want, settling in my chest like something heavy, something *undeniable.*

I shake it off.

There's no use analyzing something that doesn't need to be

analyzed. It's just sex. It's just a choice. And Henry Callahan doesn't need to be the one making me question it.

"What about your boyfriend?" he asks, and I scrunch up my nose.

"My boyfriend?"

"The one you mentioned at your parents' house at Christmas. Right after you told me that it was nice to have me there and that I'd always be a part of your family. When I was playing tea party with Addy. Remember?" My eyes just barely escape narrowing over his pointed drag down memory lane. "You're still with him, aren't you?"

Yeah, Justin. *God, I'd nearly forgotten about him.*

"Yeah. We're together. But it's really new." I shrug. I don't know what to say that isn't the fact that I literally forgot he existed, and even for me, that paints a little bit of a vapid picture. I turn the conversation back to Henry to take the pressure off myself and this pointedly uncomfortable introspection. "What about you? Are you with someone?"

He nods. "Yeah."

That's all he says, and to be honest, I'm glad. The last thing I want to hear is Henry waxing poetic about some other woman. It's not like I have any propriety over him, but…there's always been *something.*

As we walk in silence, I hold the breadfruit in front of my chest and imagine myself as Pamela Anderson. My breasts are trinkets compared to hers, and I've always wondered what I'd look like with bigger ones.

"Your boobs are fine the way they are," Henry surprises me by saying, clearly having noticed my little exercise.

"I didn't ask you."

"You're right. But they're still fine."

"Well, fine and luscious are two different things, and I've always wondered what it would be like to have the latter."

"From what I hear, the main themes are ill-fitting clothes and back pain."

"What?"

"Every woman I've ever been with who had big breasts did nothing but complain about them. As a guy, they're hot, but I imagine as a woman, they're a giant pain in the ass."

"I guess you would know. You've been with enough women."

Henry laughs. "Yeah. I have. Which is why you should take me seriously when I tell you that you don't need to change a damn thing." He looks me dead in the eyes. "You're a smokeshow. Just like you are."

A blush steals across my cheeks as I remember all the times Henry and I have kissed or come close to it in our history. The truth is, it's not a surprise that he finds me attractive or that I've spent the better part of today admiring how he looks without a shirt on.

We've been around each other for more years than most people know each other in a lifetime, and for the majority of it, I've been well aware of how much of a catch he is.

Henry Callahan has *always* been good with women. Effortlessly charming, magnetic in a way that made it impossible for people not to be drawn to him. He's never had to chase—women just seemed to fall into his orbit, like moths to a flame, eager to be the one who finally tamed him.

But Henry never stays.

I've watched it happen over and over—beautiful women on his arm, laughing at his jokes, looking at him like he's their whole world. And then, just as quickly as they appeared, they were gone, replaced by another and another and another.

It's just how he's always been.

Never attached. Never tied down. Never keeping anyone for too long.

And yet, here we are. Stranded. Alone. Tangled up in more ways than one.

I remember the exact moment I started watching Henry Callahan a little too closely. The summer I turned thirteen. The night Brandon Worley—my first kiss, my first official boyfriend—broke up with me.

That night, I saw Henry differently—like a spark I hadn't realized was there until it caught.

Because if I'm a smokeshow, Henry Callahan is the whole damn fire.

And I guess…there's a part of me that hasn't stopped looking at him since.

Chapter 8

The Past

Fourteen years ago

Avery

BRANDON WORLEY'S OLDER BROTHER PEELS OUT OF MY driveway, tires screeching as Brandon sits smugly in the passenger seat, his confession of his crush on that skankapotamus Sarah Philips still fresh in the tears streaking down my face.

Juni is busy tonight, off having a rare dinner with her dad while he's in town on a layover. As much as I need my best friend, I won't call her. All she ever talks about is how badly she wants her parents to notice her, and tonight, her dad is at least pretending he has.

So, instead, I'm here. Alone. *Humiliated.*

Ugh. I hate that I let myself get this attached to someone so stupid so quickly. But after dating Brandon for a whopping month and a half—twice as long as any other eighth grader at school—I really thought we'd be together forever.

Now? I *can't believe* I ever let that clown be my first kiss. *Gag.*

My Hermès silk scarf is drenched in tears already, so I use it to wipe at the rest before I go inside where I know my parents and my brother and all three of his dumb best friends are no doubt waiting for my arrival.

"Dating at thirteen is ridiculous," has always been my dad's take, but because it was our one-and-a-half-month anniversary, and Brandon's brother was going to be driving us, my mom convinced him to let me go by myself tonight.

I *can't* let him see me like this. One look at me in tears and he'll know he was right, and who knows how long I'll have to wait before he lets me date again.

Blowing out a breath, I finish dabbing my tears and take my compact out of my purse to check my mascara for runs. With my makeup mostly intact and the mottled red of my earlier skin starting to fade, I storm through the front door like normal, dropping my coat and bag on the tile just inside for our housekeeper Linda to put away, and head straight for my room.

My brother Beau and his friends Henry, Maverick, and Ronnie are all coming down the stairs, though, board shorts and bare chests signaling that they're headed to surf the sunset like they always do on Saturday nights, and there's no avoiding them as I'm already on my way up.

"Hey, Ave," Beau greets, his usual cheerful smile making me roll my eyes. "You're home early."

I scoff, powering past the four of them to head for my room, afraid they'll see my puffy eyes if I linger for too long. "Yeah. Because boys are *stupid*."

Beau and Henry come to a stop, Beau reaching out to halt my progress, but Ronnie and Mav keep going, laughing uproariously at something that's no doubt just as brain-dead as Brandon freaking Worley.

"What happened?" Beau asks, his protective older brother mask flaring rather dramatically. I appreciate the sentiment and solidarity, but truly, right now, I just want to be alone.

"It's nothing," I protest, but Beau's grip on my arm tightens as I try to pull away.

Henry leans casually against the curved wall of our ornate staircase, a toothpick in his mouth and his hair curling around his forehead. He's smirking in my direction but otherwise silent, and I have to admit, he looks really freaking cool.

Seriously. He's a pain in the ass pretty much every time I'm around him and their other stupid friends, but right now, he's like a teenage James Dean or something. Mr. Cool Customer extraordinaire.

"Ave, if he hurt you—" Beau starts, only to be cut off completely by Henry.

"Fuck that guy," he says, the curse making my thirteen-year-old cheeks burn. "Come out to the beach with us and surf."

"Get my hair wet?" I rebut. "Uh, no thanks."

Henry shrugs, all muscle flex and nonchalance. He's ridiculously built for an eighteen-year-old. *When the heck did that happen?*

I guess I've never even considered one of my brother's silly friends might be…like *hot* or something. It's too much of an oxymoron.

"That's cool. Come watch, then," he pushes, and between the smirk and the muscles, my brain short-circuits.

I mean, *when did Henry Callahan get so freaking fine?*

"Okay, yeah," I hear myself saying. "Let me just change out of my heels and put on some shorts, and I'll be down."

Without an answer, Henry is gone, and in his wake, I'm left with only two things—my do-gooder, overprotective brother Beau, and a new mile-long crush on his best friend.

By the time I make it out to the beach, they're already in the water. But one glance in Henry's direction and my fate is sealed—*watching Henry Callahan surf without his shirt on just became my new favorite hobby.*

Chapter 9

Avery's arm is heavy with sleep as I shift it off my abdomen and onto her hip so I can get up without waking her. The sun's not up quite yet, but I'm hoping to have better luck with fishing first thing in the morning than I have in the middle of the day.

My dad took me fishing some as a kid, and while I'm not an expert by any means, I still remember that we always left at the ass-crack of dawn to get started because of something about the fish being more active.

After tucking the leaf flap back into place on our makeshift shelter to keep the light from invading and waking up Avery, I pad softly through the sand down onto the beach, picking up the spear from its spot propped against a palm tree on the way. My stomach has stopped rumbling, despite how hungry I know my body is, and the fit of my pants, even though this is only the fourth day we've been here, is starting to get looser.

I know from my college obsession with fitness that taking your diet to zero calories suddenly won't have an immediate crazy effect, but it doesn't take long to lose a pound or two or three when you're eating twenty-five hundred calories fewer a day than usual.

Without having a way to predict how long we'll be here, or if someone is even remotely close to finding us, we need to get a rou-tine down for finding a way to feed ourselves and quick.

And, like it or not, fishing seems to be our only shot at protein.

I know netting of some sort would be much easier than having to hit them with a freaking spear, but so far, I haven't figured out a material we'd be able to make work. Once again, Tom Hanks has let me down.

Carefully scaling the rocks at the outer curl of the beach, I watch as little fish dart through the shallow water after bugs and other small debris. I take aim at one, blowing a breath through my nose to steady my racing heart, and throw my stick, striking the fish and successfully knocking it stunned for long enough to reach in and grab it.

I scream unintentionally, the victory too big not to celebrate, and Avery pokes her sleepy head out the front of the tent not five seconds later.

I wave and point to the fish, apologizing. "Sorry! I didn't mean to wake you, but I got one!"

"Woo-hoo!" she cheers, stepping out into the sand and doing a cute little twerk that makes me laugh. "Go, Henry. Go, Henry. It's your birthday!"

I chuckle and scale back across the rocks to toss the fish onto a sea grape leaf while I try to catch more. Avery surprises me by staying out of our tent and getting to work after a quick stretch. She empties the water collector into my hydration pack, seals it up after taking a quick drink, and then moves down onto the beach to stoke the fire with what we call the poker stick.

Flames lick up again, the coals still hot from last night, and a surge of pride swells my chest. Maybe it's misplaced—because I don't have any role or title that gives me the right to be proud—but I'm truly amazed at how well she's coped and adapted to the situation.

If you'd asked me a week ago how Avery Banks would han-dle being stranded on a deserted island, I'd have painted a very different picture—one that involved a lot more screaming and zero participation.

Clearly, that wasn't fair. To pretend I knew the heart of who she is as a person from the little bit of interaction we've had over the years while out at the club or in her parents' house is shortsighted. Avery has always been interesting and attractive and kind—but this island is teaching me pretty quickly that she's a lot more things than that.

I try for another fish—or seventy—for an hour and manage one more before calling it quits for the morning and joining Avery by the fire. She's already gotten the fish I caught first rinsed and cleaned as best as possible before skewering it on a stick and holding it over the fire to cook while I kept fishing. I wouldn't mind if she'd have eaten it too, but she didn't, saving it for us to share instead.

"You didn't have to wait for me."

"That's okay. I figured we could share this one and then cook the rest for later."

I laugh. "Well, the rest is one more."

"One more than I'd be able to catch," she says with a self-depre-cating laugh. "I've never even had to buy my own food at the store. I use a service."

"A service? Like they decide what to buy for you?"

"They buy it and cook it." She rolls her eyes a little. "It's, like, a personal chef thing."

"Ah," I hum. "Besides my meal prep for breakfast and lunch, I don't really eat at home. I just eat out."

"And look at us now," she deadpans, shooting me a dry look.

"Yeah." I snort. "Living the dream."

"Fine dining on charred fish, sharing a bed with bugs, and get-ting genuinely excited about rain?" She shakes her head, laughing softly. "Honestly, can't believe I didn't major in survival at U of M. What a wasted education."

"Hindsight is usually 20/20," I quip. "Speaking of careers, you're still working for Neil, right?"

She shrugs. "When I feel like it, I guess."

Such a fucking Avery Banks response. I cackle. "If you don't like working there, why don't you just get a job you like?"

"Oh, get real, Henry." Avery's nose curls. "Are we really supposed to *like* jobs? What's to like about working?"

My shoulders lift as I think about the company I've built for myself. It's not the traditional path, and I know not everyone starts with the opportunities I had, but building something based on your interests truly is the key to professional fulfillment. "They say if you do what you love, you'll never work a day in your life."

"And that's how you feel?"

"No," I admit. "That's bullshit. Of course, work is going to feel like work sometimes. But in my case, I get to spend half my time doing stuff I really love. Skydiving, rock-climbing, paragliding—I get to test new equipment to see how well it really works—"

"Which sounds like a nightmare!" Avery cuts in. "Testing a parachute? Or fall gear? To see if it works! And that's fun? Say sike right now."

I chuckle. "It's all been *tested* for function. I'm just testing the simplicity of operation or if something would make it better. It's fun."

"I'll have to take your word for it. My one experience with sky-diving is a little…tainted…I'd say."

I snort. *Uh, yeah.* "So, what *do* you like to do? I know you like to dance at the clubs, and if Beau's stories are anything to go by, I know you like Starbucks. What else do you like?"

"I like fashion. High-end stuff, obviously, but I've seen some really unique pieces coming out of the U of M fashion program, and I tend to keep up with that."

"That's cool. Why don't you try to do something with that?"

She scoffs, shaking her head. "Yeah, okay. Because *Avery Banks* trying to be serious about anything wouldn't be the biggest joke in Miami."

I frown. "Why would it be a joke?"

She lets out a short laugh, but there's no humor in it. "Come on, Henry. My entire life, Beau has been the successful one, the overachiever, the one everyone *expects* to do great things. Me? I play my part. I'm the fun one. The wild one. The one people invite to parties, not boardrooms." She shrugs like it's no big deal, but something about the way her voice tightens tells me otherwise. "No one's ever expected me to *do* anything, so I never bothered pretending like I would."

I study her for a second, catching the way she won't meet my eyes. "That's a load of shit."

Her head snaps up. "Excuse me?"

"You're smart as hell, Avery. You could do anything you wanted. And you know it."

She scoffs again, but this time, it's weaker. "Even if that were true, no one would take me seriously."

I shake my head. "You ever think maybe you don't take yourself seriously first?"

She flinches—barely, but I catch it.

For a second, she looks like she might say something. That maybe I've hit a nerve too deep for her to ignore. But then she plasters on that effortless smirk, the one she's perfected over the years, and flicks her wrist like she's brushing the whole conversation away. "Well, lucky for me, I don't *need* a job, right? Daddy's money and all."

I don't let her get away with it, though. "Doesn't mean you shouldn't do something for yourself."

Avery rolls her eyes, but I see the flicker of something else beneath the surface. Something unsure. Something that tells me maybe, just maybe, she's thought about this more than she lets on.

"We're going to get out of here," I say softly, finding her hazel eyes and holding them even when she seems like she wants to fight it. "I know sometimes it doesn't seem like it, and that it feels like we've been here forever, but I'm confident this *isn't* our eternity. We sure as hell shouldn't plan like it is."

She chews her lip, her eyes turning shiny with unshed tears. "I really hope you're right."

"I am," I say and try to make myself feel as confident as my words sound. "I mean, hell, you've got the boyfriend to go back to, right?"

"The boyfriend," she says slowly, hiding her eyes from me by looking at her lap. "Yeah. And I mean, you have someone too. What's her name?"

My chest feels tight with discomfort as I think about Ashley—my girlfriend whom I've only been with a short time and have thought about exactly zero times since we got on this island. She's a nice girl, but I know if I'm honest with myself, I'm only with her because all my friends have someone, and I don't want to be the odd man out.

Being the only single guy of the whole group was starting to grate.

"Ashley."

"Well…there you go. I'll go back to Justin and you'll go back to Ashley, and…we'll carry on. One day. I guess." She groans. "All right, enough of this. I'm going to go for a swim. Want to come?"

I shake my head. "Think I'll go ahead and cook this other fish."

She nods, shucking her sweater to reveal her bikini, and wades into the water, diving into the incoming wave when it hits.

And I find myself exhaling, scrubbing a hand down my face and wiping at my eyes to keep from staring at her perfect body in her bikini.

She's *so* fucking beautiful.

And I *really* shouldn't be thinking about that. Or the fact that I'm finding out that Avery is so much more than beauty.

But every day we're here, I feel it creeping in—this *thing* between us. This pull.

I know she's worried about being stuck here forever, but I'm starting to think about the opposite. Every day we're here together, I feel more and more like I might not know what to do without her when we leave.

Chapter 10

Avery

HENRY CRADLES MY HEAD AGAINST HIM, MY CHEEK PRESSED to the solid warmth of his chest as I trace lazy circles along his abdomen. The fire crackles beside us, its glow casting flickering shadows across his chiseled features, and for the first time since we crash-landed here, my stomach isn't clawing at my spine with hunger. The two fish he caught this morning, along with the breadfruit he gathered, have left us as full as we can get in a situation like this. And though the night air holds a noticeable chill, Henry's body heat is more than enough to keep me warm.

Normally, I'd look at my weather app to see how long the chill will last, but without technology, our only choice is to wait it out.

And somehow, cuddling with Henry has become second nature—so natural, it wasn't even a question.

Henry plays with my hair the way he does every night before we fall asleep. The motion is slow and hypnotic, like he's memorizing the texture, like he actually enjoys the feel of me against him. And my body sinks more into his, boneless and relaxed, and if I weren't so aware of the ridiculous crush I used to have on him, I might pretend this is just about survival.

Sister, that crush has never really gone away. And right now, it's threatening to claw its way back up to the surface.

"I know I'm normally in my own world," I murmur, my voice

quiet in the firelight. "But even I know I wouldn't be surviving at all right now if it weren't for you."

Henry chuckles, the deep rumble vibrating through my body. "You're holding your own, Ave."

I huff. "Please. You're the hunter, the gatherer—the survivalist guru. I'm just dead weight in a crusty sweater."

He shakes his head, nudging my temple with his chin. "You're more adaptable than you think. If I'd have guessed before we got here, I'd have put money on you crying for three days straight and refusing to eat anything that didn't come off a Michelin-starred menu."

I scoff. "Well, joke's on you. I lasted a solid hour before my first menty b."

His soft laugh makes me smile. *God, I love his laugh.*

For a while, we just exist—him stroking my hair, me melting into him, the fire crackling beside us like we're the last two people on earth. And maybe we are, in a way.

Though, if it weren't for him, I'm certain I wouldn't be alive. Henry is the whole reason we're both surviving this situation. He's my rock. My voice of reason. And maybe that's why letting him play with my hair feels so good, like I'm finally able to give him just a tiny fraction of the comfort he's given me.

"What do you think Beau is doing right now?" I ask quietly, my mind wandering to what our family and friends must be going through as time with us missing ticks away.

"Probably handling business, like always. That's part of what I've always loved about Beau being a stick-in-the-mud," Henry says with a laugh that makes his chest shake under my ear. "He's reliable. Mav and Ronnie? While a good fucking time, they'd probably be out in the ocean on Jet Skis, looking for us in the most inefficient way possible. But Beau? He's probably got charts, coordinates, a fucking spreadsheet mapping out all possible crash locations."

"My dad is really good under pressure, too. Between him and Beau, they probably have a whole search party organized, the Coast Guard, and all of Miami-Dade County on high alert."

"Definitely. I'm sure it's only a matter of time," Henry extrapolates. It's hard to know if he really believes it, but either way, he's doing a good job of pretending.

"Did Beau ever tell you all the details of how he and Juni got together?"

"Some app they were working on at work, right?"

"Yeah. Midnight. But, like, she was messaging him anonymously and he had no idea it was her, but he was still falling so hard for her that he was sending her all this dirty stuff."

"Beau?" Henry asks incredulously. "Sending dick pics?"

I giggle and pretend to gag. "I don't know about actual cock-a-doodle-doos, but they were definitely saying some scandalous stuff. I made June tell me, of course, and let me tell you, I didn't know she had it in her."

"And look at them now. One kid here and another on the way. Married. Happy. Settled."

I nod against his chest, the material of his shirt feeling softer and softer every night from being in the sun all day. He doesn't smell bad—not sure that I'd notice if he did over the stench of myself—but we've been sharing my deodorant for the time being to stave off the BO a little.

"You want that stuff one day?" I ask.

"To be married with kids?" Henry clarifies.

"Yeah."

"I guess. It sounds nice. Though, I'm not sure I'm ready for it now. I don't know. Would have to happen with the right woman, I guess. You?"

I snort. "I haven't even slept with anyone, Henry."

"Yeah. Right." A soft chuckle leaves his lungs. "I can't lie that was almost as shocking as if someone had told me we were going to be stranded on an island together."

A small giggle escapes my lips. I'm well aware there are a lot of people in my life who would be shocked to find out that I'm a virgin. Hell, the reality still kind of shocks me when I give myself time to think about it.

We fall into silence, the kind that lingers, stretching between us like something tangible. My fingers trace absent-minded circles over his chest, and I feel the deep, even rise and fall of his breathing.

When I tilt my head, Henry's already looking at me.

His gaze is steady, unreadable but intent, and for a moment, I forget about the island, the search parties, the hunger gnawing at my stomach. There's only *this*. This quiet space between us, where every-thing—every unsaid word, every lingering touch—feels magnified.

Neither of us speaks. Neither of us moves.

But I feel the shift, the subtle draw, like gravity pulling us closer. My breath catches. The warmth of his skin radiates against mine, and I don't know who leans in first, but suddenly, he's impossibly close. So close I can count the sun-kissed freckles on his nose and feel the heat of his breath against my lips.

Just a little closer—

A rustling sound from deep in the forest shatters the moment.

I jolt, eyes widening as I whip my head toward the trees. "What was that?"

Henry doesn't seem the least bit rattled, though his muscles tense briefly beneath me. He listens for a second, then shrugs. "Probably a hutia."

I blink at him. "A hu-whata?"

"A hutia. They're nocturnal rodents—think big guinea pigs. They live on a bunch of Caribbean islands."

I stare at him, my entire body still on edge. "You're telling me there are *giant island rats* lurking in the woods right now?"

Henry chuckles and shakes his head. "Not rats. More like over-sized squirrels. They're harmless."

"Harmless," I echo, unconvinced. "Big island rats doesn't feel fucking harmless to me, Henry."

"They eat leaves. Not people." He smirks, tucking a stray piece of my hair behind my ear. "I promise, they're more afraid of you than you are of them."

"That's debatable," I mutter, still eyeing the darkened tree line.

He chuckles, his hand sliding into my hair like usual, fingers threading through the strands in lazy strokes. "You'll survive. I promise. And if one of those big island rats tries to ambush us, I've got your back."

I sigh, still a little wary but too tired to argue.

Henry exhales and shifts slightly. "Come on, let's go to bed."

I nod, slowly moving my limbs from their slumber enough to pull my body off his. I move to sitting but don't get much farther before Henry scoops me up in his strong arms and carries me.

If I weren't so tired, I'd fight it.

Or maybe I wouldn't. I don't know. The longer I'm here, the less I'm starting to understand.

Henry tucks us both into the tent and lies down in the center, pulling me into what's become our position. I rest my arm across his abs and my leg across his legs, tangling at the ankles. He plays with my hair with the hand behind my back, and I nuzzle into his chest until it feels like a nice pillow.

I'm undoubtedly getting the better end of the deal—all he gets is the hard ground.

And the familiarity of it all should be comforting, but my mind keeps replaying the moment that almost was. I shouldn't still be thinking about the way he looked at me. About the heat in his gaze. About how we've kissed before, yet *this*—this almost-kiss—felt entirely different.

I nuzzle into his chest, trying to focus on the steady rhythm of his breathing instead of the chaotic beat of my own heart.

"Hush now, little bird with special wings," Henry starts to sing, the mesmerizing lull of his voice putting me directly into my comfort zone just like it has for the last three nights. *"Rest your head and your mind, for now it's time. Close your eyes, and hush now, little bird with special wings."*

I let him get through another verse, sleep tugging at my every molecule, the soft pull of his fingers in my hair, and when he's about to start over, I ask the question I've been carrying since he sang this the first night.

"What is this song, Henry?" My voice feels harsh despite the softness of my whisper because of how silent it is around us, and his fingers pause in my hair for just the hint of a moment before continuing again.

"My mother used to sing it to put me to sleep when I was little."

I nod against his chest and then venture another question—one I know I probably don't have the right to ask, but one I've wondered about for a very long time. "What happened to her?"

"She left," he says simply. "My dad said she had a history of mental health problems, and something broke in her to where she couldn't handle being a mom anymore."

My heart beats fast with heartache and a laundry list of follow-up questions, but I don't ask any of them. I don't say anything. Between my swirling emotions, Henry's singing, and the heat of our tangled bodies, this tent feels full enough. So I just hold on to him tighter, like somehow, I can make up for all the years he went without.

"*Hush now, little bird with special wings,*" Henry sings again, and I cuddle a little tighter, close my eyes, and will myself to sleep like I'm supposed to.

But I do dream.

Of a mother I can't identify with at all. Of a mother who would leave someone like him behind even though Henry Callahan is *not* the person you leave.

He's the kind you stay for. He's the kind you stay for *forever.*

Chapter 11

January 5th

Henry

MORNING WOOD POUNDS FROM MY PANTS AS I SHIFT from my spot under Avery and settle her limbs into place to keep her comfortable enough to stay asleep.

It's amazing, really. After four whole days on this Caribbean island with limited resources, limited shelter, and limited water, my hunger cues have waned and my markers for thirst are in overdrive. My body has, by and large, clicked over into survival mode, and *yet* the biological drive to fuck lives on.

Sure, I've been sleeping every night with a painfully attractive, warm female draped over me, but I still can't get over the male body's dedication to its priorities in times like these.

I'd fucking laugh if it didn't hurt so much.

And maybe if I weren't still thinking about last night.

About the way she looked at me, her hazel eyes locked on mine, the space between us thinning, my brain short-circuiting as I got caught in the pull of something I knew damn well I shouldn't let happen.

But I almost did.

I almost kissed Avery Banks. *Again.*

And if it weren't for that rustling in the trees, I probably would have.

Which is the real kicker, because it's not like I don't know better. Avery is my best friend's little sister. Avery is trouble wrapped in expensive perfume and designer clothes. Avery is the one person I should not be thinking about like this.

And yet, here I am. With a hard-on that hurts like hell and thoughts that have no business lingering.

Once outside the tent, I adjust myself in my pants and will my balls to untwist themselves as I slather on some deodorant from Avery's waist pack we keep just outside under a sea grape leaf at the bottom of the neighboring palm. I run her toothbrush over my teeth using the teeniest bit of water from our hydration pack and then tuck both the brush and travel toothpaste inside.

As I'm zipping it up, I notice her phone for the first time since the no-service debacle and Avery's subsequent all-American rage, and I wonder briefly if it has any battery left. Not knowing what the future would hold, I convinced her to shut it down when she finished freaking out, but I don't know if it's done any good.

Will a phone hold charge for four days if it's turned off? Seeing as I never power down my stupid fucker, I have no clue.

Carefully pressing the button on the side to power it on, I wait while the apple symbol appears in the center, waiting for the boot up to show the percentage, and do a silent cheer when I see it still has nearly fifty percent. I'm surprised she doesn't have a passcode on it for security—and yet, not, at the same time. It's a little annoyance like this that Avery would see as trivial despite all the logical reasons to live with it.

I know we didn't find service here, but now that we've had the time to explore a little more, I'm wondering if we might catch a rogue signal from the ridgetop.

My stomach flips over on itself at the possibility and the need to know.

I shut the phone back off to conserve the battery as the signal symbol dances to indicate it's constantly searching, tuck the phone into my pocket, and peek in on Avery one more time. She's sleeping soundly, her hands folded in the prayer position under her cheek and her knees tucked up to her chest, and her face looks as relaxed as I've seen it since the moment we arrived.

Guilt swirls in my mind and runs down the line of my spine. I want to see if the ridgetop has a signal, but I don't want to over-inflate the amount of hope inside Avery, and the thought of waking her up while she's resting so peacefully doesn't feel good either.

The fact is, this whole thing is a long shot and a half, and a fuck of a workout just to give it a try. The heat of the day is going to build to unbearable levels soon, and if I don't make the climb now, it's going to be ten times worse than getting ass-fucked by a porcupine.

Avery doesn't move or shift at all, and her breathing is even as I check carefully for signs of stirring. She's out cold. I bet if I go now, I can probably be back before she even wakes up or, worst-case, not long after. And fuck, I hate to even think it, but maybe, just maybe, I'll get to see her pretty face light up when I surprise her with good news.

Decided, I grab our poker stick to use as an extra support in rough terrain and take off for the center of the island. The ridge base is only half a mile or so in, so the hike to get there takes no time at all. The ascent, however, is another story and proves much more difficult than I thought it would be. Without climbing gear, the quickest, shortest route is way too dangerous, the risk of injury too high. Knowing what's at stake, I opt for the longer, safer way instead.

If I broke a leg or injured myself beyond capability, I have no doubt Avery would rise to the occasion, but fuck, it sure would make things a hell of a lot harder and would drive me to the point of insanity. I've always felt a strong need to provide and protect, and taking a risk that would fuck that up is irresponsible.

I pay excruciating attention to detail on every step on my route, being mindful not to roll my fucking ankle or proceed farther unless the footing is sure. It takes a little over an hour to get to the top, but when I turn on Avery's phone and it works, my whole body tingles with the possibility that this trip might be worth it.

As I wait for the damn thing to find a signal, my eyes drift down to the beach, scanning the shoreline that has become our home for the past four days. That's when I see it—the massive *SOS* I carved into the sand with driftwood and palm fronds on the first day here.

The letters are still clear, still untouched by the tide, standing as a desperate message to anyone who might be flying overhead.

I remember the way Avery had just sat there, knees drawn to her chest, staring out at the horizon in stunned silence while I worked on it. She hadn't said a word, barely even blinked, still stuck in the kind of shock I'd never seen on her before. For as much as Avery likes to act like she doesn't take anything seriously, that first day proved otherwise. She was scared. Hell, we both were.

And looking at it now, I feel the weight of just how much we've adapted.

That panic from day one has settled into something else—survival. A rhythm. A routine. It's the kind of thing that should scare the hell out of me, but instead, I just feel frustrated that we still haven't been found.

I watch and wait with bated breath as the phone searches for service, but when the signal indicator is still doing the same dance a full minute later, my chest deflates in one fell swoop.

"Fuck," I mutter, holding it in the air and moving from one side of the ridge to the other in a weaving line. I try different angles and positions, but at the end of another ten minutes, the stupid thing is still searching for a signal.

Movements manic, all the hope leaves my body in a rush of adrenaline.

Nothing. There's fucking *nothing* we can do to help ourselves get found.

My chest feels tight, my emotions almost too heavy to hold.

"Fuck!" I say again, but this time, it's a ragged yell of raw frustration that shakes my whole chest and sends several birds flying for cover.

I clutch the phone in my grip and smash at the screen with my other hand, but when none of the blinding pressure of lost hope leaves my temples, I rear back and launch the fucking thing like I'm throwing a game-ending Hail Mary pass.

It rolls and spins and flashes in the now-risen sun, and I scream at the top of my lungs like a man deranged. It was a pipe dream and a fucking stupid hope, but I carelessly let myself get attached to the idea of it working, and the reality of it not stings like a son of a bitch.

My chest heaves and my heart races as I blink into the sun and wipe the growing sweat off my forehead with an agitated hand. I look out at the perfect blue ocean and spin around, taking in the full circumference of nothingness around us and wonder if there's anyone out there even remotely close looking for us.

I scan the horizon for boats and see nothing but endless ocean and the gentle spark of the reflecting sun. Nature, in all its unmarred beauty. It should be awe-inspiring, but all it's prompting in me right now is excruciating pain.

"I have to let go of the future," I say softly to myself, knowing from experience that wishing for something that'll never be only makes things worse. It never brought my mom back from her mental break, and it sure as hell hasn't resurrected my dad after the cancer killed him. "I have to focus on the here and now. I have to focus on helping myself and Avery survive."

It's resolute and reasonable and, thankfully, enough to calm me down again. Avery's phone is good and gone forever, something I know she won't like, but when we make it back home, I'll buy her another.

She can't call or text June. She can't check in with her mom. She can't call her dad and beg him to get us out of this. It's her and me and the here and now.

For the time being, all that stupid phone was doing was taunting us.

I take a final deep breath and prepare to make the trek back down.

Avery'll be looking for me, and being there for her is one of the only things I can control.

She's my priority.

And I'm going to make damn sure I do everything I can to protect her, keep her safe, *keep her alive.*

Wet from the heat and exertion, I emerge from the underbrush just behind the beach we've been inhabiting a little over an hour later. The heat is really working today, so I'm not surprised to see the fire unstoked. Not to mention, I took the poker with me as a walking cane, so I don't know what I would have expected her to use instead.

A soft snort of air leaves my nostrils as I shake my head at myself, my anxiety to see Avery and ground myself by giving her a hug at an overwhelming high.

I'm an independent guy, but it's amazing what being trapped somewhere with no idea when or if it'll end will do to your codependency.

Part of her routine in the mornings is going for a swim and a bath all in one, so I look to the water first, rounding our fire pit on the beach to get a view of the whole cove, but even after a thorough scan, I don't see her anywhere.

I've been gone too long for her to still be sleeping, but I check the tent anyway, the gnawing feeling in my gut growing in intensity with each passing second I don't find her. There's a small chance she would have gone to gather some breadfruit, but by and large, not seeing her immediately is completely out of the ordinary.

What if she did go swimming, but she got taken by the current or pushed under by a wave? Or woke up confused when I wasn't there and wandered off?

Fuck, I can't believe I thought it was a good idea to go to the top of the ridge without her—without telling her.

Concern ravaging my nerves, I call out her name. "Avery!"

She doesn't answer right away, so I call again, this time as loud as I can manage. "Avery! Where are you?"

I run into the water, splashing frantically and searching the white sand bottom for signs of her bright-orange bikini. I don't see it, which is an obvious fucking relief, but at the same time, my gut only feels heavier.

Where the fuck is she?

"Avery!" My scream is desperate and sore, and it's so loud, it nearly bursts my own ears.

"Henry?" I finally hear in response, the soft, muted sound coming from way in the distance around the natural rock jetty that acts as a wave break at the end of our beach.

Fuck, Avery.

"Oh my God!" she yells now, the volume escalating so much, the panic at its root is impossible to deny. I have a sudden feeling of impending doom I can't shake. Leaving without waking her up this morning wasn't kind; it was cruel.

I drop my stick and break into a run to head in her direction so I can cut her distance in half, cresting the jetty just as she's coming up the other side as well. Her face is red and her eyes are wide, and fear radiates like a painful swipe of a sword in the space between us.

I feel fucking sick to my stomach over the five minutes I've been searching for her since I returned, and I've been gone for *hours.*

"Oh God—"

"Where were you?" she yells harshly, the accusation and anguish in her voice locking up my throat. "I thought you were dead or missing or really, really hurt!"

"I'm sorry," I apologize as she shoves me in the chest in an attempt to storm past me. "Avery, I'm sorry."

Her sobs only heighten as I grab her by the wrist to stop her, and she claws and scratches at my arm to get away. Her reaction is big and dramatic and over the top, but what it isn't is manufactured or uncalled for. I can see the raw terror in her eyes and hear the hoarseness in her cries, and it's all my fault.

I've been gone for close to three hours at this point. Who knows how long she's been screaming my name—how long she's been scared to death.

Even as she fights, I pull her into my chest and put my hands to her chin to lift her gaze to my own. The whites of her eyes are bloodshot and tear-filled and hurt, and I hold them anyway, letting them lash me as a reminder for the future.

"I'm so sorry," I whisper. Her lip quivers. "I didn't think. I wanted to try to get cell service at the top of the ridge and you were still sleeping, so I didn't want to wake you. It was a terrible idea, and I promise I'll never do it again."

Her neck strains to fight from my grip, but I steady her, forcing her to hold my eyes as I swear it to her all over again. "I'll never leave again without telling you where I'm going. I promise."

"I hate you," she cries, pushing at my chest with her forearms. When we've fought before, I've given her all the space in the world, but right now, I know deep down what she needs is me.

Lord knows I sure as hell need her.

To feel her. To touch her. To convince myself and her and God above that we're both here and well and alive.

"I'm sorry, Avery. Fuck. I'm so sorry."

She cries harder, her lips quivering as she finally stops pushing herself away. I deserve a million and one insults, and I know for damn sure Avery has the vocabulary to come out with some good ones, but I fill the space between us with more promises instead.

"I'll never do it again. I swear. We're in this together, and from here on out, we do everything together."

I lean down and press my lips to hers, tasting the salt of her tears. It's chaste and, given the perspective of what we've just been through, innocent. But it's also a signature on the dotted line for everything I've sworn to uphold. It's a need for human connection.

It's a reminder of how simple life used to be—of everything Avery and I have always been without saying it.

Finally, she nods, pulling free and wiping at her nose with the back of her hand. "It didn't work, did it?"

"What?"

"The phone."

I shake my head, my hands settling on my hips. "I'll buy you a new one."

I don't explain where it went, and she doesn't ask. We're both too busy with the rest of the sentence left unspoken.

I'll buy you a new one…*if we ever make it back.*

Neither of us says it aloud, but it hangs there in the silence anyway, taunting us with uncertainty. Right now, all we have for sure is each other, and weirdly enough, I'm starting to understand why fate picked her.

Which is hilarious, considering four years ago, the night of our first-ever kiss, I told her she wasn't my type.

Laughable, right?

The fact is, the most blatant lies we ever tell are the ones we tell ourselves.

Chapter 12

The Past

Four years ago

Henry

THE SHOT OF FIREBALL BURNS DOWN THE BACK OF MY throat as I slam the glass on the knee-high table in our VIP booth and dance to DJ Johnny's fire remix of the song "Forever" by Diplo featuring Malou and Yuna.

Ronnie is dancing with a woman in a tight red dress that glitters under the lights, and Mav's shamelessly flirting with a pair of Aussie girls, their accents making him eat out of the palm of their tanned, red-nail-tipped hands. I watch for a second, shaking my head. Not surprising—Australia is full of dangerous predators after all. The women, apparently, are no exception.

Not that I blame them.

Mav and Ron are swimming in their liquor, so I might as well be here alone. Beau's definitely a better companion, but lately, he's been completely uninterested in wingman duties, and tonight, he didn't have any interest in coming out for Allure's grand opening at all.

I don't know what's gotten into him lately, but I swear he's turned into a full-on fucking hermit. Always tired. Always busy. Always talking about the fucking *Midnight* app he's in an all-out war to pitch against Seth McKenzie. I get it—Seth was the fifth in our now-foursome until he fucked Beau's girlfriend Bethany right out from under him—but damn, it'd be nice to have my friend back.

I barely get the thought out before Carly, our cocktail waitress and a woman I've hooked up with a time or two when she worked at Tau Tau, tugs on my arm, leaning in as DJ Johnny cranks the bass and neon lights strobe across the floor. "You want any more bottles of anything? They're doing last call soon."

I'm already half cooked, and Ronnie and Mav are well and truly gone, so I slice a finger across my throat and wink at Carly.

She nods and sashays down the stairs to the dance floor, and I follow her with my eyes until she passes Beau's sister Avery, dancing with half the motherfucking University of Alabama football team in her tiny gold-mesh dress.

Avery throws her head from side to side, her brown hair arcing above her, and her dress rides up to the top of her tanned thighs. One guy grinds at the back of her, but she essentially ignores him, laughing and screaming with one of her girlfriends when they bump into her space with their dance partner.

I lean into the railing at the front of the booth and rub a thumb across my bottom lip as an uninvited flash of her black thong peeks out from the bottom of the back of her dress.

I tell myself to look away.

Instead, my jaw ticks.

She's hot, and she definitely knows it, which I can only imagine is what made my ego tell her she wasn't my fucking type in the elevator of her condo earlier when Beau and her best friend Juniper decided to stay in instead of joining us.

The truth is, Avery Banks is everyone's type. The real problem is that very few can actually handle her.

Self-confident, wild, uninhibited—she's the kind of strong woman who scares people.

Carly comes back with the tab for a signature, so I take it and scribble my name across it before signaling to Mav and Ron that I'm going to hit the dance floor for a few minutes before we drop out.

They both wave me off, occupied with their girls or whatever, so I go on my own, navigating the writhing bodies on the floor with relative ease until I make it to the center. Avery still dances with the football players and her friends, and I find a redhead looking for a partner several feet away.

This woman has rhythm and a banging body, and we fall into an easy cadence with each other. I like the way she moves her hips, and I tell her so as I settle my chin into her neck from behind. Her head drapes back, her hair cascading down my chest, and her eyes fall closed as she shakes against me.

From this angle, I have a view of Avery, who's no longer dancing with the football players but moving seductively by herself, her eyes focused solely on me.

It'd be easy to overthink it a million ways, but I don't.

"Thanks for the dance," I tell the redhead, stepping around her and heading straight for Avery ten feet away.

"Couldn't resist me?" Avery taunts the second I reach her, her lips curving as I grab her hips and pull her into me, making us sway together.

I laugh, conceding, "I guess not."

She grins like she just won something. "Get ready then, Henny," she says, leaning in so close I catch the seductive floral scent of her perfume. "You've never been danced with like this."

I chuckle. "Oh yeah? That right?"

She nods, backing up just enough to drag a single finger down the center of my chest, her nails grazing my skin through my shirt. Then, she moves.

Slow. Controlled. *Dangerous.*

She shakes her hips and bends slightly at the waist, and her eyes are coy as they look up at me through her lashes. It's ridiculously fucking sexy, and admittedly, I'm starting to think she's right about never experiencing this before.

And all I can see is miles upon miles of her gorgeous, perfect skin as the slinky gold dress she's wearing effectively disappears.

Her hands find their way into her hair, and she stands upright and winks, turning her back to me as she rolls her body in time with mine. She turns back toward me and presses her perfect curves against my body like it's the most natural thing in the world. And fuck, maybe it is, because I find myself pulling her in tighter, digging my fingers into her waist as we move in perfect tempo.

And then, she just looks at me.

No smirks, no games, no taunts—just Avery.

She holds my gaze for a long moment before putting a hand to my face and pulling it to her own, our lips clashing in an unexpected, tongue-filled kiss.

I feel it fucking *everywhere*. Hell, my whole damn body comes alive, and my heart pounds hard in my chest as she pulls back like nothing happened and goes back to doing her sexy little dance.

The fuck was that?

Thoughts race through my head about kissing my best friend's little sister and all the implications of that, and when she finally turns to face me again, I bring it up.

"Avery, you just kissed me."

She laughs and shrugs. "So?"

"So, you're Beau's little sister."

She smiles demurely, getting in my face and putting her lips almost to mine again. The song pounds around us, and I hold my breath, waiting to see what'll happen.

"Don't worry about it, Henny. I kiss everybody."

Evidently feeling the need to prove her point, she spins around and grabs the first football player she sees and pulls him in for a kiss.

My jaw clenches. My body tenses. And the cruel scene mocks my careless dance with potential feelings.

I take it as my cue to leave.

Because in Avery's world, it's hard to believe there'll ever be just one man.

Chapter 13

DAY SEVEN.

I know because I've been keeping track, carving small tick marks into the trunk of a palm tree near our camp. It started out as something to do—something to ground me when everything felt surreal. But now, a full week into this nightmare, I found myself staring at those seven tiny slashes this morning, trying to wrap my head around how quickly everything can change.

A week ago, I was cruising around Miami in my G-Wagon, spending my dad's money, shopping for gifts for my soon-to-be nephew, and avoiding any real responsibility.

Now? I'm *here*.

And I'm half drunk off shipwreck bourbon that made its way on shore this morning while I was sitting in the sand watching Henry fish.

Thankfully, Henry hasn't said much about my behavior, but I know he has to have noticed how closely I'm following him around these days. We're practically freaking leashed at this point, like those kids with the little teddy bear backpacks in the airport. I know it, and yet I haven't been able to stop.

He ended up catching one fish after three long hours of trying, which we shared promptly, but for as good as he is at everything else, catching these little finned fuckers doesn't seem to be getting easier.

Still, despite the hardship, we're ending the day with food and booze, and as such, we decided to have a little party tonight.

Okay, I decided to have a party, and Henry, as luck would have it, is a very captive audience.

A captive audience that is currently shirtless, sweat-slicked, and sitting right beside me. I discreetly glance at the way his muscles glisten beneath the firelight and wonder if being stranded isn't *entirely* the worst thing to ever happen to me.

Of course, there's no cushy couch, VIP section, or dark, pounding dance floor, and my get-ready-with-me routine was severely lacking in makeup and hair products, but the company is nice, *annoyingly hot*, and I look toned, tanned, and skinnyyy in my bikini, so I'm not complaining.

I unscrew the cap of the bottle of Evan Williams and take another long, slow swig. The burn races down my throat, warming my insides, loosening my limbs, and making everything feel a little too good.

Henry pokes at the fire with our stick, his bare chest illuminated by the golden-orange glow. His muscles ripple with every movement, the flames casting sharp shadows over his sculpted abs and broad shoulders. The scruff on his jaw has grown into an all-out beard, thick enough now that he looks less like my brother's best friend and more like some rugged, untamed lumberjack, ready to throw me over his shoulder and carry me off into the woods.

Goodness.

I lick my lips, tearing my eyes away before I say or do something dangerously inappropriate. Normally, when I drink, I kiss. *Lots.*

I'm also not usually a bourbon girl, but then again, I'm not usually a stranded-on-an-island girl either, and look how that turned out.

At least the company is good, if slightly lacking in volume.

"I guess our pilot liked booze enough to carry it on his plane, huh?" I question quietly, still watching Henry mess with the fire, my words half to myself at this point. I don't know that I've felt this free since before I woke up to thinking Henry was dead two mornings ago. I'm a quarter of the bottle deep, and everything feels pleasurably numbed—except for the growing heat low in my stomach every time my gaze lands back on him.

"I guess." Henry shrugs, indulging me. "I've only flown with Mario a few times, but I've never seen him drink on the job."

I hum, watching his hands, the way they move when he talks—strong, tanned fingers that could probably break me in half if he wanted to. *There's a lot of things I wouldn't mind him doing to me with those fingers of his…*

I clear my throat and force my focus elsewhere. "What do you think happened to him?" I ask. "To Mario?"

Henry leans forward, draping his forearms over his knees, his muscles tensing with the movement. "Probably a heart attack. Maybe a stroke," he says, his voice low, rough, like the subject isn't easy for him. Which I understand. It's hard to think about the fact that Mario died. I didn't know him at all, and yet there's a part of me that feels so guilty for the way we had to leave him.

"Honestly, I don't know," Henry adds, meeting my eyes for a brief moment. "I'm not entirely sure, but he was unresponsive with no pulse when I got to him. I don't think there's anything we could have done to help him even if the plane hadn't been in a dive."

I nod and swallow hard against the emotion that is now threatening to creep up my throat. I don't know anything about Mario. I don't know if he had a wife or kids or grandkids. But I do know that I wish his life hadn't ended the way it did.

Rest in peace, Mario, I silently pray and raise the bottle toward the fire in a quiet toast, "To Mario," before taking another swig of comfort to settle my always-ragged nerves.

Henry reaches for the bottle with a waggle of his fingers, and I hand it to him without complaint. As much as I'd love to down the whole thing myself, sharing fluids is an unspoken agreement these days.

He raises it to the fire just like I did, repeating my toast. "To Mario!" He takes a swig of his own and then sets the bottle down on the other side of his thigh, just out of my reach.

I narrow my eyes.

He must think I won't notice as he pretends to yawn and stretch like Mr. fucking Magoo, casually blocking my access to the booze. *Oh, hell no.*

I hold out my fingers toward him, wiggling them in demand, but he has the audacity to ignore me completely.

"Excuse me," I snap. "Are you trying to steal my booze?"

He sighs. "I know you're going to hate this, but I think you've probably had enough for tonight. Tomorrow's another day, and your stomach isn't exactly full right now."

"I'm not hungry," I protest. "You caught that fish earlier, and I had some breadfruit."

Henry gives me the look. The one that's equal parts exasperation and amusement, like he knows me better than I know myself.

"Please, Ave?" he says then, his voice lower, softer, almost coaxing. "I don't want to worry about you tonight."

I stop short.

Something about the way he says it settles inside my chest. It's completely unexpected but totally expected at the same time—*he's worried about me.*

And for some reason, that makes me feel warm in an entirely different way that the bourbon hasn't been able to achieve.

Maybe I'm turning over a new leaf or something, but I surprise both myself and him by agreeing. "Fine. I'll save it. But if we go another week here without getting rescued, I'm downing the rest of the fucking bottle, and there's nothing you can do to stop me."

Henry chuckles, shaking his head. "Deal."

I sigh and fall back into the sand, looking up at the sky, at the endless blackness stretching above us, at the way the stars are scattered across it like diamonds on velvet. "You know, for all the bullshit we're dealing with, I have to admit… This view is insane."

Henry tilts his head back, glancing up toward the heavens. "Yeah. I guess it is."

I shift my body so that I can watch him watch the sky, and my focus trails down to his sharp jawline, the slope of his nose, the cut of his throat.

God, he's hot.

I press my thighs together, heat burning low in my stomach, a mix of liquor and desire stirring up bad decisions inside me. Good grief, I need to do something with this energy.

"So, what am I supposed to do now?" I question. "I'm not ready to go to bed, and you took away the booze. I'm tired of being bored."

"We can talk."

"Ugh," I gag. "More talking. Talking, talking, talking, it's all we *do* these days."

Henry laughs. "All right, then. What do you want to do?"

I pause, considering.

Then, the best idea I've had in a long time crashes into me like a tidal wave.

I grin at him. "I know!" I say, giddy with inspiration. I sit up straight quickly, and Henry's eyes flare at the sudden movement. "Let's have sex!"

"*What?*" His voice cuts through the quiet night like a gunshot, and I have to laugh at how scandalized he looks.

Henry Callahan—seasoned playboy, known ladies' man, a guy who has undoubtedly seen more pussy than the ASPCA—is looking at *me* like I just suggested we commit a federal crime. It's like me saying I want to have sex has turned him into a schoolmarm.

I don't get it.

"*What*, what? You heard me." I tilt my head, smirking as I move closer to him, liking the way his throat bobs when I do. "We should have sex. It'd be fun, probably feel *really* good, and would definitely be less boring than sitting here watching you poke a damn fire." I gesture vaguely to his abs, his broad chest, the way the firelight twinkles against his ridiculously sculpted body. "I mean, look at you. You're a walking, talking thirst trap. And judging by your track record, I'd say you've got enough experience to make it worth my while."

His brows furrow, like he's actually offended. "Track record? How many people do you think I've slept with?"

"Oh, puh-lease." I snort. "Don't try to play innocent with me, Callahan. I have eyes. And I've known you forever." I raise a brow. "We both know you've banged your way through a whole fucking squad."

His mouth twists in amusement. "Maybe I'm an illusionist, like you. Maybe I just like kissing all these women."

I narrow my eyes. "Are you?"

"Well, no. But that's not the point."

I guffaw. "It's almost like the entire point, Henry!" I shove to my feet and hold out a hand, swaying only a *littlllle* bit from the booze. I try my damnedest to conceal it before he gets all high and mighty about being honorable and sober and responsible and shit.

The last thing I need is for Mr. All-of-a-Sudden-Honorable-and-Responsible to latch on to that and turn this into some stupid lesson about good decision-making.

"Come on, Henry." I extend a beckoning hand, grinning like I just solved world peace. "Let's go have sex."

"Avery…" He scrubs a hand down his face and sighs heavily.

"What now?" I blow out a frustrated breath from pursed lips. "What possible excuse could you have?"

"You're a virgin, Avery."

"Uh. Yeah. I know. I am the bearer of the hymen after all."

His jaw clenches. "Then you have to know it's not just as simple as saying, *Hey, let's go do it.* There are consequences. Things that it will change."

I scoff. "It's only complicated if we make it complicated. We're just two bodies, passing the time."

"We're going to get off this island, Avery." His voice has the kind of careful cautiousness that grates on my nerves. I don't want to overanalyze this shit. I just want to…escape. "And then what?" he questions. "Will you regret it then?"

I cross my arms. "Why are you making such a big deal out of this?"

"Because," he snaps, running a frustrated hand through his hair, "I can't handle the thought of you regretting it and deciding never to talk to me again." His words come out raw and unfiltered, the sharp edges of his restraint fraying. "I get that it'd be easier—that it would make this whole situation easier if you had someone to hate or blame or lash out at. But God, Avery…" He exhales, shaking his head. "I…I can't have you hating me. I can't."

And just like that, the weight of it all slams into me.

The air between us shifts, heavier than before.

I stare at him, my pulse hammering, the firelight casting shadows over his sharp features—the cut of his jaw and the heat in his stormy blue eyes.

And fuck, I *want* him.

I want him so badly it's making my head spin.

I swallow hard. "That'll never happen, Henry. I swear." And I mean it so deeply that my whole body shakes.

Two days ago, when I thought he was hurt or missing or… *dead*…I realized a lot of things about Henry I'll never be able to forget. Rich or poor, healthy or sick, happy at home or stuck on this godforsaken island, Henry Callahan is the kind of man you ride or die for. He says what he means. Does what he says.

And I can't imagine a world without him in it.

Fighting the overwhelming emotion of everything I've been working so hard to drown in bourbon, I suck my lips into my mouth, my next words no louder than a whisper. "I don't know if we'll ever get rescued."

His gaze darkens. "Avery…"

"I don't. And you don't either. But either way, this is something that's happened to both of us. Something we can't go back from." I exhale, stepping closer and kneeling before him until I slide my body between his opened thighs. "You will always be part of my life. No matter what. Okay?"

He stares at me, hard, then finally nods. "Okay."

I smile. "Good." Then, without missing a beat, I grin wickedly and waggle my brows. "Now, let's go have sex."

"Avery!" Henry lets out a strangled sound, something between a laugh and a groan, rubbing a hand down his face.

"Oh, come on!" I push, desperate for the connection, desperate for the distraction—desperate for something that'll make me feel *alive*.

I graze my fingertips down his bare stomach, and heat coils in my belly at the way his muscles tense under my touch.

"What are you so afraid of, Henry?" I question, locking my gaze firmly with his. "Do you think I'm going to fall in love with you or something?"

Chapter 14

AVERY'S WORDS HANG IN THE AIR LIKE THE MORNING MIST of yesterday, begging me to take the bait.

Do you think I'm going to fall in love with you or something?

It's a pointed question—one I know from years of experience with her personality that she's crafted with the intention of creating a challenge. She's daring me to turn down the unobjectionable, but in the process, forgetting all the other things I know.

For one, she's more than a little tipsy, and for two, I can see the mania in her eyes as a surge of dwindling hope ravages her nervous system unchecked.

She doesn't know if we're ever getting out of here, and frankly, neither do I. And while I'm not sure that either of us is falling in love, I know for a fact we're getting *attached*—I mean, I sure as hell am—and the thought of ruining that bond for one stupid night is almost unbearable.

I believe she wants to have sex; I just don't think she'll be able to stop herself from regretting it.

"I'm not afraid of you falling in love with me." I can hardly imagine Avery wants to fall in love with anyone. "But I am worried you're making a rash decision that you'll regret later, and I don't want to be forever associated with something so hugely negative in your life."

She huffs, rolling her eyes, but the way she shifts closer and the way her fingers trail along my bare stomach again, slow and teasing, tells me she's not backing down.

"You're reading way too much into this," she argues, her voice silky as she leans in, pressing her body flush against mine.

Her lips hover dangerously close to my neck, and the heat from her bare skin radiates through me like an electrical current.

"I'm not a *fair maiden of delicate disposition,*" she continues, mocking an old-English accent like she's in a damn Shakespearean play. "I'm a woman. A very sexual woman who just so happens to have avoided cashing in her V-card for entirely too long."

Fuck. I swear, if anyone else were saying this to me, I'd already be taking off my pants.

But this is Avery.

And Avery is different.

She's so close now that if I just tilted my chin forward, our lips would be touching. Her eyes dance with something flirtatious, something daring, something unmistakably Avery. They are a stark reminder of how her gaze looked during all of our almost-some-things of the past.

The way she's looking at me right now is damn near lethal.

And her body? *God help me.*

Her legs look miles long, smooth and tanned from the island sun, with nothing but a cerulean-blue bikini bottom standing between me and a terrible decision.

"I won't regret doing this with you," she says slowly, her voice clear and seemingly lucid, despite the bourbon.

She's sultry as she leans in farther, hands settling on my shoulders, her cashmere sweater gaping like a balloon away from her chest. The collar is all stretched out, making it impossible to avoid seeing her bare breasts and peaked nipples underneath.

I force my gaze to her face.

Big mistake.

Her lips are parted just enough, her breathing just a little shallow, and her gaze is locked on mine like she's challenging me to move first.

"I'd regret doing it with some skeezeball, three-balled hump machine whose sweat smells like gym socks and decomposing skunk." She shrugs. "But not you. We're friends. I trust you. You're safe."

I'm safe. It's a high compliment from a tough critic, and for the first time since she started trying to convince me, I'm actually considering if we could…*maybe*…make this work.

I don't think it's my dick talking, but to be fair, a lot of the blood supply normally finding its way to my brain is trapped in his head instead.

Without thinking, I move my hands to her legs, sliding over the soft skin of her thighs. The second I touch her, her smile grows, her eyes flickering with something victorious, wicked, *knowing.*

She straddles me, her thighs pressing against mine, and fuck, *she feels so good.*

My hands settle naturally at her hips, and she drapes her arms over my shoulders, crossing them lightly behind my neck.

I squeeze her hips, steadying her, steadying myself, but nothing about this feels steady.

It feels like standing at the edge of a fucking cliff, ready to jump without a bungee cord.

Her gaze is still locked with mine and her face is soft, and I find myself trapped in the firelit twinkle of her perfectly green-brown eyes. "Come on, Henny. The two of us together? You know it'll be good."

I laugh, but it comes out hoarse, strained. *Good?* Yeah. Between my experience and her raw, sexual charisma, it would be cataclysmic.

Which is exactly the issue.

"I'm sure it would be."

"So…" She coyly digs her teeth into her bottom lip. "What's the problem?"

"The same problem I told you before and you willfully ignored," I murmur, my fingers tightening on her waist. "Everything about this is complicated—the people, the situation...the alcohol swimming in your bloodstream."

She licks her lips with just the tip of her pink tongue, and my eyes immediately drop to her plush mouth.

"Okay," she says slowly, her voice dropping an octave until it sounds smooth like honey. "I'll give you that. And if this were a first-time encounter, I'd even agree with it. But this isn't new—this chemistry between the two of us..."

She leans in, her lips nearly brushing mine, and fuck, I almost stop breathing.

"We've walked these streets before, Henny," she whispers directly into my ear. "Remember Allure?"

I nod, my eyes narrowing slightly while my fingertips flex into the skin of her hips. "Of course I do. I remember you kissing me, telling me you kiss everyone, and then kissing some football player. You didn't choose me because I was safe. I was just a toy in the playpen."

"Fine." She rolls her eyes but doesn't pull away. "What about Halloween, then? You can't say that about that night, and you know it."

I tense.

She's right. That's a different story. Halloween four years ago, at her parents' annual costume bash, when Beau ditched me, Ronnie, and Mav for June—which none of us knew at the time—something happened between us.

Something I can't ignore.

Something I don't want to ignore.

Hell, it's something I've tried to ignore for way too long.

The concept of Avery and me isn't new.

Quite frankly, Avery Banks and Henry Callahan has been a hell of a long time coming.

Chapter 15

The Past

Halloween, four years ago

Henry

BODIES IN VARIOUS STATES OF UNDRESS LITTER THE BANKSES' living room, tucking themselves into every available corner and lounging on every empty surface.

The sexy kitten, Spider-Dominatrix, and seductive witch I was talking to when I arrived have all gone out the back door to smoke, and because I don't like to pigeonhole myself—or partake—I've decided to use the opportunity to get my bearings.

I lost Beau—dressed like some kind of fucking turn-of-the-century dude in tight pants, a ruffly shirt, and a long-ass coat—to the crowd nearly as soon as we arrived, and because of the quick convo with the skimpy trio, I haven't had a proper chance to scout the other talent either.

Beau's mom and dad, Neil and Diane, are holding court with the middle-aged crowd by the back patio doors, and a group of goblins stands at the kitchen island picking at the expensive grazing table full of finger foods, fancy cheeses, and processed meats. Because of the open concept floor plan, you can see almost the entirety of the living area at once, save the main entrance and grand staircase that leads up to the bedrooms and the half bath and utility rooms in the back, and that makes for one hell of a party house—which is exactly how this family uses it.

Beau and I have been friends since we were kids, the Bankses have lived in this house for as long as I've known them, and I've attended at least three parties a year in this very space.

I have memories in every room, and coming here always strikes me with the warmest sense of nostalgia. I spent nearly as many days here, surfing and paddleboarding and generally fucking off, as I did at home, and because of that and Neil and Diane's unbelievably welcoming nature, I'll always feel comfortable here.

I swing by the kitchen for a beer and then head into the foyer to check out another sector of the crowd, spotting Beau's little sister Avery as she comes out of the half bath down the hall.

She's wearing a saloon-style red dress that cuts up to the top of her thigh, and her long brown hair is curled and hanging down around her shoulders. Ronnie sneaks up behind her and pokes her in the side, and she squeals in terror as he runs away to high-five Mav, who's waiting at the front door so the two of them can duck outside. If I had to guess, they're headed for the tall trees by the front gate to light up a blunt away from all the Bankses' carefully placed security cameras.

Weed's never been my thing, but Ronnie and Mav will smoke the shit out of it, especially when they're drinking.

"My God, it's like *Animal House*," Avery remarks to a random girl beside her, garnering a smile and a laugh, and moving my attention fully back to her.

She pulls at the red silk gloves that reach up to her elbows, looking down in concentration as she walks toward me, so I post up on a spot against the wall, leaning my shoulders into the surface and crossing my arms over my chest. She looks up again—and even glances toward me—but doesn't immediately recognize me because of my mask. I whistle to grab her attention, and she jerks to a stop right in front of me.

"Oh my God, Henry?"

I laugh. "That's Zorro to you."

"Holy shit! Zorro?" she keens. "I wanted my date to be Zorro to go with my Elena De la Vega, but he's a stupid idiot and thought it wasn't cool enough!"

"What's not cool about a sword and Catherine Zeta-Jones?" I ask incredulously.

"Right?" She laughs. "I mean, hello!"

"Where's this tragic excuse for a man now?" I ask, looking behind her but not seeing an obvious companion anywhere.

She chuffs. "I got rid of him. He came as Hulk, and he kept getting green body paint everywhere."

"So, now you're alone?" I ask, tsking.

"Oh, Henry. I'm *never* alone." She flashes a sexy wink. "Just reopened to possibilities."

Her perspective is cute and makes me laugh. "Well, I can't seem to find Beau, and Ronnie and Mav just left to get high with some chick in a Hello Kitty costume, so if you want, you can hang out with me."

"We do look like we match," she hums thoughtfully, looking around at the same time. "You know, I haven't seen June in forever either. I wonder where the hell she went."

I shrug. "Want to get a drink?"

"Always," Avery agrees.

"What's your poison?"

"Prosecco. Tonight is a night of lots and lots of prosecco."

I laugh. "That's easy enough."

Avery leads the way, walking back to the kitchen in front of me, and I put a soft hand to the small of her back to guide her there. She smiles and waves at dozens of people on the way—all of whom have been friends of her family for years—and I jerk my chin when it's someone I recognize too.

Bottles of prosecco are lined up on the counter by the sink, so I skirt by to pour her a glass and then come back to join her by the kitchen island. It's crowded, though, and I feel surprisingly claustrophobic.

"Let's go out back," she suggests, obviously feeling the same way.

"Good idea."

Music pounds softly from the patio speakers, but the overall din of noise is much more tolerable. I find a spot to stand in the corner by the built-in grill, leaning my hip into the counter and inviting Avery to stand in front of me.

She leans in close, always flirting, no matter the occasion.

"Ave," I say in warning, knowing the last time we got this close to each other, it ended in a kiss.

She laughs. "What?" Her smile is coy. "Relax, Henny." It's a silly nickname she's used in the past to annoy me, but for some reason, right now, my body tightens at the sound of it. "We're just talking."

"Uh-huh," I reply, a grin of my own settling into one corner of my mouth. She's hard to resist; I'll give her that. "And what exactly are we talking about?"

"Life. Lust. Louboutins. You tell me."

I chuckle. "How about work? How's it feel to be out of college and officially in the workforce?"

She frowns, pouting. "Everything I said was fun. Why'd you have to go and ruin it with words like *work* and *workforce*? Ugh. Yuck."

I sigh with humor, leaning my head back a little and closing my eyes slightly.

But when I open them again, Avery's lips are on mine.

I resist, though, admittedly, it's hard, pushing her back slightly until our breath mingles and our mouths are an inch or two apart. "What are you doing, Ave?"

"Kissing," she says simply, swaying toward me and enveloping me in the scent of roses.

"You kiss everyone," I say, repeating what she told me at Allure just weeks ago.

She shakes her head and gets closer, her lips brushing mine again as she speaks. "Not tonight." She bites at my bottom lip, and my whole body spikes into a rolling tingle.

"Avery." It's a whisper. A plea. I don't know for what, but she makes her own conclusions.

"Right now, I only want to kiss you."

I close the distance this time, taking her mouth with mine and melding the front of her body to my own. She tastes like prosecco and trouble, and apparently, I really fucking like both.

On instinct, my hands find her hips, and I pull her body flush against me. Our lips caress and our tongues dance, and I get lost in the moment as everything around us fades away.

The kiss goes on and on, a perfect loop of heat and hunger, with no clear beginning and no foreseeable end. The only thing keeping me from losing myself completely is the cold, unyielding counter pressed against my back.

And then, just as suddenly as she started it, Avery pulls away.

She's breathless, her lips swollen, her cheeks flushed. But it's her eyes that stop me cold—wide, unfocused, different. Like she's just realized something big.

Her usual flirtatious, teasing smile? Gone. And with it, every bit of certainty I've ever had about anything.

She stares at me for half a second—long enough to make my heart slam against my ribs—then spins on her heel and disappears back into the house.

I don't chase her. I can't.

Instead, I just stand there, staring after her like an idiot, my pulse pounding in my ears.

What the fuck was that?

That wasn't just a kiss. That was something else entirely.

That was a whole new fucking world.

And for some reason, I get the sinking fucking feeling Avery Banks is never, ever going to let it happen again.

Chapter 16

"**I**'VE SPENT YEARS RESISTING THIS, AVERY. RESISTING YOU. But fuck, I can't do it anymore."

The words barely leave Henry's lips before he yanks me tighter against him, his grip on my hips firm and possessive. My back bows as he pulls us closer together, the hot centers of our laps matching up right along with our chests.

My breath comes in pants as the reality that I've finally convinced him hits me, and my head swims with the imaginings of what happens from here. Henry's blue eyes burn a hundred degrees hotter than usual, and, considering he's a man with a smolder that could already kill, that's really saying something.

The heat. The tension. The unrelenting, pulsing need that's been burning between us for years. All of it is undeniable now.

There's no stopping this.

"You can change your mind." His voice drops, low and steady, a whisper of raw, unshakable resolve.

He's giving me the choice, making sure I know I have an out, but his grip on me and the way his fingers are tangled in my hair are possessive in a way that screams *mine*. And hell's bells, it only makes my need for him grow to a level I've never ever experienced with a man.

"Any time, no matter how far we go," he continues. "You can always change your mind."

He's still a gentleman, still putting me first. And if that weren't already enough to convince me that Henry Callahan is the right choice, the way he's looking at me? The way his body anchors me, protects me, worships me without even touching me yet?

It's more than enough.

It's *everything*, and it confirms that he's safe.

I should've never run away from whatever this is between us at that Halloween party over four freaking years ago.

I mean, *Gah*, he was the Antonio Banderas to my Catherine Zeta-Jones, and the kiss we shared nearly put me on my ass. All of that should have been a damn sign.

I nod, our foreheads brushing, our breaths tangling. "I know. And thank you. Thank you for being everything I already knew you were."

His jaw flexes, his grip on me tightening. "Avery."

"Kiss me, Henry."

He doesn't hesitate. Lacing his fingers into the loose hair at the back of my head, Henry pulls my face toward his until his mouth claims mine. My belly feels firm and buoyant all at once, and my arms ache to wrap around him tighter.

I clutch his back as he presses our lips together, my eyes falling closed in sweet surrender as we give ourselves over to the moment completely.

I've kissed a million times before.

But never like this.

Never like this.

All the air in my lungs leaves, which is funny, because somehow, I still feel like I can breathe—feel like our connection is what's keeping me alive. Henry's fingers spasm at the back of my head, and I fight to get our mouths even closer, even though I'm fairly certain I'm already swallowing him whole.

I moan, and he disconnects our mouths briefly, sucking at the skin of my neck to the point that I know I'm going to have a hickey. *He's marking me, and I fucking love it.* But also, I can't imagine I taste good after this many days without a full-blown shower, so I try to give him an out.

"You don't have to…like…kiss me all over. I'm sure it tastes like dirt and sweat and ocean."

"Yeah. Fuck that." His voice is gritty, primal, and he leans back to force my gaze to his.

He searches my eyes for a long moment, and then he grips me snugger, pulling us impossibly close together. "If I'm going to have you, I'm going to *taste* you," he says and leans forward to nip and suck at my neck again. "Every inch, every fucking gorgeous part."

He leans back again to lock our gazes. "I don't give a fuck if you're sweaty or salty or dirty." His breath scorches my skin, his lips moving back up, hovering at my ear. "Your skin is still like fucking candy."

Holy fucking hell. With a speech like that, far be it for me to disagree. "Well, okay then."

"You're mine tonight, Ave." Henry's words are a low growl against my skin, his voice the perfect combination of rough and commanding and sex and sin. His grip tightens on my hips, and his body cages me in, holding me exactly where he wants me—so much so that I can feel the hardness of his cock through his pants pressed firmly against my already throbbing clit.

And fuck if I don't love it.

A shiver rolls through me, my skin hypersensitive, my nipples straining against the fabric of my shirt. The weather-worn cashmere of my sweater feels suddenly overstimulating, so I lean back enough to pull it off over my head, exposing the tanned skin of my chest, shoulders, and stomach to him.

Henry's gaze darkens, his nostrils flaring, his hands sliding up my ribs, his thumbs brushing the undersides of my breasts.

"Yeah." His voice is pure sin. "I hold my position on this one. Your body is perfect."

I smile; I can't help it. I fucking love compliments. I flutter my lashes at him. "Go on."

Henry chuckles, his lips curling with amusement, and his eyes flicker up to mine for a split second before he takes my nipple between his lips. His mouth is a comfort I don't expect. I don't know if it's because of the kisses we've shared in the past, but the familiarity is tangible despite the time I've spent avoiding him since that Halloween four years ago.

His tongue swirls and teases my sensitive flesh, and I swear, my brain short-circuits. It's the sweetest form of torture, and a gasp tears from my throat as my back arches and presses even closer to his chest.

I don't know how he manages it, but with little fuss or even a groan, he gets to his feet without separating our bodies, and I wrap my legs around his waist to cross my ankles at his back.

He walks us toward the tent, his movements steady, controlled, strong. I clutch at his shoulders, my fingertips sinking into the ridges of his muscles, my lips seeking out his neck, his jaw, his mouth—wherever I can reach, wherever he'll let me consume him.

Henry gently falls to his knees in front of our structure, my position around his waist unchanged. With one hand, he pulls back the flaps of the leaves, and with the other, he braces his movements as he scoots us inside on his knees. I hold on to his neck like a lifeline, kissing at the skin of his now-bearded face.

I can't even remember a time in my life when Henry's had a beard, but it doesn't matter; he makes anything look good.

Dirt, sweat, several pounds down—he's still the ultimate male specimen.

And tonight, *he's mine.*

Using care not to scratch my bare back against the sea grape leaves we have on the floor, Henry adjusts me gently into the middle of the tent and follows me in, the weight of his warm body covering me entirely.

All I can see are the care and comfort of his blue eyes. But also, there's a pure fire there that lies beneath his irises, searing into me like they've already decided, tonight, I belong to him.

And God, I do.

I rub at his dried-out lips with a careful finger, knowing he's been withholding most of the water we collect every day for me. "Thank you for taking care of me, Henry," I whisper into the quiet.

There's no music, no TV in the background—nothing to drown out the sound of our excited breaths other than the soft lull of the lapping ocean outside.

"It's been an honor and a privilege. And I know that might sound cheesy or—"

"No," I cut in before he can walk back the best thing anyone's ever said to me. "It's…unbelievably romantic and, dare I say, perfect for the occasion."

Henry's answering smile is captivating, but I can't go another second without feeling his mouth on mine again. Pulling him by the neck, I touch our lips together until he takes control of the kiss, sweeping his tongue into my mouth and running it the length of mine.

As it turns out, the toothbrush I tossed into my waist pack on a whim before we left is one of the best boons of the whole ordeal. We've shared it, keeping the hygiene of our mouths up to the point that neither of us even has bad breath.

Henry's hands cascade down the bare skin of my sides to my hips and stop, his fingers tugging gently at the now-looser straps of my bikini bottom. I raise my butt to help, and he pulls them down and off, moving his body back enough to get them over my feet and then settling back on top of me.

I should feel exposed, but I don't. I feel incredibly, undeniably secure.

Nuzzling my neck for a moment and then moving to my chest, Henry kisses my skin like it's porcelain. I can see his lips against me, and yet it feels like I'm watching someone else. Truly, I almost don't recognize myself, I'm so tanned.

"You're beautiful, Avery."

"You're pretty handsome yourself."

Henry chuckles. "I thought you were tired of talking?"

"This talking feels different."

He nods. "Yeah."

Slowly but surely, his mouth works down my body until stopping at the apex of my thighs. My situation is thankfully still pretty situated, given my Brazilian wax right before New Year's, but I have a feeling even if it weren't, Henry wouldn't mind.

He's not one of the pompous pricks I normally spend my time running around with; he's a real man. By God, has he proven that over and over since we got here.

He teases me with his tongue, and my head lolls back. My shoulders release, sinking into the ground below them, and the burden of everything that's happened over the last week leaves my body in one big rush.

"Fuck, Avery. Your pussy is even more incredible than I imagined it would be."

"Henry."

"Mhmm," he groans. "Say my name again, baby."

"Henry."

"Fuck yes," he says against me, his tongue working a circle around my clit before flicking my center and sucking.

As incredible as this feels, and as much as I'd love to come, what I need the most is to feel him inside me.

"Henry, you can eat me out later, I promise. But please, right now, I want you inside me."

He looks up at me, his mouth and beard wet from the taste of me, and I nearly swoon at the heat in his eyes. His voice is rough and almost hoarse as he says, "I just realized I don't have a condom."

"I don't care."

"Avery..." He starts to shake his head, but I cut him off before he can say anything stupid.

"I don't," I say, my voice hoarse with need. "Pull out before you come if you want, but I have to feel you inside me."

He searches my face, my eyes, and I wait with bated breath for his next move.

And I just about shriek in pure, unadulterated excitement and relief when he eventually nods, climbing back over my body and looking me right in the eyes again. There's a burn of power between us and then a flicker of change as he hands it over to me completely. "You're in control. If you tell me to stop, I'll stop."

I laugh. "There's no fucking chance I'm telling you to stop."

Ignoring me and my rambling, he leans back enough to maneuver himself and shucks his pants and shirt what feels like painfully slowly.

His muscles flex, and I find myself mesmerized by the sight of it all. When he removes his boxer briefs, his rigid length standing at attention, a thrill of excitement rolls through me.

He's beautiful. Every freaking inch of him, from the top of his head to the tip of his toes.

"Let me know if it hurts," he whispers, climbing back on top of me now that he's naked.

I nod, and his hands find the sides of my face and settle, cradling me with more care than I've ever experienced in my life. Our worlds have narrowed to this moment, and I wouldn't have it any other way. My life at home is noisy; this is comfortable silence.

Henry's movements are measured as he lines us up and pushes inside me. He takes his time, taking it inch by inch in an effort to give me time to acclimate. It's an invasion unlike any other, but I'm surprised at my body's willing acceptance and, more than that, greediness.

For every little bit he gives, I become desperate for more.

When he seats himself fully, my eyes fall closed in contentment. For the first time since we got here, I feel true peace.

He kisses one eyelid and then the other, and I rub gently at the skin of his back with my fingernails, breathing in each other. When

I'm ready, I test moving my hips to release just a little bit of him before pushing him back inside.

It's so delicious, I can't help but moan.

Henry sinks his face into my neck and repeats the motion, and my breath stutters.

"My *God*."

He nods against my skin, his voice a coarse whisper. "Tell me about it."

Little by little, he picks up the tempo into a slow rhythm, and I wrap my limbs so tight around him I'd swear my body is making a bid for absorption. He doesn't seem to mind, even when it makes it more difficult for him to move, and I grab at his face as a pleasure unlike anything I've ever experienced builds inside me.

I've orgasmed—plenty—but this feels like a thousand times that.

Henry's breathing becomes more and more erratic as his own climax approaches, and I claw at his back and thrust my hips with the desperation to take myself over the cliff before he pulls out.

It doesn't take much before I'm tumbling down, my head thrown back and a keening scream filling the silence around us, and Henry disappears, the warm weight of his climax coating my thighs not even a second later.

It's messy and animalistic and…the most perfect thing the universe has ever done for me.

I know I flit from one thing to another like a leaf in the wind. But when it came time to settle, I landed in just the right spot.

I chose Henry. I chose right.

And I'll never, *ever* look back on this night with regret.

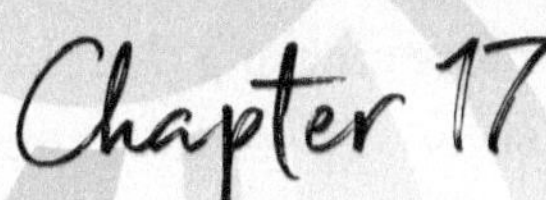

Chapter 17

January 8ᵗʰ

Henry

I STALK THROUGH THE WATER FOLLOWING A FISH WHILE AVERY tags along, our dinner procurement on our minds. We've touched and fooled around all day, but around noon, we finally decided that in the name of survival, we should probably get some work done.

Avery emptied our water collector and tidied our shelter, switching some of the abused sea grape leaves we messed up last night for new ones and making sure the roof is intact.

I stoked the fire and gathered more wood to ensure we could keep it burning, and then together, we went and collected more breadfruit. Avery's hair is wild with sex, something even her hairbrush couldn't quite fix, and I swear I've barely been able to stop staring at her all day.

Last night was fucking incredible, and we're both still riding the high.

As the fish I'm after scoots away and I search for another, several droplets of water hit me in the face, and the culprit is obvious when I turn to find Avery still mid-flick. She smiles and giggles, but I shake my head.

"Oh, you've done it now."

She turns and takes off at a run through the crystal-blue water, splashing wildly in her struggle to go faster. Thanks to my advantage in both size and speed, I catch her easily, snatching her up with an arm around the waist and spinning her in a circle that makes her squeal, and I toss my spear to the rocks that come out like a jetty.

Avery's been playful all day, and for as sure as I felt about everything last night, it's still a level of reassurance I needed to be certain she felt the same.

Sex with her was more amazing than I could have ever imagined, but it was still a risky step toward complication in our relationship. She's still my best friend's little sister and, quite possibly, the most commitment-phobic person I've ever met. Life goals, men, hobbies—they're all a revolving door of halfhearted interest and flipping pages.

The only things she's ever been sure about liking are her family, her family's money, and her best friend Juniper, and for as much as she's evolved since we landed on this little slice of the world eight days ago, that kind of stubbornness isn't the type of thing susceptible to quick change.

"Ahhh!" Avery screams again as I toss her up in the air and let go, watching as she splashes down in front of me in a cannonball position.

I expect her to come up sputtering, but she's on the attack instead, throwing herself at me bodily and taking me down in the water with her.

We both go under, and I wrap an arm around her waist, putting my lips to hers while we're submerged. We roll as a wave moves over us and come up for air together, laughing and flicking our wild hair out of our eyes.

Avery shakes like a dog before jumping up and into my arms, and I catch her by the ass as she puts her lips to mine and kisses me.

God, she tastes good.

Bright light shines behind my eyelids as the sun reflects off the water, and I stumble to keep us upright in the rolling waves. We kiss and taunt and tease, and she nips at my bottom lip with her teeth, backing off only to whisper one delicious thing into my ear.

"We should go have sex again."

I nod in agreement, our foreheads rubbing together, and carry her out of the water, one destination and one destination only in mind—Avery's perfect pussy.

She screams as I untie her bikini bottom while I'm jogging and toss it down in the sand, cupping her bare ass in my hands and skimming her center with my fingertips.

"Henry!"

"What?" I ask, laughing and spinning her around before dipping her into our shelter. "Can't handle a little teasing?" I move down her body and put my mouth to her pussy, and her back bucks off the ground. "What about that? Can you handle that?"

"More," she begs, sinking her hands into my hair and holding my mouth on her cunt. It's the hottest fucking thing I've ever experienced, and the fact that it's happening while we grow increasingly unsure whether we'll ever be rescued is the height of irony.

Reality is just around the corner, but it's fun to pretend it isn't, even if only for a little while.

And Avery Banks is the most perfect distraction.

Chapter 18

Avery

FIRELIGHT FLICKERS ON HENRY'S FACE AS HE LOOKS UP AT me. I can feel his hard cock against me where I straddle him begging for entrance, but tonight, I'm not in a rush. After three whole days of having him all over this godforsaken island, I've developed more patience.

As I pull back from kissing his eyelids, my stomach flips over with excitement, and my mind issues a correction. *Not much patience—but a little.*

"And this spot right here," I say, kissing the peeling, sunburned tip of his nose. "It's pretty cute too."

He laughs. "Oh yeah?"

"Yeah."

Ten orgasms and a whole lot of foreplay since I first convinced him to take it all the way four nights ago, and I'm still greedier and greedier to have him again every hour of the day. I thought I'd be satiated pretty quickly—like I usually am with guys when I decide it's time to drop and run. But I haven't felt even the slightest hint of pressure to bolt.

At all.

At first, I chalked it up to being the literal only male and female in existence as far as we're concerned, which, rationally, makes sense.

We're in a bubble, far-removed from reality, and I can't expect my behaviors here to mirror the ones of my home life. But I'm starting to realize the more times we're *together*—or, hell, maybe it's more admit than realize—there's a hell of a lot more driving my comfortability with attachment than proximity.

Henry's hot, funny, capable, and motherfucking banging in bed, and when it comes to options for how a girl could do in life, he's pretty firmly at the top of the list. He's patient, he's kind, he looks at me like I'm more than some passing fancy or box to check.

He looks at me for who I am, but also for the potential of what I could be if I wanted to.

He looks at me like I'm so much more than some spoiled little rich girl.

I don't know if he's just passing the time with me or if he feels a growing tether like I do, but for the sake of self-preservation, I haven't given myself more than a second at a time to consider it.

And I'm sure as hell not going to ruin how good I feel at the moment by giving it brain time now.

"Tell me something no one knows," I challenge, leaning into the need to learn more about him. For years, I've set him aside as my brother's hot friend, without setting aside space for anything more. I didn't let myself wonder.

Tonight, all the barriers are down.

"Like a secret?"

I shrug. "It can be anything. A secret. A desire. A nasty habit. Whatever you want. Just something about you you've never told anyone."

"Okay," he says, humming thoughtfully. "Let me think about it for a minute. I don't want to let you down with some bullshit like I never put the toilet seat down."

"You don't put the toilet seat down?" I wrinkle my nose. "What if I fall in?"

"Avery," he says through a laugh, and I roll my eyes. Worrying about toilet seats when I've been forced to go in the woods with nothing but freaking leaves for toilet paper for the last eleven days is the height of ridiculousness. Still, old habits and high expectations die hard, and I'd rather not drown in toilet water when we do make it back to civilization.

That is, I guess…if we even see each other enough to share toilet seats?

The thought burns my chest as I swallow it down, ignoring it for now.

"Okay, okay," I say instead. "Think about it, then."

"I guess…I've always had a little thing for Ross and Monica's mom on *Friends*. Like, maybe, if they were real, and I had an opportunity, I'd fight Jack for her."

"Oh my God! What's the male version of a cougar? A panther? A bobcat? Because that's what you are, Henry Callahan. Creeping on all the old ladies! Tell me, seriously, are you on the prowl when you go out to the clubs at home? Looking for a senior citizen?"

"I'm not on the prowl for AARP members! But you said to make it weird!" he exclaims through a hearty laugh. "And I'm sorry, but Ross's mom had this high-maintenance, the ultimate challenge, sex appeal about her."

"Oh my God!" I shriek through a giggle and pretend to cover my ears. "I didn't say make it weird, you freaking weirdo! I said to make it *good*."

"Fine," Henry says through another laugh. "You tell me one, then. What's one of your secrets, if you're so good at coming up with them?"

I think through all the things I do that people don't necessarily know about. The old ladies from The Pines I help dress in the latest fashion, the times I've volunteered at the soup kitchen in downtown Miami, and the tab I have open at Starbucks for strangers who come in there asking for food or something to drink.

They're all pretty valid secrets in the shock-and-awe department, but for some reason, I don't like how serious and vulnerable they make me sound.

I settle for something slightly more in line with the personality I present to the world, but a pretty big lack of disclosure all the same.

"Last year, when I was shopping for June and my mom for Christmas, I purposely got them gifts from Hermès so I would qualify to get offered another bag I wanted."

Henry laughs, shaking his head. "Well, I guess it's still the act of giving, so I can't fault you there."

"Well, actually..." I wince, outing myself further. "I also made sure the stuff I bought them was stuff I wanted and they didn't, so they would end up giving it to me."

Henry barks out a laugh. "Avery!"

"What?" I shrug. "It's not like the two of them aren't rich enough to get whatever the hell they want. They both have rich husbands. I'm still living off a quickly drying well from my father."

"You really are cute, you know that?" Henry asks, leaning forward to kiss the corner of my mouth and slide the strap of my bikini top down my shoulder. The skin underneath his thumb pebbles.

"Oh yeah? How cute? Cute enough to take to bed again?"

He smiles against the skin of my shoulder, and his ever-growing beard scratches at it gently. "Yes...and no."

"Yes *and* no?" I question, incredulous. "Those are opposites. You know that, right?"

"I do." He nods, looking up at me with the sexiest, saddest eyes I've seen since he dipped his wick in my ink the first time. "The thing is, I've already had your perfect pussy two times today and three yesterday, and I'm worried if I have it a third today, we're really asking for a problem infection-wise. I don't want you to get a UTI without a way to treat it."

It sucks, but he's right. I've been trying to be really careful at seeing to my hygiene after we're together, but there are some things that are a much bigger risk here than they are at home. There's no quick trip to urgent care for antibiotics. There's sepsis and a really ugly death.

Ugh.

"Okay."

He hums, pulling my face down for a kiss that makes my stomach flip over. "Doesn't mean we can't cuddle and make out."

I nod. "Yeah. Let's do that."

Ever so gently, he picks us up from our spot by the fire just like he did the first night we slept together and carries me to our shelter. I wrap my hands around his neck, and he cradles me in his arms like I'm as light as a feather.

I know I'm dropping weight just like he is, but truth be told, I've been trying not to focus on it.

I've got enough problems to worry about without considering my dwindling appearance. I cling to Henry somewhat desperately as he leans down to scoot us into our shelter, needing our already-close bodies to be closer.

Big, big problems.

Once we're tucked inside, he rolls us to our sides so we're facing each other, his eyes tracing my face and leaning forward every few seconds to take slow, lingering kisses. It's intimate and swoon-inducing, and I find myself easily lost in the magic of it all.

We could be in a daily rental cabana on the beach of a resort, in the warm comfort of my oceanfront condo's bed, or tucked away on his deep, suede couch in his cushy Miami living room. We're so locked in on each other, the simplicity of our survival has faded away, and truly, we could be anywhere.

An unknown amount of time ticks by like that, wrapped in each other's arms as we kiss and touch and explore without rushing to get to a sex-laden end. When his eyes start to get heavy, I rub at his back to encourage him to let go and fall asleep without worry or waiting for me.

Normally, he comforts me to sleep, playing with my hair and singing that same old song about the bird and its wings, but just for tonight, I take the lead at comforting him.

He's been strong and unswayable in the face of adversity. He's been generous and careful with me, and not once has he made me feel like more of a burden than a boon. He's the reason I'm not only alive, but sane.

He deserves to be taken care of.

His features, normally rugged and strong, are so soft as he lets go into a restful sleep, and I study every line as though it's a personalized, wrapped, and bowed gift.

Eleven days we've been here with only each other to lean on. I close my eyes tight and pray that we'll find a way to get out of here or that someone will find us and save us—save *me* from myself.

We have to leave.

I caress Henry's face as he sleeps and stare at his beautiful, chapped lips, pressing mine gently to his so as not to disturb his rest.

Everything inside me screams in self-preservation—a reserve that's dwindling more and more by the second.

We have to leave.

My eyes find Henry's face again. *We have to leave before I love you.*

Chapter 19

AVERY IS ALREADY UP WHEN I WAKE UP THE NEXT MORNING, sitting on the beach with her legs in the water as it washes up and around her. When I look closer, I see she's giving herself the only bath we have these days, so I leave her to her privacy and work on collecting the water from our makeshift system instead. There's not much, but something is better than nothing, and since we've been largely relying on the heavy dew since it hasn't rained since we got here, the deficiency isn't new.

But it is worrying.

I take a small drink, just enough to wet the membranes in my mouth so they aren't sticking together and save the rest for Avery. I don't know how much longer we'll be able to go on at this pace, but I shove the thought aside for now. It's not worth thinking about because, like it or not, there isn't a solution.

"I'm done," Avery calls, noticing me up here and realizing I've been purposely avoiding her.

I carry the hydration bag down to her and hold it out, but she shakes her head. "No, I'm good. You drink extra until you feel like you've gotten enough, and then I'll take what's left."

"Avery—"

"Henry, do it. You've been allocating most of the water to me this whole time, and it's starting to catch up with you. Your lips are chapped, and your eyes are sinking in. You're majorly dehydrated. Drink."

Rather than arguing, I comply. For one thing, she deserves the courtesy, and for another, I'm starting to feel like I'd do anything she asked, just to make her happy.

I'm not just noticing her now—I've always noticed Avery Banks. But this island has painted a complete picture of the woman she really is in a way our lives at home never could.

Don't misunderstand. I don't think she's *different*.

She's still entitled and on her own schedule and work-averse in an almost startlingly selfish way. She flirts her way through town and sweet-talks her daddy into giving her more money and puts herself above others a fair amount of the time.

But beneath the surface, she's always been soft in the center, a veritable statue in a blowing wind of friendships and life and circumstances. For all her quirks, she's still one of the most reliable people I've ever known and never begrudges you the space to feel your feelings. She doesn't judge, even as she's judged relentlessly.

There's a reason her friendship with June transcends decades and a reason her family would do anything for her, and it isn't because they've all got their heads in the sand. These are smart, caring people.

And they pay enough attention to know Avery is too.

Being here has acted as a highlighter, emphasizing her compassion, humanity, and humor over the rest of it.

I hope I can be what she needs until someone finds us. I hope… someone finds us.

Thirst finally satisfied—but stopping before making myself sick—I hand her the pack, and she drinks until there's a small amount left for later.

When she finishes, she closes the top, tosses it up onto the sand by our always-smoldering fire, and turns around to face the infinite water, stretching her limbs. She's skinnier than she used to be—not that she was plump to begin with—and her skin is nearly tawny.

I step forward and wrap my arms around her from behind, pressing my chest to her back, and she falls into the gesture with ease, leaning her head back on my shoulder and sighing.

"You know, this place would be beautiful if it weren't such a shitty situation."

I nod.

"I wonder how far outside of the realistic search grid we are," she remarks then, her voice flat.

I shake my head, burying my lips in her neck. "Don't go there."

"It's hard not to at this point," she argues, pulling out of my arms to face me, her expression as serious as I've seen it in a long time. "We're approaching two weeks, Henry. That's a long freaking time to be searching for someone and not find them. At some point, they're going to give up."

"We're a long way off from that. Your family?" I shake my head. "They'll look forever."

She snorts. "And to what end? Will we be alive when they get here?"

My jaw grinds. "Yes."

"But you don't know that!" she explodes, the frustration of being out of control getting to her. I don't blame her. For as good of a front as we put on, we're both ticking time bombs of anxiety and unknowns. "You don't know that they'll find us, and you don't know that we'll live! You can't! Just admit it."

She smacks my chest hard, and I grab her wrist as tightly as I can without hurting her.

"Avery, stop."

"Admit it, Henry! Fucking admit it!" she yells, pulling at my grip with noticeably weakening strength. Her muscles are eating themselves, and so are mine.

My chest explodes, the mountain of pressure I feel to make this right without an ounce of ability crushing me. "Of course! Of course, I don't fucking know! Is that what you want to hear? That I'm just as terrified as you? Because I'm fucking scared. Fucking scared I won't be able to protect you. Scared I'll injure myself and burden you even more than I already have. I'm fucking petrified, okay?"

Avery steps forward and puts a soft hand on my shaking arm, the jump in my heart rate sending my already strained nervous system into a spasm. "A burden?" Her voice is a whisper. "How can you say that about yourself?"

I shake my head, and my voice is undeniably hoarse. "I planned that jump. I insisted on it being part of the trip. I teased you that morning until you agreed to get on the plane, and if I hadn't…"

"You'd be here by yourself, and I'd be terrified at home. Sick and scared and still very much out of control. I'd have to wonder where you were or if you were okay."

"Avery…"

"There are no winners, losers, or burdens here, Henry," she says and moves her hands to my face, locking our gazes together. "It's just you and me, fighting for our lives *together*."

"Avery," I say her name again, the sting of available tears piercing a pain into my dry eyes. An unspoken line of three little words sits at the tip of my tongue, one I can't bring myself to say, no matter how much I'm feeling it.

I love you.

We've shared a lot of truths with each other that no one else knows. This one, though, I don't know that I'm even ready to share with myself.

I go to sleep at night with Avery in my arms, and I wake up wanting to stay there. And every day we're here, the feeling only gets stronger.

Avery pushes into my arms and up to her toes to seal her lips to mine, and I dig a soft hand into the back of her wild hair. We clutch each other tightly, willing ourselves to hold on to each other and hold on to hope as we wait.

Wait for a rescue we're not sure will ever come.

Chapter 20

January 13ᵗʰ

Avery

NUZZLE INSTINCTIVELY DEEPER INTO HENRY'S CHEST AS THE approaching morning stirs me from sleep. It might not be quality sleep that we're getting here, but it is comfortable and warm, and I know our bodies appreciate what little restoration we can give them under these circumstances.

Shifting softly, I peer up to Henry's hairy face to see if he's awake, but his eyes are still closed and his mouth is still lax with the relaxation only sleep can bring him.

The sun is starting to rise and our lone companions—the birds—are starting to sing, but instead of getting up, I tuck my head back into his warm chest and lie there. I listen to the steady beat of his heart and time my breathing to align with his.

Our chests rise and fall in tandem, and our heat blends together in an even exchange.

There are things I could be doing, chores we've established as a part of our routine now that we're going on two weeks of being here.

It'll be two weeks tomorrow, to be exact, and the thought is… overwhelming.

It's a milestone I never thought we'd hit, and a turning point in the faith that we'll ever be found alive. A few days…a week? Sure.

But when two weeks pass, you have to wonder if they're even remotely in the vicinity of where we are or if they'll ever figure it out.

For all I know, we were off course by ten, twenty…fifty miles. If the pilot was feeling off before or maybe if his senses were blurred, he could have been flying in a completely different direction than intended.

I, for one, know I sure as hell wouldn't have realized.

I take a deep breath to clear my thoughts of all the negativity and turn my mouth to Henry's shirt-covered chest to place a small kiss there.

As much as I want our time here to end, I wonder what that'll do to us and all the things we've become—all the things I've become accustomed to.

I turn back into my sleeping position and tuck back in, letting myself settle and drift back off into the comfort of Henry's cuddled sleep. I don't know what'll happen here. I don't know what I'll say when I get all boozed up to celebrate two weeks tomorrow night. Or if it'll expose me to both Henry and myself in ways I never dreamed of. And I don't know what'll happen when and if we leave here and go back to our lives as we once knew them.

All I know is that for a little while longer, I can pretend it doesn't exist.

I can pretend Henry and I are the only two people in the world and that my dreams are reality.

Because here, in Henry's arms, the world doesn't feel so heavy.

Here, I don't have to be afraid.

Here, in the stillness of morning… I can almost say it.

I can almost admit the truth—that whatever *this* is, *whatever we are*, I don't want to live in a world where it doesn't exist.

Chapter 21

Henry

AS THE WARMTH OF AN AVERY-NUZZLED SLEEP TUGS ME one way, an unfamiliar sound pulls me toward another, clouding the very monotone reality we've come to expect for the last thirteen days.

It's a low hum, like a distant drum or heartbeat, and it fights with the gentle rhythm of the ocean's waves. It feels like a dream—like I'm standing on top of a building vent shaft waiting to leap, no matter the consequence, and I struggle to make sense of my warring emotions.

It feels wrong and right all at once, and my body jolts as it battles to stay snug with Avery instead. Reflexively, I squeeze her deeper into myself and inhale, taking in the fading scent of roses and salty skin.

I open my eyes and blink rapidly, trying to make sense of my nightmares and reality and where the line is drawn between them. Avery stirs on top of me as the sound gets louder, and I push to sitting, taking her with me.

Her hands find my thighs as she tries to keep herself upright among my shifting.

"What is that?" she asks, her voice raw and raspy with the unshed onus of slumber, rubbing at her face.

I listen harder, flipping through a mental catalog to make sense of the buzz, and poke my head out of our shelter to take a look. The sun is up—we've clearly overslept from our normal routine—and a wavy haze cascades through the rays as they hit the water, but nothing else I can make sense of looks out of the ordinary.

She pokes her head out beside me, both of us listening and trying to track where it's coming from.

We stare at each other for a long moment and then another, and when it finally hits me, it does so with the force of a bullet to the chest.

"Holy shit!" I whisper-shout, shoving my way out of the tent and making Avery scramble to follow me as I take off at a run.

My eyes are bleary in the already-bright sun, and the reflection of the water makes it hard to focus, but I swear on the bright-blue space of the horizon, I see a small dot, traveling from left to right. It doesn't look like a bird, and it sure as hell doesn't fly like one.

"It's a helicopter!" I try to yell, my voice still hoarse from both sleep and dehydration.

Unexpectedly, the words snap something in Avery, and she takes off at a run for the water first, her lean, tanned legs eating up the distance more quickly than I've ever seen them move. I follow closely behind, waving my arms widely and wildly to try to catch the aircraft's attention, and Avery mimics me as I come to a stop beside her knee-deep in the water.

She jumps up and down and hollers and screams, and I do the same. My hand bumps her arm and knocks her to the side, and she stumbles in the water, but neither of us falters. I stare hard, afraid if I move or blink or take a breath, the vision will disappear into thin air and I'll have to face the devastation of my imagination playing tricks on me.

I don't trust that it's not a mirage, and I certainly don't trust the surge of adrenaline that's dumped into my veins not to get me in trouble.

"Heyyy!" Avery screams, her sweet voice cracking with the

effort to be loud, and my ears ring at the volume. Without anything to talk over, we've gotten quieter over the last two weeks.

Both of us jump higher as the helicopter seems to turn and come toward us, and a weird swirl makes a whirlpool in my fucking stomach.

"Help us! We're down here!" Avery screams animalistically, her voice a mix of a cry and a cheer, and for far from the first time here, I know *exactly* what she's feeling. Reality feels stretched and hope restored, and yet, in the back of my mind, I still have all the fears and questions I've been packing away for the last two weeks.

Fears of letting in expectation, fears of what's to come of us when we're no longer in this tropical bubble.

"Hey!" I yell, my voice cracking ever so slightly as I try to make it as loud as humanly possible.

Avery grabs on to my arm and squeezes, and for the briefest moment of time, both of us look away from the approaching res-cue-savior to look at each other.

Her hazel eyes are tired and withdrawn and her body frail, and I know I must look the same. It's obvious the timing of this rescue is saving us from some truly challenging times, and that if left much longer, the damage to our health might be irreparable.

And yet, there's a scariness to the idea of going back to every-thing outside of here without a handbook for how to handle it, and I don't know the right words to say to comfort her.

To reassure her that it's her and me against the world, always.

To tell her that this island woke me up to all the things that truly matter in this life—and that at the top of the list is her.

Once, Avery Banks, my best friend's little sister. But now, so much fucking more.

She turns back to the approaching help and waves her arms in the air, bouncing up and down over and over and over, her stretched-out sweater nearly falling off her.

"Avery!" I yell over the whooshing sound of the helicopter blades. They're close now, and I feel a desperation down to my bones to say something to her—anything to convey what she means to me. "Avery!"

She turns to look at me briefly and then back to the orange-and-white Coast Guard helicopter before I can get anything through the dry confines of my thick throat. Thwarted, I follow her gaze back to the helicopter as it turns to the side, revealing the relieved faces of Beau, Ronnie, and Maverick in the open side door.

They're shouting, waving, alive with relief, but within seconds, the Coast Guard crew pushes them back, stepping forward as the aircraft maneuvers for landing.

And then it hits me. A sharp, breath-stealing realization.

This is it. It's really happening.

The past two weeks of survival, of desperation, of clinging to each other like lifelines, of pretending that this island was the only world that existed—

It's over.

The weight of it slams into me all at once, and my knees buckle.

I collapse into the water, my chest heaving, my senses overwhelmed, and my mind unable to catch up to the reality we've spent days chasing.

Avery falls next to me, pulling me into a crushing hug and burying her face into the hollow of my neck. I cling to her, one arm tight around her back, the other shielding her from the crushing wind of the blades.

I should be looking at the helicopter. I should be watching as it descends to the sand, kicking up embers from the dying fire.

I should be feeling nothing but relief. But all I can see and feel is her.

It's really happening. They found us. We're rescued.

But somehow, it doesn't feel like I'm being saved.

Chapter 22

Avery

BEAU HUGS ME TIGHTLY AS THE SOUND OF THE HELICOPTER roars around us, his genuine cries of relief slicking the skin of my shoulder with a sheen of tears Henry and I have long since lost the ability to produce. I know he's overwhelmed—and I even appreciate it, seeing as I've been freaking missing for nearly two weeks and this is the proper response to that—but my insides feel hollow, my emotions nearly empty.

A coastguardsman takes my pulse from behind Beau's back before smiling and shoving away to head for the front, and another works over by Henry, doing much the same.

I try desperately to draw from my normally quick-trigger well of tears and tantrums, but no matter how hard I try, I can't seem to feel anything. I don't know if I'm too tired or too hungry or too traumatized, but my body is in overdrive, and even the feel of my rib cage as my abs try to stabilize with the motion of the helicopter is overstimulating.

"Avery, my God. Oh, Ave, it's so fucking good to see you," my brother rambles on, his heart so far down his sleeve it's practically painted all over his hand. He rubs at my back, and even though the feeling is abrasive against my sun-worn skin, I don't tell him to stop.

It feels nice to be loved and missed and appreciated, and he smells so familiar and clean and real.

Still, it's so strange to be with other people, so weird to have a barrier between me and the man I've spent the last thirteen days surviving with.

My eyes dance behind Beau, trying to find Henry, but Ronnie and Mav both block my view by crowding in front of him. Though obstructed, I know he sits on the other side of the helicopter by the door, his knees to his chest and his head in his hands as Ronnie and Mav both slap and rub at his shoulders with relieved aggression. There's a salve on his dry, chapped lips, courtesy of the medic who was working on him, and a blanket is wrapped lightly around his shaking shoulders. I'm glad he's being loved on and taken care of like I am, but I feel almost jealous that it's coming from someone other than me.

It's crazy and startling and doesn't make a lick of fucking sense, given how readily I would have taken the avoidance just two short weeks ago. But we've barely left our island, and yet I miss him.

Beyond that, not being able to meet his eyes is painful and scary, and I'm nearly desperate to know how he's feeling or what he's thinking. This is everything we've dreamed of since we crashed, but I know both of us had reached a point where we truly didn't think it was going to happen. It's not as simple as it could be—as it probably should be. Instead, it's much, much more complicated.

Beau finally pulls back and holds me at arm's length, studying the changes in my face and body with incredulity. "How are you feeling? Do you hurt? Are you hurt? What do you need? What can I do?"

I shake my head, barely registering his questions as I try to get a look at Henry again, only to be foiled. I just need to see his face—to hold his eyes and bury myself in the comfort I know I'll find there. I *need* it.

Beau's concern grows as I don't answer, and I can't blame him. Being at a loss for words isn't even remotely my normal MO. I talk and I yap and, right now, I should be railing the whole lot of people on this helicopter with complaints. "Ave. Honey. I think you might be in shock. Are you in shock?"

I shake my head slightly, willing myself to say something, anything to comfort my brother, but preoccupied with Henry, I can't seem to find the words.

Mav and Ronnie are pulling full-time duty on the other side of the helicopter, too, trying to assess Henry for needs or injuries, and unlike me, it seems like he's managing to at least answer.

I know because his voice is the only thing I can pick out among the sound of the rotor blades as we cruise over the brilliant, sunny blue water of the Atlantic Ocean, bound for Miami. It's not loud; I'm just attuned.

"Avery!" Beau yells, his normally calm speech grating on panicked. "Look at me! Are you okay?"

My focus restored with a snap of his fingers right in front of my nose, I meet my brother's honey-brown eyes and nod, forcing myself to do right by him the way he's always done right by me. I cup his cheek with a gentle hand to emphasize my point, and the difference in the color of our skin is pointedly obvious. While our tones are normally similar, today, I'm at least ten shades darker.

"I'm okay, Beau." It's a promise to both him and myself as I sort my thoughts.

Ready or not, in just a short while, we'll be back on land and bombarded with ten times the number of people on this small helicopter. If I can't handle the attention of my brother by himself, I'll never manage in the raw, rushed attention of my parents and June and everyone else.

"Oh, thank God," he cries again, slamming me back into a hug that rocks my body backward, thanks to a deteriorating and weakening muscle structure. "My baby sister." His cries are loud and unchecked, and I rub at his back with a calming hand. "June and Mom and Dad and the geriatrics, as you call them…" I laugh internally at the thought of my band of grandparents that do every single thing in their lives together. From cruises to doctor's appointments to trips to the grocery store—they do everything as a fierce foursome. "We were all so worried. Addy asked about you constantly too, but we tried everything we could to keep her from worrying."

Aw, my sweet little niece Addy. God, I've missed her so.

I nod into Beau's shoulder, but once again, without even meaning to, I'm seeking out Henry again. Sure, he has Ronnie and Mav and Beau and me…but with his dad having passed a few months ago, he has no family to go back to.

No parents or grandparents or distant cousins even—no one to welcome him with open arms and unconcealed fanfare and all the tender, loving care he so desperately deserves.

Pushing Beau back, I cup his face one last time before leaning in to kiss the apple of his cheek, and then I crawl across the helicopter, the way it looks or the shock it may cause be damned. I need Henry, if only for a little while longer.

Through Ronnie and Maverick and straight into Henry's arms, I hug him tightly without a care in the world for who's looking on, though I know they must be noticing with curiosity. I hiccup on a sob, the dam of untapped emotion finally overflowing, and break into cries. My face smothered in his warm, familiar chest, he rubs a hand down my back until I stop.

When I finally get it together, I move to sit beside him, tucking my body against his and holding his hand. Ronnie, Mav, and Beau all stare at us with wide eyes, and I find myself cracking a joke to lighten the tension.

"I'm sorry… I just… I can't wait to take a shower."

Beau laughs and jumps forward to kiss my forehead, and despite my position against Henry, everyone's behavior finally returns to normal.

Except me, of course. Ronnie, Mav, and Beau gab and chatter and celebrate in front of us, and I sit quietly, listening and taking it all in.

I squeeze Henry's fingers tight—as tight as I can—trying and failing miserably to prepare myself for the moment when I'll have to let go.

"Seventeen islands, fifty square miles of ocean," Beau regales, going over all the details of the search mission they've lived and breathed for the last thirteen days. "June tried to reach out to Avery to see how the skydive was, and then we heard from the news and the FAA that air traffic control lost communication with a plane somewhere off the coast."

I look at Henry when he squeezes my hand, expecting his eyes, but he's looking at the three stooges and listening carefully before explaining, "The pilot had some kind of medical emergency, and the plane went into a dive. I tried to revive him and considered trying to take control, but I wasn't confident we even had any lift left. I made the decision to get us out of there." He shrugs thoughtfully. "I didn't know where we were either, besides an estimation based on how long we'd been in the air. I wasn't paying close attention."

Beau nods from his position on the floor at the back of the helicopter, his arms draped over his knees. "The plane didn't have a working transponder, so we had no clue where you actually crashed. The sheer area to search was daunting. All we knew was that no one on the coast saw the plane go down, and no ships reported it either. We've been working your path every day, all day, but it took us this long to get this far out."

I glance behind us to the window in the door, watching as the sparkling blue water zooms by below us. *All this ocean with no idea where to start.*

It's a miracle we weren't lost forever.

It's a miracle we survived as long as we did.

If it weren't for Henry Callahan and all the things his dad taught him, we sure as hell wouldn't have. Thank God he's the man he is.

Thank God he exists.

It almost makes me laugh that there was a time, not that long ago, when I didn't feel that way. A time when Henry's very presence was the thing that could send me into a spiral.

A time when I actively wished for the disbandment of the four stooges and, if I'm honest, conspired to make it happen.

Chapter 23

The Past

Almost two years ago

Avery

ADDY SMELLS LIKE ALL NEWBORN BABIES DO—LIKE addiction and powder and curdled milk in the folds of their neck—as I cuddle her close to my chest, lifting her up higher every once in a while to kiss her little button nose.

June sits on the rocking chair across from me that Beau moved into the living room at her request, and my brother sets down a duffel bag on a kitchen island stool behind her.

I eye him with unconcealed malice. "I can't believe you're fucking leaving my best friend, six weeks after giving birth, to go on a golf trip with your stupid friends. Like, hello? Can you say *grow up*?"

June laughs, her slightly inflamed face curling up into a smile. "It's no big deal, Ave. I gave him permission to go."

"Which was a dumb move on your part. I mean, Juni, this is the time for you to milk it, my God. You just pushed this adorable little bowling ball out of your vageen. The Arby's Roast Beef will never be the same, and you're just letting him *leave*? I could *never*."

I look from her back to my brother. "Does she have a fresh mani? A fresh pedi? A massage appointment every week? Do you have daily flower delivery and Starbucks DoorDashes coming every day? Because if not, dear brother, you're not doing enough."

June laughs again. "I don't need my nails done to take care of a baby, Avery. All I'm doing is sitting around the house and soaking it in."

"And whose fault is that?" I ask, spearing my brother with daggers again. He comes to sit at June's side, his face now worried.

"Maybe she's right, Juniper June. It's only been six weeks. I don't have to go on this trip," Beau says, his eyes searching June's face. "I can stay. The guys will understand. You and Avery could go out to dinner or have a girls' weekend or something."

"Yes! That's a much better idea!" I clap my hands behind Addy's little baby back, but Juniper cuts me off with an annoyingly diplomatic glare.

"Don't be silly!" Juniper protests, rolling her eyes. "It's my fault that I'm just hanging at home because that's what I *want* to be doing. I'm soaking in every minute of this maternity leave I can and smelling as much baby skin as possible."

I smell Addy again and sigh. She *does* smell good.

"Well, that's fine. You can hang out and do nothing, but Beau should do the same." I shrug one nonchalant, I-don't-care-if-I-just-offended-you shoulder. "What? He can just go on working and galivanting like he pleases because he has a penis? I don't think so. Drop the dead weight of all three of those friends and be a man, Beau."

My brother shakes his head, exhaling like he doesn't have the energy to fight me on this. "They're not dead weight. They're good friends."

I chuff. It's not that they're *not* loyal or trustworthy or occasionally fun, but they're *always* around. They practically live in his pocket, like a trio of golden retrievers who refuse to go home.

Things would be a lot easier if they'd just keep to themselves a little more. *Then I wouldn't be tempted to go around kissing some of them all the time.*

"Plus, Henry really does need this trip," Beau continues, his tone a little heavier now, a little quieter. "They just diagnosed his dad with cancer, and it's...not good."

My stomach drops.

"Henry's dad has cancer?" My voice comes out too sharp, my spine snapping straight as a strange, unwelcome pang rolls through me.

"Yeah." June's nod is sad. "They just found it, but it's already spread. They're saying a couple years at most, you know?"

I force myself to swallow past the sudden lump in my throat.

"That sucks," I say, staring down at Addy, watching the gentle rise and fall of her tiny chest, willing my focus to stay there instead of on the heaviness settling deep inside me.

Because the truth is, I don't like being wrong, and I don't like the idea of Henry being sad, as much as I hate to admit it.

He's never done anything dishonest or unjust to me, the stupid fucker. In fact, I don't know that he's ever done anything wrong to anyone, really.

"He's handling it okay," Beau updates, but there's a tightness to his voice, like he's trying to convince himself just as much as us. "We just figured we'd get him away for a couple days before all the treatments start. It's just him and his dad, you know? And yeah, we'll help all we can, but..."

He winces, scrubbing his hand over his jaw, and I fight the sudden urge to pick up and run out of the house screaming, even with the baby in my arms.

Some people get such an unfair shake at things, and from everything I know, Henry is one of them. I don't know the full story of his mom. Just that it's been him and his dad for as long as I can remember.

And now, the one person who has always been there for him is slipping away.

I try to shake off the sadness that threatens to clog my throat again. My gaze drops back to Addy, my fingers tracing soft circles over the warm, delicate skin of her cheek.

Henry's stuff probably isn't any of my business anyway.

I mean, he's just…a guy I've kissed twice.

Just my brother's best friend.

And that'll probably never change.

Right?

Chapter 24

Henry

MIAMI STANDS TALL IN THE BACKGROUND AS THE helicopter lowers slowly toward the ground at the Coast Guard station right on the south end of Miami Beach, the air heavy with the scent of seawater and jet fuel. The reflective glow of skyscrapers and glass windows is almost as strong as the water of our cove, and if I close my eyes, I can practically hear the waves lapping up on our beach in the background.

Two hours ago, we were cuddled in each other, a restless sleep driven by the unknown. Now, we're back, right in the middle of the action, as if life didn't pause at all.

Avery's hand clutches mine tightly as Beau, Ronnie, and Mav all look out the window to the waiting crowd full of reporters, family, and friends, and my heart takes off at a gallop.

Fuck, it feels strange to see civilization after thirteen days of nothing but ocean and sand…*and Avery.*

The sound of the blades winding down is a pulsing timer toward chaos as we make contact with the ground and the whine of the engine quiets to a dull roar. Ronnie wastes no time sliding open the door at the side of the helicopter and climbs down first, and then the coastguardsmen follow suit. I doubt they ever have their passengers opening their doors and climbing down out of their shit without permission, but Ronnie wouldn't be Ronnie if he were worried about following the rules. He stands his ground even as they try to usher him out of the way so they can do their jobs, taking up a position at the side of the door and holding up a hand to help the rest of us jump out.

Mav goes next, moving to the edge and launching himself down, but Beau turns back to us, waving a hand for Avery to go before him. She looks to me, her eyes wide and scared and confused, so I give her the nod of encouragement she needs and follow it up with a smile.

"Go ahead, Ave." My voice is soft and ragged with weariness. "Your family is all waiting to see you."

She nods and scoots forward, her grip on my hand just as tight as mine on hers, and I smile when she looks back once more.

It's okay.

Beau ushers her forward when she gets within reach, grabbing her free arm and pulling her to the edge to hand her off to a waiting Ronnie. Her outstretched arm behind her still holds tight to me, but there comes a point of impossibility, and in one smooth motion, our grip is ripped apart.

Time speeds up and slows down all at once as Avery is ushered out of the helicopter and across the tarmac, and I scoot to the edge, where Beau and Ronnie help me down all the same.

I'm not normally one to need help with anything physical, but my body is very obviously weakened from the malnourishment and dehydration, and I don't fight their hold on my hands.

Avery tries to wait for me, but overwhelmed as we are with people, it's an impossibility. We aren't the only two people in the world anymore.

Not even fucking close.

My body is stiff from exhaustion, my mind still spinning from the whirlwind of survival. But the ache in my chest isn't from dehydration or hunger—it's from the sight of Avery disappearing into the crowd without me.

Cameras flash and voices call out, frantic and eager for a

glimpse of the "island survivors." Several journalists shout questions in my direction, and my stomach twists. I don't know what I expected to happen once we were safely rescued, but it sure as hell wasn't this. We're not celebrities or rock stars or billionaires—we're just a couple of people who got lost in the fold of the universe for a brief moment in time.

Normally, I'm not opposed to having a moment in the spotlight, but normal is on the bottom of the ocean in a banana-colored plane.

Being on the island wasn't easy, but it was real. And yet, with the distance between Avery and me growing by the second, it's starting to feel like it didn't happen at all.

All these fucking cameras and reporters and people waiting to see the infamous "island survivors" feels faker than a porn star's tits. They don't care about us—they care about ratings. Our story is bound to bring them.

I don't have any use for them turning what happened between Avery and me into some cheap, money-grab headline when it was… so much more than that.

Using a hand to block the light from the cameras and ignoring them otherwise, I scour the crowd for Avery.

I can still feel the warmth from her hand in mine, but she's long gone, tucked into the waiting arms of her family. They've been frantic, I'm sure, though the two of us have worked really hard not to let ourselves go there.

Neil and Diane are the best of the best. They love their kids— and even their kids' friends—fiercely and are the most generous and kind and compassionate two people you'll ever meet. Their worry and well-being while we were gone wasn't something we could control, and if we'd let it, the need to do something to fix it could have driven us insane.

My father was always that way with me too, so in some really weird, fucked-up way, I'm glad he didn't live to see this.

I catch a glimpse of Avery's brown hair, still frizzed and matted in parts, as her mom pulls her into a crushing hug. Diane's sobs are soft but audible, and Neil and June end up latching on in a pile, unable to wait for their own turn. Beau stands back a foot, his little girl Addy on his hip and his four grandparents, Phil and Bev and Bill and Judy, at his side, and waits, having taken his moment on the helicopter ride back. His face is tight with stress and worry, and his hand grips Avery's shoulder like he's afraid she might vanish again.

They've missed her. *Of course they have.* I've spent the last two weeks alone with her, and right now, I miss her too.

"Henry! Henry! Over here!"

The shout of my name startles me as reporters rush closer, microphones and cameras aimed directly at my face. Questions fly at me like bullets.

"How did you survive?"

"What happened to the pilot?"

"What was it like being stranded for thirteen days?"

"Was this a stunt you pulled for Adrenaline Junkie marketing, or did you really get stranded on that island?"

A fucking *stunt*? Getting stuck on a remote island with no food, water, or way to reach the outside world? *Give me a break.*

Before I can open my mouth or flip that last reporter the middle finger, a Coast Guard officer steps in, holding up his hands to keep the media back. "Give him some space," he barks, his voice firm.

"Henry!"

Ronnie's voice snaps me out of my thoughts, and I turn to find him and Maverick jogging over with four bottles of Prime, my favorite electrolyte drink. Ron holds out one of the bottles and pushes it to my chest, and I crack it open and take a swig without thinking.

The taste is overly sweet as it hits my tongue, and I lick my dry lips to spread some of the moisture around, pulling the bottle away to stare at it for a moment.

Cracking open a bottle. I shake my head. *I can't fucking believe it's that easy.*

"Man, you're the talk of the fucking town!" Ronnie's laugh is hearty, but his eyes are creased with concern. He watches closely as I take another drink from the bottle and then another, and only when I finish the whole thing in one long gulp do his shoulders fall from his ears.

He pulls me into a bear hug, clapping me on the back. "Still can't believe you fucking survived a plane crash and living on an island for two fucking weeks straight."

The memory of Mario slumped over the controls and Avery's high-pitched screams as the plane dove for the water assaults me first, followed by the eerie sound of the plane hitting below us while we watched from our canopy ride down. "I didn't have much of a choice," I say, my voice almost too quiet for Ron or Mav to hear over the crowd.

"Just look around, Hen," Maverick says, shaking his head in incredulity. "You're a goddamn hero."

Truth be told, the word "hero" feels wrong. I'm not a hero. In those terrifying moments of survival, I thought of nothing but Avery and myself, and I didn't hesitate to choose us over Mario when the shit hit the fan.

I'd like to think I would have acted differently if he'd shown any signs of life whatsoever, but I'm not entirely sure. All I know is that I would have done anything to protect Avery, including sacrificing myself if I needed to.

Leaning my head to the side, I try to get another look at her, but too many people are in the way—too many reporters pointing their cameras in her beautiful face and snapping as many fucking pictures as their fingers can manage and too many family members fighting to hold her tight.

"You know, maybe I should buy some stock in Adrenaline Junkie," Ronnie adds, the teasing in his voice bringing my attention back to him and the big-ass grin on his face. "Surely that shit is about to fly to the goddamn moon after all this."

Mav snorts. "Adrenaline Junkie CEO proves he's legit by getting stranded on a remote island and surviving for thirteen days."

I roll my eyes. "One of those asshole journalists asked me if it was a fucking stunt I pulled for marketing."

"What the fuck?" Ronnie narrows his eyes. "Which one?" he questions, looking toward the boisterous crowd of media with scrutiny. "Point him out, Hen. Point that motherfucker out."

I clap a hand to his back. "Don't worry about it, man."

"Yeah, Ron," Mav chimes in. "Now isn't the time for you to start a fucking brawl. That shit would go viral. Too many cameras."

"All right," Ron agrees. "But if you need a distraction to get the fuck out of here, you let me know." Before I can nod or tell him that that's actually a good idea, he pulls me back into a bone-crushing hug. My back aches with the pressure, all screwed up from sleeping on the ground for two weeks, but I don't say anything. For Ronnie Damon to be this emotional means something. "Fuck, Henry. I'm so fucking glad you're okay. We've all been worried sick."

"Thanks, Ron," I say, my voice rough. It's exhaustion. It's emotion. It's everything. "It's good to see you guys."

Mav follows suit, giving me another hug with a hearty clap to my back. "You scared the shit out of us, man. I swear I've never seen Ron cry so much."

"Fucker," Ron whispers under his breath as I laugh.

"It's good to be back." It's a dichotomous statement—both true and false at once. Being back is everything I prayed and hoped for every day, and yet I haven't felt right since we got here.

Avery's hugging Beau now, her face pressed into his shoulder and her niece Addy patting her hair. June is holding Avery's hand, tears streaking her cheeks, and Neil has an arm around Diane, both of Avery's parents looking like they've aged a decade in the past two weeks. And her grandparents watch on—Phil and Bev standing sentry behind Neil, while Bill comforts Judy over to the side.

Avery turns her head slightly, and for a split second, our eyes meet. My whole body locks up tight. The need to hug her, hold her—it's so fucking overwhelming. I've spent the last thirteen days with this woman. Every single minute, second, hour was spent together, trying to survive and cope and find a way to get through it all.

We're bonded.

The urge to go to her, to tell her I'll never forget the nights we spent together on the island, to tell her that I don't want what we shared to stop now that we're home, is right there, so close to fruition I actually take a step.

"Henry!" a familiar female voice yells from the opposite direction, stealing my attention and sending my stomach to my toes.

Ashley. *My fucking girlfriend.* She's running toward me, her blond hair flying behind her, tears streaming down her face as she busts through the line of reporters and shoves Ronnie and Mav to the side. She throws her arms around me before I can react and sends my weakened body back a step with the impact of her weight.

"Oh my God, Henry! I thought… I thought I'd lost you!" Her voice cracks, and at the sound of her anguish, I feel like the world's biggest asshole. The only time I thought about Ashley in the last thirteen days was when Avery asked me about her, and upon arriving here, it stings to admit, but I didn't even think to look for her.

She's a nice woman and an innocent victim in a conflicted situation, but right now, her body against mine feels like the enemy. A betrayal to the nights I spent cuddled with Avery and the very real sex we had on the island—my cock deep inside her and my eyes locked on her face when she came.

It's so fucking ironic that the reality is the exact opposite.

"God, Henry. I was so worried," Ashley chokes out. "S-so scared."

"I'm okay," I say, my voice hollow. "I'm here."

Ashley pulls back just enough to look at me, her hands still gripping my arms. "I can't believe you're actually here," she says, her eyes searching mine. "I've been praying for you every single day, Henry. Praying that you'd come back to me."

Come back to her.

Ashley's grip tightens, and she presses her face into my chest.

I wrap my arms around her out of reflex, but my eyes keep drifting back to the crowd, searching for Avery. She's nowhere to be seen, and the ache in my chest deepens.

For thirteen days, it was just Avery and me. *Together.*

Now, there's another woman in my arms, and I'm not sure where we stand at all.

Chapter 25

I F MY ISLAND TAN WERE JUST A LITTLE BRONZIER, NOT ONLY would I feel like a goldfish in a bowl being ogled by an entire city, but I'd look like one too.

My ears ring from the helicopter, and my heart pounds in percussive harmony with the sound. The cameras haven't stopped flashing, and my body hasn't breathed air since we got here, smothered instead by the desperate hugs of my parents and grandparents and Beau and June and Addy, and now, to make matters worse, there's a woman fondling Henry Callahan like she owns him, and she is *not* me.

"God, Avery!" June cries into my neck, still worked up fifteen minutes into our arrival. I barely manage to keep my balance as she clings to me. Her tiny baby bump presses against my stomach, and she's sobbing again like a water main break. "I can't believe you're here! You're really here!"

"Relax, June," I say, patting her back as gently as I can. "I'm fine. See? All in one piece."

She pulls back, mascara streaking her cheeks, and glares at me like I just insulted her unborn child. "Relax? Relax?! You were missing for two weeks, Avery! I thought I lost you! I thought I was never going to see you again! And you want me to relax? Are you kidding me!"

Oh boy.

"Juni, honey," I say, gently putting my hand on her shoulder. "I think you need to calm down. You're pregnant, and there's no way it's healthy to be this worked up. I mean, I know how scary a life without me in it sounded…" Beau and my mom both bark little laughs, obviously relieved to find I'm still the same Avery they know and love. "But I'm here. I've been here for fifteen minutes."

"You're impossible," she huffs, swatting my arm away before pulling me into another hug. "I hate you. Don't ever do that again."

"I love you too," I mumble into her shoulder.

When June finally lets me go, my gaze latches on to my dad's face. He's crying actual tears—something I haven't seen him do in years, and a pang of serious discomfort runs through me. If he's feeling things this strongly, they truly must have thought I was dead.

"Dad, are you crying?" I ask, my voice dripping with disbelief.

"Shut up, Avery," he says, sniffing loudly. "Shut up and give me another hug because I thought I'd never see you again."

I roll my eyes but step into his arms. His hug is tight, almost crushing and a little painful, but it's comforting. There's never been a problem my daddy couldn't fix—or, at the very least, would try to with all the money and resources at his disposal. I can't imagine the lack of control he felt not even being able to find me, let alone save me.

"Okay, okay, Neil. Release the vise grip, or else you're going to break my ribs," I say, laughing softly.

"Good," he mutters, eventually letting me go. "Serves you right for scaring me half to death."

My mother pulls me into another hug, her forty-seventh, if I recall, squeezing me a tiny bit less tightly because her breast implants make it tough to get as close, and then Beau is next, his expression a mix of relief and annoyance. "If you ever pull a stunt like this again, I swear…"

"You swear, what?" I retort, quirking a brow at him. "I only went on this trip because of the two of you, remember? *You can't back out. It'll still be fun,*" I mock, using my best version of his and June's voices.

I don't mean to place any blame or renew erroneous guilt at all—it's a joke, at best—but good intentions or not, the words do not help June's emotions. My niece Addy tries to console her with a few pats to her shoulders, but I have a feeling the pregnancy hormones are running this ship now. "Oh my God!" she wails. "I did this to you. We did this to you! We—"

Beau cuts off her tormented tirade by pulling her and Addy into his arms and pressing a soft kiss to June's forehead. "It's okay, Juniper June. Don't focus on the what-ifs, baby. Focus on the fact that both Avery and Henry are safe."

"Avery and Henry!" June wails into his shoulder. "That's all I've heard for the past two weeks. *Avery and Henry* have been missing for forty-eight hours. *Avery and Henry* have been missing for five days. Ten days and the rescue teams have still not been able to find *Avery and Henry.*" She sobs harder and pulls me back into her arms, and with a quick glance over her shoulder at my brother's tired eyes, I start to wonder if he's had it harder than me after all.

Sure, I was hungry and thirsty and I missed my creature comforts, but for thirteen days, he's had…*this.*

"Don't ever do that again!" June yells at me, but her face is pressed into my shoulder, and her voice is muffled through her sobs. "You're never allowed to travel anywhere, Ave. And if you go anywhere, you need to tell me first. I don't care if it's to your stupid Botox appointment. You need my permission."

My poor June. She's a mess.

"I love you. I'm safe." I squeeze her tightly, gently rubbing my hand up and down her back. "And I promise I won't travel anywhere without your approval, okay? You can even come to my pap smear appointments and hold the speculum if it makes you feel better."

"Okay." She nods and sniffles, which makes me smile. Volunteering for OB-GYN duties without a degree is the definition of *being in a bad way.*

Eventually, she leans back, shaking her head as she does, and Beau reaches forward to swipe a few tears from her face. He also takes Addy from June's hip, and June releases me from her Hulklike hold and steps into Beau's side.

"You's okays, Auntie?" Addy asks, and I rush to press a kiss to her cheek. This has to be so confusing for her, and I imagine I look nothing like she's used to either.

"Yes, Addy. I'm okay. Promise."

Addy smiles and even holds out her hand to give me a high five.

My grandma Bev shoves out of my grandpa Phil's arms and wraps me in a hug clogged with expensive perfume. It's a popular older ladies' scent apparently, as I've learned over the last year.

I hug her back, squishing into her plush, blood-red sweater and breathing her in. My grandparents are the ritzy type—not the cookie-baking, sleepover-holding, lollipop-doling-out kind I've heard of online—but their love and loyalty is immeasurable, and I can't imagine the strain of watching their own children long for me.

"Love you, Grandma," I whisper into her ear, and she just purses her red-stained lips and pokes the tip of my nose before retreating back to her posse.

I know my other three grandparents are dying for hugs, too, but staying back to keep from smothering me, so I go to them instead, pulling them each into my embrace and holding them as tightly as my arms will manage.

My grandfathers both pull back quickly, trying to conceal the shaking embodiment of their tears. My mom's mom, Judy, though, she lays a wet kiss on my cheek so moist, I'm pretty sure if I spread it around, I could use it as a shower.

"Never scare us like that again," June threatens as I step into my own space, a jack-in-the-box on repeat, and I smile at her.

"No more island adventures. I promise." It's a truth and a reminder at once, urging me to find my source of comfort in the crowd now that I can breathe again.

It doesn't take long to find Henry where I saw him last; I'm too attuned to him at this point to struggle. The woman I can only assume is his girlfriend, Ashley, clings to him even tighter.

She's pretty—blond, petite, and well-dressed—and very clearly emotional over him. She cares. Maybe even loves him. And I can't even fucking blame her.

Henry Callahan is the real deal.

He leans in, speaking softly to her, and the visual feels like someone has buried a knife straight into my chest. Which is stupid... right?

She's his girlfriend. I'm just the woman he survived with, the woman who coerced him into taking her virginity even when he fought it because he's a *good* fucking guy. *The woman who wishes she were right there, in his pretty girlfriend's place.*

Before I can dwell on it further, another voice cuts through the chaos, a raging bellow of an irritable man who I find quickly fighting with Coast Guard security to get through. "Avery!"

Oh God. Justin. My...boyfriend. Even if I did blame Henry for clinging to me while we were there and then running back to Ashley upon arrival—which I don't—it'd be the literal definition of calling the kettle black.

I didn't just forget about Justin while we were there—I willfully ignored him. *You're a total bitch, Avery Banks. A total fucking bitch.*

In a full-blown cry, his face red and blotchy, Justin pulls me into a hug that sends my small, frail body reeling. "Thank God you're okay! I was so worried about you, Avery!"

"Uh, hey, Justin," I say, my voice awkward as I pat his back. "I'm fine. Really."

He pulls back, his hands on my shoulders, and looks me over like he's inspecting me for injuries.

"I thought I'd lost you," he says, his voice thick with emotion. "I've been so worried, Avery. I feel like it's been a year since I last saw you, baby."

My mind struggles to remember the last time I even saw Justin.

I mean, in my defense, we've only been dating for a short time. A month. Two months, tops. *I think…*

The point is, clubbing with Justin and making out on the dance floor feels like an entirely different lifetime ago.

"I'm good, Justin." I know my tone is a little too light for the situation, but hell's bells, I don't know how to react to someone I completely forgot existed. I've always been the type of girl who wears her emotions on her sleeve, so hiding the fact that I can hardly remember why I was even dating this guy in the first place is really damn hard.

He leans forward to press a kiss to my lips, and it's a shock to my system. I've kissed hundreds of guys in my lifetime—in clubs, at random, and without second thought—but for the first time ever, the very act feels wrong.

Even as Justin talks, my eyes search for someone else. *The only someone else.*

"God, Avery, I've missed you. And going through the past two weeks thinking I'd lost you for good has put everything into perspective for me," Justin says, taking my hand into his.

Behind me, I hear my dad whisper to my mom, "Who is this guy?"

To which she answers, "That's Avery's boyfriend, Jamie."

"It's Justin," June corrects quietly.

Beau laughs.

I'm distracted easily, but Justin doesn't hear them at all, rubbing at the backs of my hands with his thumbs and staring into my scattered eyes. "When I saw you were being rescued, I knew what I needed to do. What I *wanted* to do. Life shifted, you know? Got put into perspective."

Releasing my hand, he sinks his own into his pocket and bends notably at the waist, his knees flexing forward. My eyes narrow as he gets shorter and shorter, his body looking increasingly, frighteningly, like he's about to get down on one knee.

Oh my Gawd. Yep. The knee just made contact.

My eyes go wide. "No. No, no, no, nooooo," I rush to say,

putting my hands to his biceps and lifting with all my strength. But I'm arguably weaker than normal, he isn't budging, and his stupid fucking knee might as well be glued to the tarmac.

My mom gasps, and June shrieks. My grandpa Phil clears his throat like he's choking.

Panicked, I lean forward and get close, my words urgent. "Not right now, Justin," I whisper toward him, shaking my head maniacally. *Not ever, for the love of everything.*

Justin's brow furrows.

"What is he doing?" Beau questions, stepping closer. I turn to him quickly, praying to all that's holy to keep him from drawing more attention to this.

"Nothing," I say quickly. "He's doing absolutely nothing. Right, Justin?"

Justin looks up at me, confused. "Avery?"

"Justin," I say, trying to keep my voice steady. "Now is not the time. Seriously. Get up."

Reluctantly, he stands, his face a mix of hurt and confusion. "I...I just wanted to—"

"Don't," I interrupt, putting a hand on his arm and then gentling my voice as much as I can manage. "We'll talk later, okay?"

Justin nods slowly, stepping back, and I let out a breath I didn't realize I was holding.

I glance frantically to Henry, and for the first time since we've arrived, thank God for the blonde clinging to his every word and distracting him.

I don't want to go back. To the heat and the hunger and the uncertainty.

But I can't avoid that some things *were* simpler.

Better, even.

On the island, I didn't need an excuse to keep Henry to myself.

Chapter 26

Henry

"**I** THOUGHT I LOST YOU," ASHLEY CRIES, HER VOICE CRACKING. She grips me like she's afraid I'll disappear again, and I fight every instinct in my muscles to do just that. The contact is awkward and forced on my end, but the guilt of feeling that way is enough to keep my arms awkwardly around her.

"I'm okay," I murmur, but I'll be the first to admit, the words are empty. They're a comfort to a fellow human being, and no more.

For thirteen days, Ashley didn't even cross my mind. Not when I was fishing for our next meal. Not when Avery and I were laughing under the stars. Not when we were tangled together, finding comfort we didn't know we needed.

And I know right now, as I can't help but search for Avery over the top of Ashley's head, that's never going to change.

It might make me the biggest asshole on the planet, but as soon as I find an appropriately private moment, I have to cut Ashley loose. It's a little cruel—but not nearly as bad as making her think there's something here to hold on to when, to me, there isn't.

"You scared me so much," Ashely whispers, pulling back to look at me. Her mascara is streaked, and her eyes are red and puffy. She's beautiful, despite the despair, but she's not Avery.

Not even close.

"I'm sorry," I manage, though it's not enough, and it probably never will be. Whether I like it or not, at the end of today, I will be the villain in Ashley's story.

I own that.

"Man, look at you." Ronnie shakes his head, grinning, before giving my shoulder a hearty pat. I welcome the distance it makes Ashley give me, if temporarily. "You're, like, actually alive."

"Right?" Maverick smirks. "It feels like a fucking miracle. Thought we'd be telling your story on a podcast by now…maybe even get a Netflix doc out of it."

"You two with a podcast?" I snort, my lips twitching upward despite the weight on my chest. "Really?"

"Hey, it's the age of content," Ronnie says, shrugging. "Might as well capitalize."

"Hell yeah," Mav chimes in. "Plus, Ronnie has that Theo Von vibe, you know? The wild shit that comes out of his mouth would be sound-bite heaven."

I laugh. "Well, sorry I've ruined your big ticket to fame."

"It's okay," Maverick says, clapping me on the shoulder. "I think I'd rather have you here than be catapulted into the spotlight and make millions of dollars and shit."

"You think, or you know?" I question, an eyebrow quirking.

Mav just shrugs. "Just give me another day or two to ponder it."

I laugh. "Oh, I see how it is."

Ronnie cracks up and wraps his arm around my shoulder to jostle me back and forth a little. "Really? I'm not sure you can see at all. I mean, you look like total shit, dude." He shakes his head, pretending to be embarrassed.

I snort. "Yeah. I don't smell so great either."

These guys are the closest thing I have to family now, aside from Avery and the Bankses. Ashley tries to comfort me by telling me I look rugged, but I just shrug it off. I know Avery thinks the way I look and smell is just fine, which is really all that matters to me.

I spot her, standing in another tight circle of hugs and tears and smiles with her family. It's exactly how it should be, and yet a pang of loneliness twists in my chest.

"You okay, man?" Maverick asks, his brow furrowing.

"Yeah," I say quickly, brushing it off. "Just tired."

"Of course you're tired," Ashley says, having to remind me of her presence yet again, and wraps her arms around my waist. "I'm just so happy you're here, Henry. So happy you're safe."

Avery's head tilts as she says something to Beau, her smile faint but genuine. She looks safe. She looks…loved. It makes my chest ache and settle all at once, even with some meathead douchecanoe standing next to her.

Justin, I have to assume.

The guy's tall and decent-looking, with an earnest expression that grates on my nerves. I can handle the opportunists and the good-time chasers—but a guy who seems like he sincerely cares about her can fuck right off.

That's my job. It's a crazy, unbidden thought, but I'll be fucked in the head if it isn't true. The man who got on that plane is not the same man I am now, and I don't give a shit. I don't want to go back.

Justin holds her hand, his body angled toward hers like he's staking a claim, and something cold and sharp knots in my stomach.

Desperate for an escape, I move my attention to Beau, redirecting my focus. He's walking over, his expression tired but relieved. "How you holding up?" he asks when he arrives at our little huddle, pulling me into a quick hug and relieving me of Ashley's hold once again.

"I'm doing good," I lie. "I mean, I'm here, right?"

"Damn right, you are," Beau says, clapping me on the shoulder.

"How's Avery?" I question, unable to hold back my curiosity.

"She's good. A little rattled, maybe." Beau laughs. "I can't be sure, but I swear her boyfriend almost proposed to her. Which would be fucking wild because my parents didn't know jack shit about him. Frankly, the only reason I knew anything was because Avery tells June everything."

"He was going to *propose*?" My stomach sinks, then flares with something that feels a lot like jealousy. "You're fucking kidding me, right?"

"Dude, I don't know," Beau says, shaking his head. "All I know is he got down on one knee, and then Avery told him to stop."

Before I can respond with a fist pump or scream into the ether, a Coast Guard officer approaches, a clipboard in hand and his eyes on me. "Mr. Callahan?"

"Yes," I say, giving Beau a jerk of my chin before stepping away.

The officer nods toward a man in scrubs standing nearby. "This is Dr. Matthews. You'll have to go to the hospital for evaluation, as it's standard protocol after an extended survival situation. He'll travel with you to a private wing, and those police officers behind him will escort you until you're there for security purposes."

Security purposes. Like I'm some kind of A-lister or politician. It sounds absolutely ridiculous on the surface, but seeing as the press hasn't stopped taking pictures since we got here, I guess it isn't a bad idea.

I glance back at Ronnie and Maverick, then at Beau, who gives me a small nod. "Go," he says. "We'll catch up later."

My gaze drifts to Avery one last time. She's still with her family, her arm looped through June's as her dad rubs her back. Justin stands a few feet away, looking like a kicked puppy. Avery's expression softens as she glances my way, and for a moment, our eyes meet.

My chest tightens, the need to be close to her omnipresent.

"Mr. Callahan?" the coastguardsman asks again.

"Yeah," I say, tearing my gaze away. "Let's go."

The good thing about protocol is that it leaves very little room for exceptions. If I'm required to go to the hospital, so is Avery.

And maybe, just maybe, we'll be away from prying eyes long enough for me to talk to her.

Chapter 27

Avery

YOU'D THINK AFTER SPENDING THIRTEEN DAYS STUCK ON an island, I'd savor the feel of a bed and fresh linen, but even with the blankets piled high on my lap and the warm saline solution pumping into my veins through the IV, this hospital room is too white, too sterile, and too cold for my liking. I can't shake the chill.

The doctor has already come and gone, telling me everything looks fine except for mild dehydration and that I'll need to stay overnight for observation. But otherwise, I'm good to go.

Physically, anyway.

Mentally, I'm still stuck on that island. With Henry.

Sure, it wasn't easy, but the air was warm, the sun bright, and at the end of each day, I knew what to expect. Now, I don't know if I'll ever feel the comfort of Henry's arms or hear the soft lull of him singing me to sleep again, and everything about not knowing last night might have been the *last night* makes me uneasy.

And to make matters worse, I haven't seen him since the tarmac. It's been hours, but my mind keeps replaying every glance, every word, every touch we shared over the last two weeks, and it silently cries out in desperation to know if any of it will ever happen again.

My family—Mom, Dad, Beau, and June—are crowded around my bed, trying to fill the silence with laughter and questions and

June's occasional hormone-fueled emotional outbursts, and Justin is around here somewhere in the gift shop or something—though, if I'm honest, I lost track—but my head is someplace else. Specifically, in an island fog of unanswered questions about Henry freaking Callahan.

My grandparents went home under the assurance that I'd call and see them soon, the excitement of the search and rescue and seeing me again an overwhelming thing for their well-worn nervous systems, and if I can manage it soon, I'm hoping to convince everyone else to leave too.

Normally, I'd love this level of attention, but right now, I just feel overwhelmed.

"So, what's next?" Beau asks, breaking my train of thought. "Do they just let you out tomorrow or what?"

"Pretty much," I say, taking a sip of water. "Just some fluids and observation and a couple of hot meals. Nothing major."

"I swear, this all feels like I just woke up from a nightmare." Mom sniffles and hugs Addy closer to her chest. "I'm just so happy you're here, Avery. So happy you're okay. I can't even imagine what could've happened. What if—"

"I'm fine, Mom," I cut her off before she can get herself worked up all over again. "See?" I wiggle my fingers for effect, trying to lighten the mood. "I mean, besides the fact that I'm in serious need of a fresh mani." My hands are rough, my cuticles dry, and my polish chipped. My nail tech, Marty, will be horrified when he gets a look at these daggers.

Unfortunately, my joke goes over like a batch of botched filler. My mom's bottom lip trembles, and June starts to get all teary-eyed again.

"She's right, Avery." June grabs my hand, a fresh wave of tears streaming down her cheeks. "We thought we lost you. I thought I lost you!"

"Relax, June," I say, trying to sound breezy. "I'm here, okay? I'm not going anywhere."

"Relax?" she exclaims. "You were missing for two weeks, Avery! *Two weeks!* I thought I was going to have to name my kid after you or something!"

I snort. "I mean, Avery *is* a great name for a baby…"

June narrows her eyes at me, but her lips twitch like she's trying not to smile. "You're impossible."

I shrug, leaning back against the pillows. I don't want to be sad. I don't want to cry or wail or complain. I just want to feel warm. My gaze drifts to Beau, and before I can stop myself, I ask the only question truly burning me. "Have you seen Henry? Is he doing okay?"

"He's on another floor because Mom bribed the nurses to give you this room since it had the best view," he answers.

My head jerks to my mom petulantly. "And you didn't bribe them to give Henry a good room too?"

She frowns. "Of course I did. They only had one room with a good view on each floor."

I shake my head lightly, trying to seem nonchalant, but my chest is much tighter than I let on. *I wish she would have kept us together.*

Is he alone? I know it shouldn't matter, but it does. Henry doesn't have family anymore. Just Ronnie and Maverick and Beau—but one of them is in my room with me. My throat feels dry, and I swallow hard against the uncomfortable sensation.

"Is…is anyone with him?" I ask, my voice quieter than I intend.

Beau shrugs. "Yeah, Ronnie and Maverick and Ashley. Ron says they're still doing evaluations, but so far, so good."

"Good," I manage to squeak out. "I'm glad someone is with him, at least." *Even if one of those someones is his dumb girlfriend.*

June laughs. "Honestly, I'm surprised there weren't more girlfriends waiting for him on the tarmac. You know Henry and women. As soon as news of your plane disappearing hit the papers, I figured they'd be crawling out of the woodwork like roaches."

Beau chuckles. "Ah, but the news of his survival is fresh. There's still time."

"Henry is such a nice young man," Mom says, dabbing at her eyes with a tissue. "I hope one day he'll decide to settle down."

"Doubtful," Beau snorts. "He's always been a bit of a lone wolf when it comes to long-term relationships. He only turned semi-monogamous when he realized he was the only one left without a girlfriend."

Their words sting more than I'd like to admit. Henry might be a lot of things—restless, unpredictable, a little reckless—but for the past two weeks, he's been my everything. I don't like feeling like an outsider in this conversation, and I don't like feeling like someone knows him better than I do. At all.

I gave myself to him. Completely. Something I've never done with anyone else, and even with the uncertainty of all this, I don't regret it. But I don't know where we stand. I don't even know if he wants to stand anywhere with me at all or if it's a long-lost memory stuck on the island we aren't on anymore.

"You know," June says, breaking into my thoughts. "It's kind of funny Henry and Avery were stranded together."

"Why?" I ask, sitting up a little straighter. There's an edge to my voice I don't mean to add, but it sure sounds like the very thing I'm crying over internally is about to be the butt of a joke.

"Because he's like the male version of you, you know?" June says. "I mean, I didn't even know much about your boyfriend Justin. Hell, today was the first time I actually met him, even though I'm pretty sure you've been dating for, like, two months."

"A boyfriend who apparently wanted to propose," Beau chimes in.

"Ju…he wasn't going to propose," I argue, but even as I say it, I have to work to remember his name. *Justin, Avery. Your boyfriend's name is Justin, for fuck's sake.*

"I don't have the best eyesight these days, but the boy got down on one knee, sweetheart," Dad says, crossing his arms.

"He needed to tie his shoe," I lie.

"He was wearing loafers," Dad counters.

"Which is clearly a fashion offense punishable by jail and not the sort of thing a man I'd consider betrothal to would *ever* do," I say, pointedly rolling my eyes and glancing down at my father's favorite Gucci leather loafers that he's currently wearing. They're from ten seasons ago, and the leather is so worn it looks like he attempted to hike Mount Everest in them.

"Nice deflection," my dad muses, and I roll my eyes again. Though, I know he's not wrong. None of them are. Justin *was* about to propose, and while stringing guys along while they jump to fulfill my every whim isn't new, it also isn't right. I need to cut him loose as soon as possible.

As if on cue, the door swings open, and Justin walks in with a massive bouquet of flowers. Red and white and pink roses bundled together in an arrangement so large, he has to bend at the hip to show his face. Several sets of wide, amused eyes turn in my direction, beaming against my embarrassment like a spotlight.

Not only was this fucker about to propose before, but I'm starting to grow concerned he's going to do it *again* if I don't act quickly.

"Avery, baby," Justin says, his voice soft and emotional as he sets the bouquet on the table beside me. "How are you feeling?"

"I'm good," I say awkwardly, glancing at the flowers. They're beautiful, but all I feel at the sight of them is a sharp pang of discomfort. This feels wrong. He *is* wrong—like a chapter I should've closed before it even got started. "But we need to talk."

"Talk. Yes, of course. Let's talk," Justin says, sitting in the chair beside my bed. His eyes are full of genuine concern, which is truly appreciated, but if I could scratch his eyes out to make it stop without making a scene, I would. "You really scared me, Avery."

I open my mouth to say something—anything to ease the tension—but before I can, Beau's smothered laugh and my mom's responding chide remind me I'm not alone. Not even close.

My mom, my dad, June, Beau, Addy—the whole fucking Brady Bunch is here, watching my every move. Thank God my grandparents left, or there'd be an even bigger audience to this shitshow.

"Hey, guys," I say, gritting a smile to make the request feel less abrasive. "Could you…buzz off for a little bit? Justin and I need a moment."

I just catch Justin's misguided smile out of the corner of my eye before my dad nods, rustling the herd with a wide sweep of his arms. "Of course. Come on, come on, guys. Let's give Avery a minute to decompress."

"I don't want to go," June says then, fighting the gentle pull of Beau and my parents and bursting through to come to my bedside. I smile and cup my best friend's panicked cheek, knowing if our roles were reversed, I'd be a basket case in the exact same way.

"Oh, Juni. I'm okay. Promise."

"I just want to stay here with you tonight. Know for sure."

I nod. "I know you do. But you need rest. I can see it in the god-awful circles under your eyes, sweetie. And so do I. Go home, take a bubble bath, send Beau out to get me a new phone…" I eye my brother, and he nods his compliance without complaint. If I can get a phone, maybe I can figure out a way to get in touch with Henry. "And take care of my best friend the way she'd expect me to take care of myself. Okay?"

She finally nods, leaning forward to kiss my forehead before shoving off the bed and melding immediately into Beau's waiting arm. "I'll be back first thing in the morning."

I shrug. "I'd expect nothing less."

A blissful silence befalls the room as my family shuffles out, and Justin shifts to lean a hip into my bed in the spot June just vacated.

He's still smiling, oblivious to the fact that his presence feels like a weight pressing down on my chest and the bomb I'm about to drop to relieve it.

"I just want to make sure you're okay," he says. "After everything you've been through…it's the least I can do."

"You don't have to stay," I say finally, my voice softer than I intend. None of this is his fault, and that makes it harder than it should be.

"I want to…" Justin's brows knit together, seemingly clueing in to my stiff shoulders and gritty frown. "Unless you don't want me here?"

I swallow hard. This is the moment. I could let him stay, maintain this facade just to feel less alone knowing Henry is somewhere in this hospital with his girlfriend Ashley, but it would be a lie. And I'm so tired of lying to myself, even if it's easier.

"Justin," I start, my voice firm. I take a deep breath, steeling myself to hurt a nice person's feelings. "You're a great guy. Really. And I've appreciated you being here for me. But there is no future for us."

His face falls, and for a moment, I hate myself for being so concise. "What do you mean?" he asks, his voice low.

"I mean us," I say. "I…I don't think we're right for each other. And it's not fair to you for me to keep pretending otherwise."

He's quiet, his jaw tightening as he processes my words. "But I thought we had something, Avery. I'm in lo—"

"No," I cut him off, holding up my hand. "Don't go there, Justin. Please, do not go there."

"But I do, Avery!" he exclaims, shoving off the bed to stand to his full six-foot-three height. "I lov—"

"You think you do," I cut him off again. "But you don't really know me. And honestly, I don't really know you." *Let's face it, I fucking forgot about you while I was on that island.* "We were only dating for a very short time before everything happened, and I'm grateful that you're here and I'm sorry for all of the stress I've put you through, but we're not right together."

"How can you say that?" he questions. "How do you even know if you don't try?"

"Justin, I just know, okay?" I retort. "I just know." *I know how it feels when it's right.*

"I can't believe this," Justin mutters, running a hand through his hair. "I thought…I really thought this was going somewhere."

I shake my head, staring down at my hands as I knot my fingers together. "The truth is, Justin…no relationship with any man, for me, has ever been going anywhere."

Being stranded on an island with Henry is just what made me re-alize why…

His brow draws together as he tries to make sense of it all—what I'm saying, how he's feeling, maybe even how everything he thought we had was a lie. "Are you saying…"

I nod.

"Are you saying you're a lesbian?"

"Ye—wait. What?"

"You said it's never been going anywhere with *any man*."

I'm not proud of it, but I almost go with it, just to spare his feelings. In the end, though, I think it really is time that I grow up enough to hold myself responsible for my choices, good or bad.

"No. I…I'm sorry I wasn't clear. I'm just not the right fit for you, Justin. I…have a lot of personal growth to do, some of which started in the last thirteen days, and it's taught me a few things I can't ignore. I would love to stay friends, if you think that's something you'd be okay with, but romantically, this is the end of the line."

He sighs, settling his hands on his hips and looking thoughtfully away before turning back to me. "I guess I should have seen this coming… I was just hoping it wasn't."

I nod and shrug. Not to make light of the situation but to put on the punctuation all the same. There isn't anything that could happen in this room to change my mind because of everything that happened somewhere else. "I'm sorry." Because truthfully, I am sorry. Sure, I love attention and adoration, but I don't love the idea that this guy was pining for me—fearing that I was dead—while I was stranded on an island. That doesn't make me feel good. And that says a lot because, usually, just about every type of attention makes Avery Banks feel good.

"It's okay. I'll…I'll just have to get back to you on the being-friends thing. I'm not sure I'm ready for that."

"Of course. I understand."

"Well…" He shrugs. "Goodbye, I guess."

"Goodbye, Justin."

Ironically, now that I've cut him loose, I'm having a lot less trouble remembering his name.

He doesn't say anything after that, instead searching my eyes for one long moment. Eventually, he leans forward to press a kiss to my cheek and walks out of my room, and I take the first full breath I've had since the helicopter landed at the Coast Guard station.

The door clicks shut behind him, and just like that, all my guilt over Henry is gone.

In its place, an intense yearning I can't quite shake. The room feels bigger now, colder. I sit back on the bed, staring at the door like I'm expecting someone to walk through it.

But no one does.

My thoughts scour memories of Henry, pausing on his crooked smile and the way his eyes softened when he looked at me on the island. To the way he made me feel like I wasn't just beautiful, but… enough.

I close my eyes, leaning back against the pillows. Life on the island was hard, but it was simple. With Henry, everything felt clear. Here, in this hospital room, surrounded by the mess of reality, I'm not sure of anything anymore.

Except for one thing: I miss him. And it doesn't feel like there's a damn thing I can do about it.

Chapter 28

Henry

THE HOSPITAL ROOM IS QUIET IN COMPARISON TO THE Coast Guard station, but it feels anything but peaceful. It's sterile and empty, the faint beeping of machines the only sound, and in some weird way, it feels as if I've been dropped off on a new island to start all over again.

Maverick and Ronnie left about an hour ago after making their usual jokes to lighten the mood, but now it's just me and Ashley and my tortured thoughts.

She's sitting in the chair by the bed, her fingers fidgeting with the edge of the sheet draped over me like she's trying to smooth out wrinkles that aren't even there. I should say something, but I don't know what, and even when I try, nothing comes out. I've been quiet since they brought me here, my mind running circles around everything and nothing.

Mostly, though, around Avery.

I shouldn't be thinking about her. Not right now. Not with Ashley sitting a foot away, her eyes red from crying. But I can't help it. Thirteen days on that island… It was like nothing else existed. Just us. And now, sitting here under the harsh fluorescent lights, it feels like a dream I've woken up from too soon.

I pull out my phone—the new phone my assistant Cara dropped off for me after a rigorous fight with security to be let through—and scroll to Beau's number. My thumb hovers over the screen for a second before I type out a quick text, my question simple on the surface. In reality, it's a thought mined from deep roots in a healthy system of weeds.

> Me: How's Avery?

> Beau: Just being kept overnight for observation. Little dehydrated, but she's fine. She kicked us out and sent us home—and sent me to get her a new phone. I guess she's antsy to have her connection to the world of Starbs and nail techs and online shopping back.

I let out a breath I didn't realize I was holding. She's fine. Of course she's fine. Avery's tougher than anyone I know. Still, knowing she's just a floor away and not being able to see her feels like some kind of punishment I didn't earn.

I poise my thumb over the keyboard to tell Beau I've already sent Cara back out to get Avery a phone and deliver it to her too, but I am interrupted by a quiet, unsure voice belonging to a woman I hate to admit I've completely forgotten about again.

"Henry?"

I look up to see Ashley staring at me. She's stopped fidgeting with the sheet, her hands now clasped tightly in her lap, and there's a question in her eyes—one I'm not sure I'm ready to answer.

"Yeah?" I say, forcing my voice to sound even.

She hesitates, her teeth catching on her bottom lip. "Are you okay? You've barely said a word since they brought you here, and I understand what you've been through is…well, it's unimaginable. And I don't want to pressure you, but…"

"I'm fine," I say automatically. It's a lie, but not for the reasons it should be. I'm not traumatized beyond repair and mute from the experience. Just the opposite. I've got things to say—millions of words and phrases and declarations—but my head's so tangled up in thoughts of Avery that I can't focus on anything else.

"Henry," she says softly, leaning forward. She reaches out her hand, resting it lightly on mine. "You can talk to me, you know. About anything."

I look at her, really look at her, and guilt hits me square in the chest. She's trying so hard, and I... I don't feel anything. Ashley may as well be a stranger off the street for how emotional I am to see her, and even though my reasoning is complex, it's still fucked up.

She doesn't deserve this shit, and I need to do the compassionate thing and set her free.

"Ashley," I start, but the words get caught in my throat. I take a deep breath and try again. "I appreciate everything you've been through since I went missing, and I can't explain how touching it is that you care this much that I'm back. But...enlightenment is a switch I can't turn off, and I..."

Her expression shifts, worry flashing across her face. "What's wrong?"

I sit up a little straighter, the IV tugging uncomfortably at my arm. "We're not right for each other. You are amazing. And so, so right for *someone*. But you're not right for me, and I am *not* right for you."

Her eyes widen, and she pulls her hand back like she's been burned. "What are you saying?"

"I'm saying we should end this," I say, forcing the words out before I can second-guess myself. "It's not fair to you at all because I can't give you what you deserve."

She's silent for a long moment, and then she laughs, but it's sharp and humorless. "Is this about her?"

"What?" I ask, caught off guard.

"That girl you were stranded with," she says, her voice rising. "Avery."

I don't answer. I don't need to. My silence says everything. I wish I could say I'm surprised by her supposition, but I'm not. Anyone with eyes and an inclination could tell that Avery was the *only* person I cared about upon arrival.

Ashley stands abruptly, her chair scraping against the floor. "I waited for you. I was worried sick about you. And you were what? Fucking her?"

It's both true and completely discrediting at the same time. Avery and I weren't *fucking*. We were each other's everything. Still, I know I've brought this on myself, so I don't bother with words that won't help to ease the sting in the least. I keep it simple. Succinct. Truthful. Transparently final.

"I'm sorry," I say. "I never meant to hurt you."

She stares at me for a long moment, her chest rising and falling with uneven breaths. Finally, she grabs her bag and turns toward the door. There's no goodbye, no look back.

The door clicks shut behind her, and just like that, it's done.

What was once peaceful quiet feels heavier now, pressing down on me like a weight I can't shake. It's sharp, and I ache.

Sure, my muscles are sore and my skin abused, and the inflammation from the sudden influx of fluids doesn't help either.

But it's not what I'm feeling physically. It's deeper. Dirtier. *Much more complicated.*

I miss her.

And I wonder if she misses me.

Chapter 29

Avery

THE SHOWER FEELS AMAZING. MY SKIN IS PINK AND RAW from scrubbing off layers of dirt and island grime, and I can feel the warmth of the scalding-hot water all the way down to my bones. The tiny hotel-sized shampoo and conditioner in the bathroom don't do much for my hair, but at least it's no longer tangled and greasy.

If I close my eyes to avoid the mirror, I almost feel like myself.

There's no sound in my room, all my alarms and machines turned off to free me for the shower, and moving my arm without an IV for the first time since yesterday afternoon is surprisingly liberating.

It's still early, the beginning of the shift with my new nurse, Elizabeth, but with the scant amount of sleep I got last night, it might as well still be yesterday.

Perusing the bag of skincare my mom had delivered, care of a Neiman Marcus salesperson, along with a fresh set of clothes this morning, I settle on a simple moisturizer and call it a day.

Normally, I'd work my way through a painstaking one-hundred-step routine, complete with serums, moisturizers, treatments, and makeup, and I'd blow-dry my hair section by section and smooth it out with the precision of a stylist.

But this morning, I just…don't care.

I towel off my hair until it's damp and let it hang loose around my shoulders. My skin feels tight from the shower, but I can't muster the energy to do anything about it. Thirteen days on the island stripped away a lot of things, and apparently, my meticulous grooming habits were one of them.

As I pull a sweatshirt over my head and walk out of the bathroom, I'm hit with a memory of Henry's handsome bearded face, cherishing the peeling skin of my nose and chest. I hadn't brushed my hair in days, my face was bare, and my body crusted with building salt and sweat, and it didn't matter.

He could see *me*. Looking at myself in the mirror, I find it hard to imagine how.

I shake the thought away as I step back into the hospital room and tuck my tattered sweater into the hospital-provided plastic bag with my other belongings. It isn't much—a dirty orange bikini, the waist pack I packed in vain, and an utterly ruined pair of Golden Goose shoes.

The door swings open after a manic set of knocks, and June, Beau, and both my parents trail inside in a single-file line. Juniper is the first to pull me in for a hug, and now that I'm standing with two entirely free arms, I don't hesitate to wrap my arms around her shoulders in return.

"Good morning," I say with a small laugh when she doesn't let go.

Beau pulls her gingerly away, and I search the two of them carefully, my eyebrows pulling together. "Where's Addy?"

"We left her with a sitter this morning. I wanted to get up and go get your phone as soon as the store opened, but then Henry called and said his assistant Cara was already taking care of it."

"You talked to Henry?" I ask, my voice undeniably hopeful.

"Yeah. Last night and then again this morning. He's been asking how you are."

"He has?" I want to know more, to ask what Beau's told him

about me and if there's any way we can arrange to go to his floor and see him, but before I can, the door swings open again.

Five older women—whom I know *very* well—march in, armed with balloons, flowers, and gift bags. I'm surprised to see them, given how tight I've been told the security is to get in here, but knowing their connections with the whole Miami judicial scene, I shouldn't be.

I doubt there's a single door in the whole county these bad-ass geriatrics couldn't get in if they wanted to.

"Oh, Avery!" Ethel exclaims, rushing to my bedside. "We thought we lost you! But we saw you on the news! The news, Avery!"

Blanche, Dottie, Joanne, and Sarabeth follow close behind, all dressed to the nines in Chanel tweed, Burberry trench coats, and Yves Saint Laurent blouses. I know their wardrobes by heart because I picked out every piece.

"We had no idea what happened to you, Avery!" Sarabeth exclaims as the five of them hover around me so tightly, I end up pushed back into sitting on my bed. "We all tried to call you a hundred times, and then Blanche saw you on the news—saying you were missing!"

Dottie moves to grab my hand. "Honey, we were so worried about you."

"So worried," Ethel adds as she reaches out to run her hands through my hair.

"Well, there's no need to worry," I tell them. "I'm back and I'm okay."

"Goodness, Avery," Blanche says on a dramatic exhale of air while she clutches her pearls—literal Tiffany pearls. "You gave us such a scare."

"Don't you ever do that again," Dottie chimes in, wagging a finger at me.

"Never again," Ethel agrees. "I swear, you must have one thousand missed calls and text messages between the five of us."

"I would," I answer with a shrug and smile. "But I no longer have my phone. It's…lost." My voice shakes involuntarily, no doubt a trauma response to the morning Henry pitched it. I thought he was gone, dead, hurt. I thought…

A throat clears from behind my five elderly gal pals, and it's only then that I realize my family is standing there completely bewildered by their presence.

My mom leans toward my dad, whispering, "Who are these women?"

"Oh, you must think we're so rude!" Ethel answers before I can. "I'm Ethel and this is Joanne, Sarabeth, Blanche, and Dottie," she introduces each of them. "We're Avery's clients."

"And friends," Dottie adds, and Ethel nods.

"Of course, Avery is such a dear friend to us all. It's just icing on the cake that she's been our stylist for the past year."

"Stylist?" Mom repeats quietly, her confusion deepening, but none of my elderly gal pals seems to notice. They're more focused on giving me hugs and shoving their handkerchiefs at me as they realize how upset I've gotten.

I'm trying to keep it together, but not being able to find Henry now, even in this crowd of people, while the memory of that morning on the island replays in my head has me feeling some kind of way.

"You okay, honey?" Dottie asks, taking the lead, while the other women look away in what I know is an attempt to keep from overwhelming me.

I nod. It's all I can manage.

"Now that we've seen you're okay with our own two eyes, we're going to let you rest, Avery," Ethel says, arranging all the flowers and balloons and gift bags they brought to my room on the nightstand beside my bed.

"Yes, honey, you get some rest," Blanche says, pressing a kiss to my forehead. "You check in with us soon, okay? Let us know when you're out of the hospital and settled?"

I nod. "Once I get a phone again, I'll text you."

"Good girl." Dottie smiles.

They all give me hugs and kisses and pats of my hands a few more times. Ethel even mentions something about a new resident at The Pines named Darla, who's a walking fashion disaster and needs my help. But eventually, they offer their goodbyes to my family and head back out of my hospital room, only leaving a trail of their Shalimar perfume in their wake.

When they're gone, my family stares at me, dumbfounded.

"Who was that?" Beau asks.

"Just my friends," I say, shrugging.

"Your friends?" my mom repeats. "They look about fifty years too old to be your friends."

"And they said you were their stylist," my dad adds.

I sigh, knowing this conversation is inevitable. "That's probably because I am their stylist."

"But, Avery, you're not a stylist," Beau says flatly.

"You don't know everything about me, Beau." I shrug and stick out my tongue at him. "And for the record, I am their stylist. Like Ethel said, I have been for about a year now."

"Excuse me? You're their stylist?" Dad asks, crossing his arms. "How the hell did that happen? Last I knew, you were an employee of Banks & McKenzie."

"Clearly, I'm good at multitasking, Daddy." I lean back, crossing my arms too. "And I met Ethel at Nordstrom's last year. She was in this horrid Kate Spade getup, and I couldn't stand by and let her buy last season's leftovers from some clueless salesclerk. So, I helped her."

"And that makes you a stylist?" Beau asks, raising a brow.

"Oh, c'mon, Beau. I think we all know that my sense of fashion and style pretty much makes me a stylist. I mean, it's one of those talents that some people just have. Like, Edward Einstein and all his number stuff."

"Albert Einstein, Avery," Beau corrects like he's saying stuff I actually care about. "Albert."

"So, let me get this straight…" My dad still looks baffled. "You just help them pick out their clothes?"

"I don't just help them pick out clothes, *Daddy*. I guide them on their wardrobe, shoes, hair, makeup. I *style* them."

"And they pay you for that?" he asks. "As in, it's a job?"

I laugh. "No."

His face falls. "What do you mean, *no*?"

I scoff. "You don't get paid for charity work, Daddy."

"Charity work?" Dad repeats, his voice rising. "They live in The Pines, Avery. Those women have money. A lot of it."

"Daddy, you know I don't judge people on their money."

"Do they at least pay for their clothes?"

"Again, it's charity work," I say, annoyed that he's clearly not getting the point. "You can't expect people to pay for stuff when it's charity."

"Then who is paying for it?"

I shrug. "I guess whoever pays my credit card bill."

My dad's jaw drops. "You mean me."

"And doesn't that make you feel good, Daddy? Helping those women like that?"

He stares at me, completely flabbergasted. "Avery, I swear to God…"

June snickers. "Oh my God."

"It's official." Beau smiles. "Avery is back."

Neil sighs, runs a hand through his hair, but eventually, he just smiles at me too, laughing softly as he wraps his arms around my mom's shoulders.

"I love how it took Avery going missing for thirteen days for me to find out that she's a charity stylist to the rich women of The Pines and I'm footing the bill," he muses, and June bursts into laughter.

But then her hormones get the best of her, and she starts sobbing.

"June?" my mom asks, and June just lifts her hand in the air briefly.

"I'm fine," she stutters out between tears, "just happy my best friend is back," before turning her whole body to bury herself against Beau's chest.

Beau smiles down at June like she hung the stars and the moon—the way he always looks at her—and my chest squeezes.

I want to see Henry. I want to see him badly.

And as of this moment, I'm done waiting to do it.

"I want to see Henry. Can someone take me to his room, please?"

Beau's forehead creases with both confusion and apology as he shakes his head. "They discharged him a little bit ago. Ronnie and Mav are driving him home. No one told you?"

No. No one told me.

Evidently, all references to Avery and Henry as a set ended the minute we landed in Miami.

Henry is just Henry, and I'm just me, and I'm starting to wonder if the two will ever get the chance to mix again.

"Speaking of discharge," my mom says excitedly. "They said you can go home too."

I nod, considering what that even means. I'm not so sure anymore.

I used to think home was a place. Now, I'm wondering if it might be a person.

Chapter 30

Henry

THE DOOR TO MY APARTMENT CLICKS SHUT BEHIND ME, THE sound echoing in the empty space. It feels surreal to be back here. Ten days ago, I'd have killed for this—a hot shower, a bed, clean clothes, and all my comfortable shit.

Now? It feels…hollow. And truly fucking lonely. Which is hilarious, seeing as I practically bribed Ronnie and Mav to leave not ten minutes ago.

I drop the bag my assistant Cara dropped off at the hospital near the door, kick off my shoes, and take a look around.

I bought this condo three years ago—a certified penthouse bachelor pad with an incredible view of the ocean. It was a celebratory purchase when Adrenaline Junkie reached eight figures in revenue and, at the time, a picture-perfect home base for everything I wanted out of life.

Nothing has changed—not the decor, the leather sectional, nor the expensive artwork I let some popular interior designer pick out for me because I thought it'd impress whatever chick I brought home for the night—and yet, it all feels incredibly fucking different.

Crazy how it can be exactly as I left it two weeks ago, down to the massive marble dining table filled with adrenaline-packed posters for our next big marketing campaign scattered across it like badges of honor, and feel, today, like I've been dropped off on another planet.

The faint hum of the refrigerator buzzes, the noise freshly grating after nothing but waves, birds, and Avery.

I sink onto the couch, pulling my phone from my pocket. It lights up with a flood of notifications. Texts, emails, missed calls. I swipe through them mechanically, my thumb scrolling past dozens of messages from journalists, clients, and employees. Everyone wants a piece of the story.

> **Unknown: Henry, can you comment on your survival experience?**
>
> **Cara: Hey boss, hope you're feeling better now that you're home. New phone is being couriered to Avery Banks's condo as we speak. Call me when you're ready to debrief. By the way, Larry Meadows from NewsSource (among several other journalists) is requesting an in-person interview. Are you interested in that?**

Larry Meadows is one of the most popular journalists on national television. Clearly, he wants the inside scoop on the "the island survivors," but I can't deal with any of it right now.

Don't want to deal with any of it right now.

How can I give some kind of interview about what happened between Avery and me on the island? That feels wrong in every kind of way. It feels like…I'm letting someone else in on our secret. Like I'm being disloyal to Avery.

I turn off the phone and toss it onto the coffee table. My head falls back against the couch, and I close my eyes. For the first time in twenty-four hours, there's no one around to ask how I'm feeling, no doctors poking and prodding, no friends cracking jokes to distract me. It's just me.

I don't need the crowd—can't fucking stand it right now, to be honest. But I am undeniably missing one person.

She's still in the hospital, I think. Or maybe she's been

discharged. I don't know. I should have made Ronnie and Mav take me by her room when they let me out, but the iron-fist nurse kept insisting that I take the wheelchair all the way to the door in accordance with hospital policy and left no room for argument on it.

I reach for my phone again, hesitating for a moment before powering it back on. The screen fills with more notifications as the device reconnects, but I ignore them, going straight to my text inbox to find my message thread with Avery. The last messages we sent each other were from months ago, when she was asking me about the New Year's Day trip and trying to talk me out of the skydiving portion.

My snort is audible as I consider how fucking right she was about it being a stupid idea.

I laugh to myself at her horrified reaction to my telling her she had to leave her suitcase behind that morning in the hangar as my fingers hover over the keyboard, unsure of what to say.

According to Cara, there's a chance she doesn't even have the fucking thing yet, and still, I know I would have to be fucking dead to wait another minute to try.

Eventually, I type out something simple.

Me: Hey. Just checking in. How are you feeling?

I hit send and stare at the screen, waiting for the little bubble to pop up, signaling she's typing back. But nothing happens.

Minutes pass, and still nothing. Even though I know that she might not even have the phone yet, the possibility that she does and just doesn't want to talk to me is too ubiquitous to ignore.

I…I don't know what I'll do if that's the case. On the island, it felt like we were in this bubble. Nothing else mattered but surviving and each other. But here, in the real world, everything is different. She has her family, her life.

And me? I have…this. An empty apartment and a phone full of demands.

I set the phone down again, running a hand through my hair.

Was what we had on the island real? Or was it just the circumstances? Two people clinging to each other because there was no one else?

I don't want to believe that. Every moment with her felt real. The way she laughed, even when everything felt impossible. The way she looked at me, like I was more than the reckless guy everyone else sees. And the night she gave herself to me... I'll *never* forget it. I don't want to.

I wish I knew where we go from here.

It's ironic, I guess.

There, we had no option but to sit and wait, and while I thought that ended yesterday, it didn't. It shape-shifted and morphed into something a lot lonelier, but the feeling of waiting is the same.

Waiting to know. Waiting with hope.

My own metaphorical fucking stranded island.

I get up and wander to the kitchen, opening the fridge out of habit. It's empty except for a few takeout containers that have to be weeks, if not months, old. I grab a beer, ignoring the taunt of the morning clock on the stove, crack it open, and lean against the counter.

My mind fixates on the way Avery's hair looked under the sunlight, messy and tangled but perfect, and the way she challenged me and called me out on my bullshit. I see her smile and her frown, and I feel the tears she cried in my arms.

She is unlike anyone I've ever known and has always been that way, even when she was a knobby-kneed thirteen-year-old.

Because of Beau, she's indirectly been in my life for as long as I can remember. And because of the island, she's burrowed into my life in ways I never ever imagined.

And the thought of not having her in my life anymore... It's unbearable.

I grab my phone again, staring at the screen. Still no response. My chest tightens. I've always been the guy who's good at bouncing back, at moving on to the next thrill. But this? This feels different. This feels like something you don't move past.

I take another sip of beer, the cold liquid doing nothing to ease the ache in my chest. For the first time in a long time, I feel lost and not the kind you can fix with a GPS or a map. This is deeper. This is the kind of lost where you don't even know where you're supposed to be looking.

And the worst part? The only person who might be able to help me find my way again isn't here.

And I fucking miss her.

Chapter 31

Avery

"**I** KNOW. YES. YES, I'M LEAVING NOW." JUNE TURNS BACK TO me, her eyes pleading from the sliding door. "Unless Avery thinks I should stay tonight."

I catch myself before I laugh, not wanting to hurt my bestie's delicate pregnancy feelings, but shake my head. "That's not necessary, Juni. Go home to your husband and daughter."

Spinning back to the railing of my balcony, I close my eyes and breathe in the breezy, salty air coming off the water. I've lived in Miami my whole life, and in this specific condo for several years, and I've never appreciated the view as much as I do right now.

It's peace and memories and just enough Henry to keep myself from going stir-crazy in my newly revolutionized world now that I'm officially home from the hospital after being discharged this afternoon.

June's been hovering over me all day, long after Beau left to get Addy from the sitter and my parents went home to their house. And despite lots and lots of trying, I've not been able to get my contacts to load into the new phone that arrived with a simple note from a courier shortly after I got home.

I've synced to my computer and reloaded and restarted and practically bribed the fucking tech gods on Best Buy's website with sexual favors, but nothing, and I mean nothing, has granted me access to my numbers.

June gave me hers and Beau's and my parents, but I've been too embarrassed to ask for Henry's so far, much to my own detriment.

Opening my eyes and taking a deep breath, I take my phone out of my shorts pocket and start messing with it again, toggling all the settings switches like a maniac.

June touches my shoulder, startling me, and I fumble the phone so hard, I just narrowly miss dropping it off the balcony in a dangerous tumble.

"Shoot, sorry," she apologizes. "I didn't mean to scare you. I just… I guess I'm going to go for now. Unless—"

"Don't you dare say it, June. Go home. For the love of God, go home."

"Fine!" She huffs. "Whatever. Just know that I could have fixed you a whole-ass meal if you'd let me stay. Five courses!"

God, she's the best. I smile. "I love you, truly, but once you deliver your newborn several months from now and look back at this time, you'll understand how crazy you're being."

She leans forward and kisses my cheek and then pulls me into a hug. "Call me if you need me."

I nod. "I will." *If I can ever get this phone to work.* I don't dare mention the technological troubles to her, though. She'll never leave.

"What are you going to do?"

I shrug. "Sleep, I guess."

She considers me closely for a long moment, and I pause intently, waiting for the scrutiny to pass.

I know I'm different. *I know.*

But the last thing I want to get into with June right now is all the reasons why.

Ten minutes of begging later, I finally get my best friend out the door, waving goodbye as the doors to the elevator close in front of her.

I shut the front door of the condo and lock it, and then I retreat to my room, climbing into the comfort of newly washed sheets, courtesy of June's neuroses.

It's plush and warm and all the things I longed for during the chilly, uncushioned nights on the island.

And yet, it's all wrong.

I toss and turn, back and forth from one side to the other, karate-chopping my pillow over and over in the dark room until giving up with a groan. I'm tired, almost desperately so, but sleep eludes me anyway.

Sitting up and grabbing it from my nightstand, I toggle all the switches in the settings of my phone again, connecting to the Wi-Fi again when I'm done, and finally, everything loads in a startling flourish.

Texts, calls, emails, and notifications roll in by the hundreds, and I drop the crazed thing on my bed and wait as it struggles to catch up.

It feels a little like a ticking time bomb when I pick it back up, but I scroll furiously to Henry's number and open the message thread, only to find one from him already waiting.

Oh my God. When did he send this?

I sit up straighter in my bed.

Henry: Hey. Just checking in. How are you feeling?

I stare at his message, the words pressing heavy against my chest. My fingers hover over the screen, desperate to answer, but for as much as I want to say *all the things*, I can't settle on a single one. I set the phone back on my nightstand and roll onto my side. The weight of his text lingers, mixing with the endless swirl of thoughts that keep me from sleeping.

The bed feels too big. Too empty. All fucking wrong.

Henry had this way of grounding me, of making me feel safe even when everything around us felt impossible. The sound of his breathing, the warmth of his body next to mine, the low hum of the song he'd sing when I couldn't sleep. It became my anchor. My calm in the chaos.

I turn back toward my nightstand, grabbing my phone without thinking. My thumb hovers over the screen again, but instead of typing, I get out of bed and throw on my favorite Prada sweats before slipping on a pair of Hermès slides and grabbing my purse.

Maybe I can't decide on what to say because fucking typing something out on a stupid phone isn't the answer at all.

I close my door and lock it behind myself quickly, jumping on the elevator of my building and riding it to the basement garage with unconcealed urgency.

My G-Wagon is in its assigned spot like magic, even though the last time I saw it was at the airport hangar on New Year's Day morning, and I climb in and fire it up without hesitation.

My lip gloss is in one cupholder, an old empty Starbucks cup in the other, like artifacts of a woman left behind.

I strap on my seat belt and floor it out of the spot, rolling down my window despite the nighttime chill. The wind grounds me on the drive over, blowing in my hair and tangling it wildly.

On autopilot, I pull into a parking spot outside his building, shutting off my engine and laying my head on the steering wheel as I try to muster the courage to climb out.

This is crazy. I know it is. And so at odds with the twenty-seven years of life I've lived up until the start of this all. But on another wavelength, in a parallel universe, it feels so, so right.

I climb out and head inside, and after a short ride up in the elevator, I'm standing in front of his door. I pause, my mind finally catching up with my surroundings and working to prepare me for an outcome I can't foresee.

What am I expecting him to say?

What am I expecting him to do?

My heart pounds as I lift my hand and knock lightly, and for a moment, all I can hear is the sound of my own breathing.

Then the door swings open.

"Avery?"

Henry's voice is low and rough from sleep, and the sight of him… God, the sight of him steals the air from my lungs. He's standing there in gray sweatpants and a T-shirt that clings to his chest, his hair mussed, his eyes soft with sleep, and his beard still intact.

Maybe it's wishful thinking, but it's the first positive sign that maybe I'm not the only one holding on to the island's alternate reality.

Relief floods through me, so overwhelming that I feel like crying.

I've missed him.

Not just his presence, but everything about him. The way he looks at me, the steadiness of his voice, the way he makes me feel like I'm not alone. Being here, seeing him, it's like finally taking a breath after being underwater for too long.

In that moment, none of the questions matter. *Has he been thinking about me the way I've been thinking about him? Does he miss me, even a fraction of the way I've missed him? Is he still with the blond woman named Ashley?* I need him and his arms more than I need answers to anything.

I shove inside, slamming into his chest and pushing him back until his door falls closed behind us.

"Avery," he says my name again, his voice a soft balm for the rough uncertainty I've become twisted in since we got back.

I open my mouth, but the words catch in my throat. The jumble of feelings I've been carrying threatens to spill out all at once, but I don't know where to start.

So, I say the only thing I can.

"I can't fall asleep."

He pulls back slightly to look me in the eyes, his crinkling carefully at the corners as he brushes my hair behind my ear. Then, without a word, he grabs my hand and guides me through the darkened space on gentle feet. It's such a simple touch, but it sends a shiver down my spine.

His bedroom is dimly lit by the soft glow of a lamp on the nightstand. He pulls back the covers of his currently empty bed, motioning for me to lie down, and I do. The bed is warm, and it smells like him—clean and familiar. He climbs in beside me, his movements careful and deliberate, like he's afraid I might shatter.

But I don't hold back. I curl up against him, tucking my head into his chest.

He wraps his arms around me, pulling me close, and for the first time in two days, I feel like I can breathe again. He slips his hand into my hair, threading his fingers through it in slow, soothing strokes.

"I've got you," he murmurs, his voice rumbling against my cheek.

Tears prick at my eyes, but I blink them away. He moves his hand to my back, tracing soft patterns there, and I feel the tension in my body start to melt away.

Then, softly, he starts to sing. The same song he used to hum on the island. It's not perfect—his voice cracks a little on the higher notes—but it doesn't matter. It's him. *It's us.*

And for the first time since we left the island, I feel like maybe, just maybe, everything will be okay.

The room is still dark, bathed in the faint glow of the moonlight spilling through the blinds of Henry's bedroom. I wake slowly, warmth seeping into every part of me. Henry's arms are wrapped around me, his body pressed firmly against mine. His chest rises and falls steadily, the rhythmic sound of his breathing lulling me even as I stir.

I'm so warm, so perfectly warm, and the hard muscles of his body are a comfort I didn't realize I'd been craving. Being with him like this feels good. Too good.

And the growing ache between my thighs makes one thing clear—*I want him.*

If I'm honest with myself, I've probably wanted him for far longer than I ever allowed myself to realize.

Memories of him flash behind my closed eyes, like an old movie reel playing scenes of my life with him always lingering somewhere in the background.

Him as a sixteen-year-old, all lean muscle and tanned skin, surfing on the beach with Beau while I sat on the sand, pretending not to stare. The day he graduated from college, standing on the stage with that crooked grin that made my stomach flip. I was there for my brother, but my eyes never left Henry.

So many memories. So many moments. And the realization hits me like a freight train. It's not just that he's my brother's best friend. It's so much more than that. I've been into him. *Really* into him. For years.

It's probably why you never noticed June crushing on Beau. You were too busy crushing on Henry.

The thought almost makes me laugh. How inception-y is that? My best friend was pining for my brother, and I was pining for my brother's best friend while being oblivious to the obvious.

I shift slightly, reaching up to run my fingers through Henry's hair. It's soft and thick, curling slightly at the ends. His face is slack with sleep, his features relaxed and unguarded. This man is so handsome, I swear, *GQ* should call him for a front-page profile. Even like this, in the middle of the night, with his lumberjack beard, he's freaking drool-on-myself stunning.

Eventually, his lashes flutter, and his eyes blink open. The startling clear blue warmth of them locks on mine, and we just stare at each other for a long moment.

So many men I've dated, and never once did looking into their eyes feel like this. There's no awkwardness. No pressure. The air between us feels charged with something I can't quite put into words.

"You okay?" he eventually whispers, his voice low and rough.

I nod. "Are you okay?"

"Now that you're here, I am."

His words burrow deep inside me, settling somewhere beneath my rib cage. My heart skips a beat, my eyes dropping to his mouth. Those perfect, full lips. I can't stop myself from remembering how it felt to kiss him. How it felt to let myself give in to him on the island.

You want to kiss him again.

"Henry?" I whisper.

"Yeah?"

"Are you with that girl?"

He doesn't hesitate. "No." He shakes his head, like he already knows exactly who I'm talking about. "Are you with that guy?"

The question makes my stomach flip, but I shake my head. "No."

We could say more. We could explain who Ashley and Justin are, why neither of us seemed to care much about them on the island. But it doesn't feel necessary. There's a trust between us, an understanding that doesn't need words. It might seem crazy to anyone else, but to me, it makes perfect sense.

Henry's proven himself in every way that matters. He saved me when the plane went down. He took care of me when I thought I wouldn't survive the island. In every extreme moment, he's shown me that if there's anyone I can trust in this world, it's him.

Do you want to be with me? The thought flits through my mind, but I don't say it out loud. Instead, I lean forward and press my lips to his.

The kiss is everything I remember and more. His lips are soft but firm, moving against mine with a mix of tenderness and urgency. He tastes like Henry, like warmth and safety and something I can't quite define but never want to let go of.

He tightens his arms around me, pulling me closer, and I sink into him, letting everything else fade away. It's just us, and for the first time since we left the island, I feel like I'm exactly where I'm meant to be.

Chapter 32

January 15th

Henry

AVERY IS HERE. IN MY APARTMENT, IN MY BED, IN MY ARMS. And I finally feel like I can breathe.

Thank fuck.

Her lips are on mine, soft and warm, and it's like the rest of the world disappears. There's no hospital, no tarmac, no island—just Avery. My hands cup her face, and she leans into me, her body pressing closer, like she's trying to merge us into one. And hell, I'd let her if it were a physical possibility.

Because you'd do anything for her.

I pull back just enough to look at her, to make sure this is real and not some vivid dream I'll wake up from. Her eyes meet mine, wide and searching. Her clothes are long gone—leaving her body at some point, just like mine, while we were kissing. Her hair is messy from sleep, slightly curling around her face, and she's not wearing a trace of makeup.

This is Avery in her rawest form, and she's fucking perfect.

"Avery," I murmur, brushing a thumb over her cheek. "Are you sure?"

She nods, her hands slipping up my arms and over my shoulders. "I'm sure," she whispers.

I kiss her again, deeper this time, and she responds with a

hunger that matches my own. I slide my hands down her back, pulling her even closer, until there's no space between us. Every touch, every sigh, every soft sound she makes fuels something in me I didn't know existed two weeks ago.

"Fuck," I groan, flipping her onto her back. "I want you."

She kisses me harder, her nails digging into the skin of my back with a delicious zing, while her legs wrap around my hips. She pushes her bare pussy against my bare cock, grinding herself against me in a way that makes another groan leave my lips.

"Put your cock inside me," she whispers, her voice a combination of a demand and a plea. "I need to feel you, Henry."

I can't say no. Truthfully, I don't even try. I just slide my cock inside her perfect pussy, my eyes practically rolling to the back of my head as I feel her warmth stretched tightly around me.

It's beautifully familiar, and the only thing that feels exactly the same as it did while we were stranded. It's grounding.

"God, Avery, you feel so good," I whisper and take her mouth in another deep kiss. "How do you always feel so fucking good?"

A moan escapes her throat when I start to thrust my cock inside her, filling her all the way up before slowly pulling back and doing it all over again. Her perfect tits brush against my chest with every panting breath, and I can already feel pleasure building at the base of my spine.

Her hands explore my body, her touch igniting a fire under my skin. I've been with women before—plenty of them, if I'm honest—but nothing has ever felt like this.

Nothing has ever felt like *her.*

Previously, I had the stamina of legend—I could always fuck for hours. But Avery feels too fucking good, and I have to make a concerted, focused effort to hold back my climax. I refuse, however, to come before her.

Her pussy clenches around me, and I grit my teeth as I flip onto my back and adjust her body above mine. "Ride me," I tell her, my mouth parted as I watch her seat herself fully. "Make yourself come on my cock, Avery."

She moans, but she doesn't hesitate to brace herself with her hands on my chest and get to work. Her hips move in the sexiest fucking way as she finds her rhythm, taking what she needs and leaving me with the scraps.

It's so hot, so uninhibited. I swear, I could watch it all night.

"God, Henry," she whispers through a moan. Her head falls back, and her breasts bounce softly up and down as she rides me.

I can't look away. All I can do is watch her and do my fucking best to hold my climax back until she comes.

Her lips part and her eyes fall closed and her body trembles as waves of her own pleasure consume her. I bite the tip of my tongue to stave off finishing, the beauty of her climax deserving of every last vestige of my attention. She moans and screams, and my heart races at a gallop as her neck bends back with no control, my entire world focused at the center of her tanned thighs. *She's so fucking perfect, and I can't take it anymore.*

When the urge to come grows too strong, too all-consuming, I flip Avery onto her back again and thrust my cock as deep as I can go. Her pussy grips me tightly as I plunge toward my climax recklessly, raucously, like a runaway, million-ton train. At the last possible fucking second, I pull out and paint her perfect fucking skin with my come.

Her hair fans out on the white of my sheets, her hands above her head and her eyes narrowed with satisfaction. She's sated, safe, and her belly is covered in my come.

My God, I feel like a warrior, a caveman—so fucking possessive, the sound of a low growl accompanies my blood as it rages through my veins.

She's mine. She has to be.

I make a quick trip to the bathroom for a towel, wiping Avery's belly to the sound of her soft giggle when I return, and then chuck it to the side to climb into the cocoon of my bed with her. She snuggles up to me again, her head resting on my chest as I run my fingers through her hair.

The room is quiet except for the sound of our breathing as we come back down to normal, and I can't stop myself from pressing a tender, greedy kiss to the top of her head. She's warm, her body curled against mine like she belongs there, and it feels so right, all sorts of things start making sense.

She *does* belong here. She is the missing piece to my puzzle, and nothing is right in this world without moments exactly like this.

"Henry?" she murmurs as her fingers trace lazy patterns over my skin.

"Yeah?"

She hesitates for a moment, then shakes her head. "Nothing. Never mind."

"Hey." I tilt her chin up so she's looking at me. "You can tell me anything."

She bites her lip, her eyes searching mine. "I'm just…really glad I came here tonight."

"Me too," I say, my voice firm. "More than you know."

She smiles before settling back against me, and I hold her close, just like I did on the island. I stroke her hair and I sing, ever so softly about a special bird, until her breathing evens out and she falls back asleep.

I stay awake for a while, just watching her. The way her lashes rest against her cheeks, the easy rise and fall of her chest.

God, she's beautiful. I want her to be mine, but I'm *already* hers.

I don't know when it happened exactly—somewhere between getting stranded on the island and watching her hold it together when everything else fell apart.

But there's no going back.

Chapter 33

MY EYES CRACK OPEN, THE OBNOXIOUS SOUND OF HARRY Styles singing about watermelons and a familiar warmth wrapped around me—Henry's arm draped lazily over my waist—mixing in a confusing way.

I flail the covers off my legs in a panic at first, and then I realize it's just my phone's new ringtone, and the bewilderment, of course, is because the last time I was wrapped up in a man, I didn't have a phone at all.

Henry's still asleep, his breaths slow and even, my initial jolt of movement somehow not rousing him, and because of that, I decide to ignore the call entirely.

Henry's still completely naked beside me, his big, strong, muscular frame looking like something out of my wildest fantasies. My mind latches on to the fact that I'm also naked, my clothes still gone from the sex we had late last night.

The most perfect, soul-link-affirming, pleasure-bringing sex—

Mid-thought, Harry sings again, the ringing getting incessantly louder by the second. Worried my obnoxious phone is going to wake Henry, I Gumby-stretch my arm over to grab my cell off his nightstand without moving otherwise.

The screen is bright and offensive to my still-sensitive eyes, but with focus, I see **Incoming Call June** quickly.

Shit. If the last two days are anything to go by, I'd say there's a seventy percent chance she's on her way to my condo right now.

"Hello?" I mumble, my voice still involuntarily thick with sleep.

"Where the hell are you? Why aren't you here?" June's voice is frantic, and I instantly sit up a little straighter. *Okay, maybe she's not on her way anymore and, instead, standing at my door.*

Henry's arm slides off me, and he finally stirs, his brow furrowing in sleepy confusion.

"Are you at my place?"

"Of course I'm at your place," she says, her words tumbling out in a rush. "Where the hell else would I be, and why aren't you also here?"

"Listen…" I hedge, glancing back at Henry briefly. "Let yourself in with the key—"

"I'm already in! I still have my own key!" she cuts me off on a yell. "You didn't answer the door, didn't answer my phone calls or texts, so I decided to come inside and make sure you're still alive, but you're not here! Thank God, you finally answered my freaking call! I was starting to fear the worst! I thought I was going to have to call the cops again and tell them you're missing, Avery! Can you imagine what that's like? To think your best friend is missing for a second—"

"*June,*" I quickly cut her off, deciding that I've let her maniacally ramble long enough. "Relax. I'm fine. I'm not missing, okay?"

"*Relax?*" she screeches, and I rub my forehead, already bracing myself for the hormonal storm.

Uh-oh, here we go…

"Relax?" June screeches again. "Avery, you were missing for two weeks! Do you have any idea what that did to me? And now you're just…not at home? Without telling me where you are? Where are you, Avery? Tell me right now."

Henry's watching me now, his head propped up on one hand, his lips twitching like he's trying not to smile at what he's probably overhearing from my conversation with a very *loud* and worked-up June.

But I'm here. In Henry's bed. *The very last place a lot of people would expect.*

Truth be told, I'm not sure if Henry would want my brother Beau to know this. I don't even know what Henry wants out of this. I mean, *I'm* the one who came to his apartment in the middle of the night, not the other way around.

Clearly, something happened between us on the island, but I'm not entirely sure either of us has wrapped our heads around it yet.

I don't want to assume and make an ass out of you, me, and our entire families, for Pete's sake.

The whole concept of a committed relationship is a foreign adversary in enemy territory with limited resources. I'm used to flitting from one guy to the next and never settling down, and even though I'm fairly certain I've gone and caught a serious case of feelings for Henry, all of that conditioning doesn't just disappear.

I glance at his handsome face, the realization undeniable. *Yes, I have feelings for him.* But fuck, that's kind of scary.

"Avery? Hello?" June is in my ear again, impatience dripping from her voice. "Are you there? Where are you?"

"I'm here," I answer quickly. "And I…I had an early massage appointment," I lie, the words just kind of rolling off my tongue before I can even think them through. "Self-care, you know? Obviously, I have to get back on track after…" I stop before I can say anything about my being stranded on an island. Clearly, that's a trigger for my best friend.

There's a pause on the other end of the line, and I can practically see June narrowing her eyes. "A massage?"

"Yes, June. *A massage.* You know, for sore muscles. Probably a smart idea after having to survive off breadfruit and an occasional fish for thirteen days, don't you think? Or would you prefer I walk around with a constant kink in my neck and end up, like, out of alignment so I can answer your calls?"

"Ugh! No! But you could've told me you had an appointment!" she huffs. "I was about to start another freaking search party!"

"Juni, honey, do you think it's possible you're being a little controlling?" I tease, hoping to lighten the mood.

"I do not care, Avery Banks," she snaps. "You need to keep me updated at all times. Do you hear me? All. Times."

"Fine, fine," I say, holding back a laugh. "I'll text you my every move from now on."

"You'd better," she mutters. "And don't you dare joke about this. I'm serious."

We exchange a few more words, her tone gradually softening as the panic subsides. When we finally hang up, I shoot her a quick text.

> Me: Just want to keep you updated on my every move. I just got off the phone with my crazy best friend. Our conversation lasted exactly 5 minutes and 43 seconds.

Her response is immediate.

> June: I know you're being a sarcastic biotch right now, but I don't care. Keep doing this.

I set the phone down, feeling Henry's gaze on me. When I turn back to him, he's smirking, his head resting on his hand. The sheet is slung low on his hips, and I try not to let my eyes wander. Much.

"So…you're at a massage?" he asks, his brow furrowed as we lock eyes.

"What was I supposed to say?" I counter, crossing my arms. "'Oh sorry, June, I'm actually at Henry's apartment. Naked.'"

He chuckles, but his expression softens. "Why didn't you just tell her you were here?"

I bite my lip, looking away. The truth is, I don't know. Or maybe I do, but I'm not ready to say it out loud.

"Oh, I don't know, Henry," I eventually answer, a little sharper than I intend. "Maybe because no one knows about what happened between us on the island. Beau certainly doesn't know that we hooked up."

Henry's expression shifts, his smirk fading. "Hooked up?" he repeats. "C'mon, Avery. I think you and I were a little more than a hookup. Don't you?"

Relief floods through me at the unexpected lash of hurt. If Henry doesn't want me saying things are casual, maybe it's not *casual*. My heart races with hope I wish I could control. I don't want to be at the will of emotion—it's vulnerable and not at all on-brand for Avery freaking Banks.

Unfortunately, that doesn't make my very real feelings any less true.

"Then what do you think we are, Henry?" I ask softly, searching his eyes for any signs of bullshit so I can backtrack quickly if I need to.

He doesn't hesitate to respond, his eyes open and unguarded. "Well, we're not a *hookup*. And I definitely think we shouldn't be seeing other people. And we should be seeing each other a lot. Maybe constantly. Especially naked, but not naked as well. It's a pretty even percentage, though, so if pushed, I'd probably give a few extra points to the naked side."

My heart skips a beat, and a smile curves one corner of my mouth. He's so freaking cute, I can hardly stand it. "So, we're together?"

"Yeah," he says simply, no reluctance at all. "We're together."

I'm quiet for a moment, mulling it over. I usually tell June everything, and her, me. Though, when she first got together with my brother, I definitely wasn't at the top of the list for shared information. I've earned a little bit of privacy on this—especially given how quickly I got over my anger when I found out about them.

Truly demure of me.

Henry's track record with relationships is even worse than mine, but holding him to that standard would be just as bad as holding me to mine, and given how much I forgot my last boy-friend existed, I don't think I'd like that.

I have to give this a chance, and yet…it'd be the worst kind of experience to go all in with Henry and then for him to decide he doesn't want to be with me.

Where would that leave me? He's Beau's best friend.

And if we tell everyone we're together, what if it didn't work out?

I need a compromise. At least for now. "Okay, we're together, but I think…just for a little while…we should keep it between us."

Henry raises an eyebrow. "So, we're together, but in secret?"

I shrug, wanting it to sound a little less clandestine. "Not secret. But…just a little more of our island bubble, but off the island, you know? I want the chance to get to know you, on my own, without you sticking your dick in other women and without my family and our friends making it the biggest deal, like you and I both know they will. Neither of us has committed before. They're going to have a whole freaking circus act to say about it."

Henry's laugh fills the otherwise quiet room. "You have nothing to worry about, Avery." He pulls me into his arms, his lips brushing against mine. "I understand your hesitancy, and I'm willing to play along. But just so you know, I'm all yours, bubble or not."

He kisses me again, slow and deep, and I melt against him.

I'm all yours, bubble or not. Oh boy. I probably like the sound of that way too much.

Chapter 34

THE OFFICE HUMS WITH ENERGY AS I STEP THROUGH THE glass doors of Adrenaline Junkie four days after getting home, my face still bearded and my stride undeniably different.

The open floor plan is alive with chatter, phones are ringing, and the occasional burst of laughter from one of the creative teams reminds me of what a fun environment I've managed to build with my own blood, sweat, and tears. It's good to be back. Truly.

But I'd be lying if I said my whole point of view isn't directed through an entirely different lens. Prior to all this shit, I saw Adrenaline Junkie as a freedom-seeking, good-time-having company. We were about the thrill and the chase, but I know now, with renewed energy and a new vision, we could be so much more.

A tool for survival. A center for learning and preparedness. A partner in both good and bad and for every situation in between.

On my way in, I had to bypass a small army of journalists and paparazzi camped outside the building, waiting for my arrival. In reality, they're a large part of why I'm still sporting the beard. It's a camouflage or a shield of sorts, and a comfort when I start to think I'm emotionally overreacting to what we went through. That didn't stop their cameras, though. They flashed like fireworks, questions being shouted at me from every angle.

"Henry, can you tell us about the island?"

"What was it like surviving for thirteen days?"

"Did you think you were going to die?"

I'm hoping all the fanfare will end soon, but I'm not naïve enough to think it'll be instantaneous. The headline is too good, the sensationalism too powerful.

By the time I make it to my office in the back corner of the building, I've been stopped and flagged by every employee, slapped on the shoulder at least twenty times, and pulled into a hug by at least five people I wasn't expecting. It's overwhelming, if touching, and when I close the glass door, my skin itches with discomfort.

It's not the attention in general I don't like—but the attention and scrutiny on this particular set of life-changing weeks with a woman I'm now dating without anyone knowing that I could do without. The glass walls of my office don't offer much privacy, but at least I can shut the door and pretend the world doesn't exist for a little while.

Unfortunately for me, Cara, my assistant, is already hot on my heels, striding into my office behind me with a stack of folders in one hand and her tablet in the other.

"Good morning, boss," she says, stopping at the edge of my desk. When her eyes meet mine, I note how her mouth is slightly turned down at the corners. "I heard from Mario's family. They're going to be doing a memorial for him on Sunday."

Instantly, my chest tightens with a poignant combination of sadness, grief, and guilt. It's hard to wrap my head around the fact that Avery and I survived but Mario didn't. "Do you think I can attend? Pay my respects?"

"I know for a fact they would like that." She nods. "One of his sisters already sent me the information. Address is only about thirty minutes from downtown Miami. Just on the outskirts of Fort Lauderdale."

I didn't know Mario well, but from what Cara has been able to find out for me since Avery and I got rescued, he was a single guy in his early sixties with two sisters who loved him dearly and several nieces and nephews who adored him. I know the Coast Guard is still technically trying to find our plane and Mario's remains, but the odds of their being able to achieve that are slim at best.

Which, I can't imagine, is an easy thing for his family to face.

"Find out if there's anything I can do to help his family," I tell Cara and she's already making a note on her iPad.

"On it." And while she's still tapping her fingers across the screen of her tablet, she drops the stack of folders in her other hand onto my desk. I swear, she must have an extra arm somewhere. Either that or she's a goddamn wonder of the world how she can multitask a million things at once. "By the way, you have three meetings this afternoon. One with the production team about the new commercial, one with the finance department about quarterly projections, and one with—" she glances at her tablet "—some new investors. Oh, and by the way, several journalists are still requesting interviews about 'the island survivors.'"

"Defer all the interviews," I say, already done with these fucking journalists. I'm not telling them jack shit about what happened on that island with Avery. "Tell them I'm busy."

Cara's eyes narrow, and she plants a hand on her hip. "You're always busy."

"Yes. I am. So, maybe just keep that in mind for future meeting and interview requests," I reply with a grin.

She huffs. "And here I thought you'd be a changed man after surviving off coconuts for thirteen days."

"Technically, it was breadfruit." I laugh, leaning back in my chair. "And sorry to disappoint, Cara, but I'm still me. Though, I'll be at all my meetings today. Promise."

"Fine." She rolls her eyes but heads for the door. "But I've got my eyes on you. If you try to go MIA for any of those meetings, I'll come in here and drag you out myself."

"Noted," I call after her.

Most people might be annoyed with how bossy Cara is, but

I know better. She's been with me for over three years, and I'd be lost without her. As the door clicks shut behind her, I make a mental note to talk to HR about giving her another raise and scribble down a few notes I want to make sure to bring up to the team about expanding our potential to include more than a regular adrenaline fix.

I turn to my computer, but instead of diving into the flagged emails Cara left for me, I open my phone and pull up a popular celebrity gossip site. Sure enough, my face is plastered all over the fucking home page. A photo of me walking into the office this morning, looking pissed off and ignoring the cameras.

But what catches my eye the most is another photo farther down the page—of Avery.

She's heading into Banks & McKenzie, her dad's marketing firm. She's smiling and waving at the cameras, her attire looking nothing less than effortless, tanned, and completely, fashionably put together once again. I don't miss the fact that it's noted within the short article that she declined any questions or comments, though, and for as insignificant as that may seem, it brings a smile to my lips.

Maybe we're both feeling covetous over what happened on the island.

Immediately, I find myself switching over to my messages, and I type out a quick one to the one woman I can't get off my mind.

> **Me: I see my fellow "Island Survivor" is also declining to answer questions from these fucking journalist hounds.**
>
> **Avery: My lips are sealed, Henry. They can fuck right off because I'm not telling them anything. It's none of their business.**

Her words settle something deep inside my chest. There's just something that puts me at complete peace knowing she feels the same as I do. That she wants to keep everything that happened on the island just between us.

> Avery: Though, I don't mind them taking pictures of me. I mean, it does the bitches in Miami good to see what true fashion looks like.

I laugh. I can't help it. Only Avery would say shit like this. But then my laughter fades as my brain connects the dots between the island and the information Cara gave me about Mario.

> Me: My assistant got in touch with Mario's family. There's going to be a memorial service for him on Sunday. It's only a half hour away from us. You want to go?

> Avery: Is that even a question? Of course I do.

> Me: Good. We can go together, then.

> Avery: Is it just me or…whenever you think of Mario…do you feel guilty in some way?

> Me: Because we got to come home and he didn't?

> Avery: Yes.

> Me: Yeah, I definitely feel that. The psychologist who came in to check on me at the hospital said it was common. He called it survivor's guilt.

> Avery: Mine said the same thing. When I let myself really think about it, it just feels so fucking sad. I feel like I'm compartmentalizing it all most days.

Before I can even respond, another message comes through.

> Avery: Now, hurry up and change the subject. I don't have waterproof mascara on today.

To an outsider, to someone who didn't go through what Avery and I did, they might think it's cold or callous. But I get it.

And I also have a quick trigger when it comes to conversation.

Me: What are you wearing?

It's clichéd as fuck, but I know it'll do the trick. Plus, for as much as I could give a fuck about clothes, she loves them. And since I'm not some dusty, fucking crusty pussy, her interests are now my interests.

Avery: Pretty sure you already saw this when you were stalking my paparazzi photos but…Dior Ecru jeans. Gucci white tank. Yves Saint Laurent pumps. Very "old money" take on sophisticated but casual.

I shake my head, a grin pulling at my lips. That's Avery, all right.

Me: That's nice, honey. But if I'm not mistaken, you forgot to include your panties… What about those?

Avery: You saw my panties when I left your apartment for work this morning.

My grin widens, my mind flashing back to this morning, waking up with her in my bed, her warm body pressed against mine. We didn't waste any time before tangling ourselves back up together—twice. I'm convinced there's not a single better way to start my day.

Me: I think you should take your lunch now and come to my office and show me your panties again.

Avery: I don't know. I'm very busy today, Henry.

Me: Yeah? Planning on doing actual work today over there at Banks & McKenzie?

Avery: Ha. No. I'm not busy at all. I can be there in an hour.

A laugh jumps from my lungs.

Me: An hour?

Avery: I can't leave in the middle of my mani/pedi.

I have the strongest sensation I have no fucking clue what I'm getting myself into with this woman, and yet…I like it. I don't think I'll ever know what to expect, and for an adrenaline junkie like me, there's nothing more exciting.

Me: See you in an hour.

Avery: An hour. But get your tongue ready, okay?
My pussy's feeling greedy.

Fuck me. Yep. I'm *never* going to know what to expect.

Chapter 35

THE ELEVATOR DINGS, AND I STEP OUT ONTO HENRY's office floor. My freshly manicured nails gleam ballerina pink, the exact shade I chose because I thought it'd look best when I…well, when I wrap my hand around Henry's cock later. I'm nothing if not thorough in my color coordination.

The space is as sleek and intimidating as I imagined. It's all fucking windows, the sunlight pouring in from every angle, bouncing off the polished floors and high-tech. I've been to Adrenaline Junkie's headquarters before but never to this floor. And now that I'm here, I can't help but feel like I've walked into a king's domain.

And there he is, the king himself, sitting behind his massive desk—in a sleek black suit jacket, perfectly-fitted black T-shirt, and black slacks—like he owns the world. Which, in a way, he does. It's pretty fucking sexy, to be honest. He's successful—at what he loves and because of his own drive and determination.

I've never showcased any of that same ambition, but if I'm going to live the lifestyle I'm accustomed to while maintaining that attitude, I'm going to need a man who's the opposite.

A man who can take charge and take care of me—a man who's already shown me in spades he's more than capable of those things and, beyond that, can do it with a tenderness in his heart I'd never expect.

Henry looks up just as I'm walking toward his office, his lips curling into that wicked, knowing smile that makes my stomach flip.

Before I can reach him, his assistant intercepts me at her desk. She's efficient and polished, her dark hair pulled back into a sleek ponytail. "Hi, Ms. Avery. Can I help you?" she asks, her tone polite but firm.

"I have an appointment with Henry," I say, my voice breezy.

Before Cara can question me any further, Henry steps out of his office, still smiling. "Hold my calls, Cara," he says without missing a beat. His eyes lock on mine, and he tilts his head toward the hallway. "Come on."

He places a hand on the small of my back, guiding me away from his office and down the hall.

"Where are we going?" I ask, glancing over at him.

He smirks, his eyes glinting with mischief. "It's a secret."

We stop at a private elevator, and he punches in a keycode before the doors slide open. I step in beside him, my curiosity piqued. The elevator ascends smoothly, and when the doors open again, I'm greeted by bright sunlight and the sound of the ocean breeze.

"Wow," I breathe as we step out onto the roof.

The space is stunning. A rooftop oasis perched high above Miami, complete with a pool, a Jacuzzi, glass balustrades that make the view of the city and ocean seem infinite, and a luxurious sitting area with plush couches and pillows. The smell of sea and salt is an immediate comfort.

The old Avery would've hated what this might do to her hair. So weird.

"This is a new addition to Adrenaline Junkie," Henry explains, slipping his hands into his pockets. "But it hasn't had the official reveal to my employees yet."

"And what are we doing up here?" I ask, turning to him.

He smirks again, that same infuriatingly sexy look that makes my knees weak. "I thought you'd enjoy the view while I enjoy you."

Before I can respond, he's closing the distance between us. In one smooth motion, he lifts me into his arms, making me squeak in surprise.

"Henry!" I exclaim, but he just chuckles, carrying me over to the sitting area. He lays me down on one of the plush outdoor couches, the cushions soft beneath me. The bright blue sky stretches out above us, but my focus is entirely on him.

He doesn't waste any time. His hands slide to the waistband of my pants, and he tugs them down with deliberate ease. I'm already aroused, my body responding to him like it's second nature.

His gaze travels over me, dark and hungry, and he leans down to press his lips to mine. The kiss is deep and demanding, and I can't help the way my hips arch toward him, seeking more. His hands trail down my thighs, his touch igniting every nerve ending as he moves lower.

"You're so beautiful," he murmurs against my skin, his voice thick with desire. "And I miss having you around all the time."

I reach up, threading my fingers through his hair, and pull him closer. My heart races, the heat between us building with every touch, every kiss, every whispered word. Up here, high above the city, it feels like we're the only two people in the world.

Back in our precious bubble.

I whisper the truth because saying it any louder might shatter me. "I'm ridiculously attached to you too."

Chapter 36

I^{T'S EARLY ON} SATURDAY MORNING, THE HOUR WHEN THE CITY is still quiet and the light filtering through the blinds is faint, and the soft sound of running water pulls me toward the bathroom.

Avery stayed over again last night, and not just because we can't seem to get enough of each other, but because June has a key to her place and is driving her crazy. She does phone check-ins, surprise drop-ins, coffee dates, bed turndown service, and everything in between, still reeling from the scare of having Avery missing for two weeks. Avery says, and I quote, "For all I know, she'll show up and try to offer assistance while I'm inserting your cock."

Considering our current keeping-it-a-secret status, June's handy-dandy hand service seems like a step too far. Not to mention the implications of my best friend's wife putting her hand on my cock, in an assisting capacity or not, are a wee bit uncomfortable.

Personally, I'm ready to be out in the open, but Avery's not and I understand why. Our friends and family are a lot.

Just this morning alone, I've gotten three texts from Ronnie and Mav offering to stop by on their way home from the bar, a text from Beau checking in while he makes an early breakfast for Addy, and several missed calls from Cara about shit I don't even want to think about on the weekend. And Avery's got her parents, grandparents, and a whole other set of friends on top of that.

The door to my bathroom is cracked open, steam curling out and filling the air with the scent of Avery—sweet and floral, like sugar and fresh roses. As I step inside, the sight of the counter makes me smile. It's covered in Avery's things. Little jars of face creams, a bottle of lotion she religiously applies to her legs before bed, leaving her skin impossibly soft and making her smell like a goddamn dessert. Even her silk eye mask is folded neatly to the side, which she claims is essential for preventing wrinkles.

It's ridiculous and endearing all at once.

Avery is what a lot of men would call "high-maintenance," and much like them, I used to find it intimidating. Women's minds and emotions are complex enough on their own—add in a fifty-step routine you can't interrupt or mess up with your own shit, and you're talking about climbing a mountain of understanding. But it's funny what a little perspective shift can do, and after spending every minute, awake and not, with Avery on that island, I feel like I understand her better than ever.

Just as the wind blows for adventure and high adrenaline for me, fashion and beauty do it for Avery. She's passionate, and in my newly formed opinion, passion can't be misplaced. She cares about it, and I care about her, so that's all that matters.

Plus, it's always but always a fucking adventure. The other night, she came to bed with this fucking hockey-mask-looking, Halloween-Jason-esque thing over her face and nearly gave me a heart attack. She told me it was red-light therapy, and before I knew it, she had me wearing the damn thing for the required twenty minutes to help heal any sun damage I got when we were stranded on the island.

"Thirteen days without sunscreen, Henry, is just asking for skin cancer," she told me. *"You need red-light therapy. And probably a skin peel, so I'll work on getting you an appointment at Fredrick. Oh my gawd. I swear, that man has magic hands or something. His facials are heaven."*

I, of course, made the small mistake of asking who Fredrick was, and that led to her telling me all about her aesthetician Fredrick who does Botox and all sorts of other shit I can't remember.

I told her that I was down for her to do whatever she felt she needed to, but that it wasn't necessary for me to get to know Fredrick because I'm a man. But I got some kind of text message confirmation last night saying I have an appointment with Fredrick for a fucking face peel next week, so I'm pretty sure that boundary didn't hold at all.

And you'll probably end up going, too.

I laugh to myself as I glance toward the shower, the glass fogged but not enough to obscure Avery completely. She's standing under the stream of water, her head tilted back as she rinses shampoo from her hair. Her skin is still tanned from our time on the island, her body etched into my memory in a way I'll never shake.

Without hesitating, I strip off my boxers and step into the shower with her. The warm water hits my skin, and she doesn't notice me at first, her eyes closed as she massages her scalp.

"Let me do it," I say softly, my voice cutting through the sound of the water.

Her eyes flutter open, one brow arching as she peeks at me through the curtain of water. "Do what?"

"I know I probably don't have Freddie's magic hands, but..." I grin, stepping closer and gently turning her around so her back is to me. "Let me help."

"Fredrick," she corrects through a snort.

"My bad," I tease and give my best—*aka horrible*—French accent. *"Fredrick."*

"Oh my God, you're so dumb." Avery laughs. "Fredrick is from Jersey."

I shrug and get to work on tangling my fingers into her hair. The strands are silky and warm beneath my palms, and I take my time, massaging the shampoo suds from her scalp and working my way down. She lets out a soft hum of approval, and it's enough to make my chest tighten.

"Damn, Henry. You're actually good at this," she murmurs, her voice lazy with contentment.

"I have many talents," I reply, my lips quirking into a smirk she can't see.

When her hair is free of suds, my hands drift to her shoulders, kneading the tension there. She sighs, her head tipping forward slightly, and I take it as permission to keep going. My fingers trail lower, massaging her neck and then her back, tracing the delicate tan lines left by her bikini. Her skin is soft and warm, and I'm reminded of all the nights we spent together on the island cuddled together like we were the only safe thing in each other's world.

I move my hands to her hips, brushing my fingers over the curve of her waist, and I'm hit with a wave of something I can't quite name. It's not just lust—though, judging by the hardness of my cock, there's plenty of that too. But it's something deeper, something that roots itself in my fucking bones and refuses to let go.

Avery glances over her shoulder at me, her eyes half lidded and soft. "You're quiet," she says, her tone light but curious.

I lean in, pressing my lips to the damp skin of her shoulder. "Just thinking," I murmur against her.

"About?" she prompts, turning slightly to face me.

"About how you've taken over my bathroom," I tease, gesturing toward the counter outside the shower.

She laughs, the sound easy and unguarded, and it's one of my favorite things about her. She's not embarrassed or unsure. She is who she is, take it or leave it. "You're welcome," she says, a playful glint in her eyes.

I grin, pulling her closer and letting the water cascade over both of us. "Don't think I'm complaining," I say, my voice low. "I like having you here."

Her expression softens, and for a moment, the playful banter fades into something quieter, more intimate. She doesn't say anything, but the way she looks at me says enough. She reaches up, her fingers brushing against my jaw, and I lean into her touch without hesitation.

This…whatever it is between us, it's new, but it feels like it's always been there, just waiting for the right moment to surface. And now that it has, I'm not sure I can ever let it go.

My hands find their way to her shoulders and neck again, and I massage my fingers into the skin some more, silently loving the way her body relaxes into my touch. And I keep going until the urge to touch more of her body is undeniable.

I trace my fingers along her tan lines, until I use just one gentle index finger across her hips. I turn her body around, still using that one index finger to trace across her back until both of my hands caress her perfect ass.

It's round and firm and plump in ways that go straight to my fucking head.

My cock grows harder at the feel of her plush body in my big hands, and I slide that one finger over the curve of her ass until it rests right between her thighs. A little moan leaves her lips.

I press my chest into her back, my finger still precariously hovering at the one place I'm desperate to slide my hard cock into. "Mine," I whisper gruffly into her ear.

She moans again.

I reach up with both hands and grasp the curves of her breasts, my fingers gently pinching at her nipples while my hard cock presses against the curve of her ass.

"*Mine,*" I whisper again.

Avery moves her hips, rubbing her ass into my cock, and my head is swimming with need for her. We had sex last night. We even had sex this morning before she got in the shower. But when it comes to her, I never feel like it's enough.

I want her. All of her. All the time.

Avery spreads her thighs a little, urging me on, and I press the tip of my cock inside her. I'm hard, so fucking hard, and when another little moan leaves her lips, I'm so insanely tempted to push myself all the way in until I'm pressed to the hilt inside her.

But I'm bare. *Completely* bare. And that reality is not lost on me.

"I don't have a condom," I admit, a gruff rasp to my voice.

"So? That's never stopped you before."

She's not wrong. On the island, we had lots of sex without protection, and since we got back, we haven't been great about remembering a condom either.

But I've pulled out. It's *important* that I pull out. But fuck, I'd give a lot of things to know what it feels like to come deep inside her.

"Please, Henry," Avery begs.

How can I say no to that?

I slide myself inside her, droplets of water still splashing onto both of us from the showerhead. I grip her hips and turn her toward the glass shower wall, pressing her body against it as I thrust myself inside her tight pussy. Both of her hands move to the glass, bracing herself, and my eyes catch sight of the erotic display in the reflection of the bathroom mirror. Her breasts are pushed against the glass, and her lips are parted in a way that makes my cock grow even harder inside her.

I can't take my eyes off us. Off *her*.

The way her mouth forms a little O when she moans. The way her eyes are heated with arousal. The way strands of her wet hair hang over her shoulders and her breasts bounce with each thrust of my cock.

She's so tight and so warm and damn near pulsating around me, and the urge to come starts to build at the base of my spine.

"Fuck, you feel so good. Too good," I say, practically grunting out the words. *You're everything.*

Avery whimpers.

I drive myself deeper and deeper. Over and over and over again.

And I can feel her body grow tight like a bow with pleasure. It's as if each thrust of my cock is pushing her closer to the edge. It's like her pleasure is my pleasure, and there's no in-between. If she feels good, I feel fucking good.

"Keep going," she moans. "Don't pull out."

"Fuck, Avery. Don't say shit like that."

"Don't pull out," she repeats. "I'm back on my birth control. Come inside me."

The combination of her words and her pussy wrapped around me like a vise is almost too much. I grit my teeth. *"Avery."*

"Please, Henry," she pleads through panting breaths. "I want it."

There's no logic in her words. But when it comes to her, there's clearly no logic for me at all. Whatever she wants, I want to give it to her.

She's an all-consuming force that I can't refuse, and she's the one and only woman on the planet I'd do anything for.

I drive my cock inside her, over and over, until I feel her pussy clenching around me in rhythmic waves and hear pleasure-filled moans escape her lungs.

And then, I come. Deep inside her. And it's the best thing I've ever felt in my fucking life.

There's no going back from this. There's no going back from her.

Chapter 37

January 22nd

Avery

WEDNESDAYS ARE THE ACHILLES' HEEL OF THE workweek, but I can't deny that spending every night at Henry's place has turned the usual monotony on its head. Though, it hasn't been easy keeping nosy, borderline-stalker June out of the loop.

The only night I was actually honest with her about my whereabouts was when Henry and I drove to Fort Lauderdale for Mario's memorial service.

It was emotional, meeting his two sisters and his two brothers-in-law and his nieces and nephews, but I'm glad we went. If anything, it's given me a small piece of closure on the tragedy.

When the sounds of busy office chatter filter into my ears, I realize I'm just sitting here at my desk. My computer screen stares back at me with its uninspiring spreadsheet—some stupid thing June sent to me to look over—on my desk at my dad's company, and I scan the area for something, *anything*, more interesting than this.

Goodness. This shit is bor-ing.

Frankly, I don't have a clue what I'm supposed to be looking at, and after spending the past few nights staying up way too late having hot sex with Henry, I'm too tired to care even as much as I normally do, and it's safe to say that's not much.

A yawn escapes my throat, and I tap my pen against the edge of my desk in a sad attempt to keep myself awake, taking a swig from my second cup of Starbucks this morning.

The office hums with the usual background noise—keyboards clicking, phones ringing, and distant murmurs of conversation—but it's not enough to distract me from the monotony. There's no drama, no secret flings, no fights or anything.

Gah, I miss the era of Bethany *the Bitch* Williams and that snake Seth. Sure, it was a little miserable for Beau, being around his ex-best friend and ex-girlfriend all the time, but things were *exciting*.

Last I heard, Bethany and Seth's dad Chris were traveling the world together or some shit, and Seth had gone to Hollywood to fake an acting career. Evidently, they took the fun with them, because now all people do here is work.

My phone buzzes on my desk, and I eagerly snatch it up, hoping for a reprieve from the dullness. It's a text from Ethel, one of my old lady friends from The Pines.

> **Ethel: Avery, darling, are you coming by today to help our little fashion disaster Darla? She's sweet as pie, but I simply cannot witness her spandex sweatpants for another day. My eyes are burning at just the thought of it.**

A smile tugs at my lips as I read her message. Ethel's always dramatic, which is what makes her one of my favorite people. I can easily clear out today's schedule for a trip to The Pines. Lord knows I'm more likely to stay awake there than here in this god-awful cubicle.

Before I can type out a reply, my phone buzzes in my hand with another text. This time, it's Henry. I nearly rub my hands together with glee.

Finally, things are getting stimulating!

> **Henry: Want to meet for lunch?**

I grin to myself, leaning back in my chair as I tap out a quick reply.

Me: Is this a booty call?

"What are you doing?" June's voice pops up behind me, startling the life out of me. I turn slowly to find her leaning over my cubicle wall. "Who are you texting?"

I quickly tilt my phone away, hiding the screen. "Jeez, stalk much?"

June rolls her eyes. "You want to go get lunch? I'm starving."

I smirk. "Juni, you're always starving."

"Because I'm pregnant," she argues back, a small frown line forming between her eyebrows.

I laugh. "I'm not judging. I mean, that baby growing inside you is a boy, and as we all know, men are soul-suckers," I say matter-of-factly, leaning back and crossing my arms.

"Shh," June shushes me. "Don't say that too loud, Ave. Everyone in the office could hear."

"Oh yeah, I forgot," I respond with a snort. "Not only are you puking *and* hungry all the time, you're also losing your mind ninety percent of time. Seriously." I drop my voice to a whisper. "Only a man would do this to a woman."

"I am not losing my mind," June refutes, pointing a stern index finger in my face. I playfully swat it away.

"June, I love you, but at Christmas, you were all excited, not only to tell us you were pregnant, but that you're also having a—" I start to say, but my words are cut off when June slaps her palm over my face.

It's my turn to roll my eyes. And also, promptly remove her hand from my mouth.

"Just curious, but why are we acting like we don't know what you're having even though we do know what you're having?"

Apparently, while Henry and I were stuck on the island, June decided that she wants to pretend they don't know what they're having—even though they clearly do know. It's all very confusing, and honestly, I think she's the only one who truly understands it.

"Because that's what I did with Addy. And everything with Addy's pregnancy and delivery was perfect and I don't know… I just… I want everything to go smoothly. I don't want anything bad to…" She pauses as tears start to well in her eyes.

"June," I say, my voice the kind of tender she needs right now. I reach out to take her hand into mine. "Everything is going to go smooth, okay? You and that perfect little baby inside your belly are healthy and happy, and nothing is going to change that."

She nods, sniffles, and I hand her a tissue from my desk to wipe her tears away.

I'm not therapist, but there's a large part of me that wonders if her new fixation on pretending she doesn't know she's having a boy and planning an actual gender reveal party has everything to do with how out of control she felt when Henry and I were missing for two weeks.

And as I sit there and watch my best friend struggle to pull herself together, I make a conscious decision to give her whatever she needs. Even if that means pretending.

"So, anyway," I say, making a point to raise my voice so anyone around us can hear. "I honestly think you're having a boy." I toss a secret wink in her direction. "Only a man would make a woman feel this awful on the regular. But what do I know, right?"

June laughs, the sound soft and genuine. Then her eyes get all dreamy, and she rests a hand on her still-small bump. "I guess we'll find out soon enough, huh?"

"We sure will. And may God help your poor vagina."

"Avery!" June chastises through a laugh.

"What?" I grin at her. "I think it's sweet that I'm praying for your hoo-hah. That's best friend shit, Juni."

"You know what else a best friend would do?"

"Don't even try to ask me to rub olive oil on your taint. That's a step too far, June."

"Olive oil? What? No, you psycho." She practically chokes on her own saliva. "I was going to say watch Addy for an entire night so Beau and I can get some sleep."

"She's still not sleeping through the night?"

"Oh, she's sleeping, all right," June answers with a sigh. "But she's sleeping in our bed with her feet in Beau's chest and her arms punching me in the face."

"That girl." I laugh. "And yes to your request. I'll keep Addy for the night soon."

June's eyes light up. "Yeah?"

"Of course." I nod.

June's expression collapses into a weep of gratitude, and she tucks her face into her hands. I reach for her wrist in comfort, but when my phone buzzes again in my hand, I also use the opportunity to discreetly glance at the screen.

> **Henry: It wasn't a booty call, but now it's starting to feel like your subtle way of saying you'd like me to have your pussy for my meal…**

Truthfully, I wasn't being subtle. I'm always greedy for Henry these days, and getting my pussy licked for lunch seems like a grand plan.

Unfortunately, there's no time or room to reply because June is starting to get it together, and, evidently smelling her tears in the air, my brother has now arrived.

"What's going on over here?" he asks, throwing an arm around June's shoulders.

And, because this is my life, Neil is right behind him. *Perfect.*

"Avery says she's up for watching Addy all night for us," June announces with glee, making Beau's mouth curve up and my dad's eyebrows pull together.

"You sure you're up for a whole night, Avery?" my dad asks, tilting his head like he's inspecting me for clues of a drug addiction or impairment.

"Good grief, it's like a family reunion and interrogation all rolled into one," I say, grabbing my purse and standing up. "And I'd love to stay for it, truly, but I gotta run."

"Where are you going?" Dad asks, narrowing his eyes.

"I have plans," I say, slinging the strap of my bag over my shoulder.

"In the middle of the workday?"

I give him a pointed look. "Daddy, do you really want to be that kind of overbearing boss to his employees? That's so Boomer." Before he can argue, I press a quick kiss to his cheek. "Love you, Daddy. I'll do work stuff again tomorrow."

Then I turn to June, rubbing her belly affectionately. "Bye, my future little nephew…or niece." I wink at June. "Auntie Avery loves you so much, even though you keep making your mama puke all the time."

June rolls her eyes but smiles, and I glance at Beau. "Later, loser."

Their laughter follows me as I make my way toward the elevator. Just as the doors begin to close, Dad calls out, "Wait. Tomorrow? Are you coming back to work today?"

I flash a cheeky smile. "Not sure if I'll have time. Love you!"

The doors shut, and I pull out my phone, an idea forming in my head. I quickly type out a message to Henry:

Me: If you want to see me, you can find me here.

I attach the address and hit send, a grin tugging at my lips as I step out into the sunshine. It's no booty call, but it is a headfirst dive into a deep end of a different kind.

I can't wait to see his face.

Chapter 38

Henry

I PULL UP TO THE ADDRESS AVERY SENT ME, HALF EXPECTING some trendy new restaurant or boutique or plastic surgeon she scheduled to repair my supposed sun damage, but find instead an ornate, gated entrance with a gold sign that reads **The Pines: A Luxury Retirement Village.**

I see several multiunit condo buildings when I first pull in, their backsides planted square on the beach, and if I crane my neck, I can see some more private residences through the back end of the parking lot.

I pull into a space in front of the first building, not knowing exactly where I'm supposed to be and why the hell anything would be in a luxury retirement village in the first place.

I blink, glancing back down at the message on my phone to double-check the address, and then smile as I confirm it's correct. I swear, I'm *never* going to know what's coming.

Typing fast, I send her a quick message.

> **Me: I can't tell you how exciting it is to be with a woman who keeps me on my toes, but if you tell me we're swinging with a bunch of senior citizens, I'm going to have to draw a line.**

Her reply comes almost immediately.

Avery: HAHAHAHA. Just meet me in condo 305,
you idiot.

Shaking my head, I shut off the engine and make my way to the specified building. The whole place screams money—pristine landscaping, valet golf carts, and a fountain in the courtyard that probably cost more than most people's homes—and old wealth, at that. These aren't the new, modern tech bros I see out at the clubs; this is wealth a la the *Titanic*.

I knock on the door of condo 305 with a small knot in my stomach and a gleam in my eye. I'm not sure what the hell Avery Banks is up to, but I'd be lying if I said I wasn't thrilled she picked a place without paparazzi—an unfortunate reality I'm growing increasingly annoyed with since we arrived back from the island nearly two weeks ago.

When the door swings open, I'm greeted by an elderly woman with perfectly coiffed hair and a mischievous glint in her eye. She fits the location, but she doesn't fit anything else. Not unless my girlfriend found a way to shape-shift or teleport the two of us about fifty years ahead in Earth's timeline.

"Avery? Is that you?" I question a little teasingly, and the woman, thankfully, laughs. I suppose I can mark the possibility of dementia-related charity work off the list.

"Oh my, aren't you just a tall drink of water?" Her gaze sweeps me from head to toe. "The news made you look a little shorter. Less rugged. I mean, my God, sweetie, you're *something*." She giggles again. "I would have broken your heart back in my day."

I chuckle a little and try to smile, leaning to look around the random old lady who seems to know me without me knowing her. "Um, thanks…I think. Is Avery here, by any chance? I'm supposed to be meeting her."

"I'm Ethel." She grins and holds out her hand. "It's a pleasure to meet you. Come on in, honey."

The thing is, she still hasn't said if Avery is actually here or not.

She steps aside but not before giving my bicep a little pat. "I'll get you a nice glass of lemonade if you flex for me just—"

"Hands off, Ethel," Avery's voice finally calls from inside, sending a zing of relief down my spine. "He's mine."

He's mine. At ease with those words instantly, I smile again, placating Ethel a little. "I don't know about flexing, but if you play your cards right, I might be able to lift something heavy."

Ethel grins. "God, I love young people. You have so much energy and spunk."

I step inside with a newly renewed bounce in my step, and my smirk only widens as I take in the scene. Avery is standing in the middle of the living room, surrounded by a group of older women draped in clothes and jewelry, makeup strewn all over the coffee table. To her right, a rack of expensive clothes is set up, and one of the women is admiring herself in a floor-length mirror.

"Ladies, this is Henry," Avery says, turning to face me and then blushing a little before turning back to the women. "The one I was… telling you about." They all hem and haw a little extra, raking me with their eyes and cooing until Avery slices a hand across her throat for them to cut it out. "Henry, meet Ethel, Blanche, Dottie, Joanne, and Sarabeth. And this lovely woman here is Darla. We're working on getting her set up with a new wardrobe."

"Oh, he's even more handsome up close," Dottie says, peering at me over the rim of her glasses.

"Like a modern-day lumberjack," Sarabeth chimes in. "That beard is impressive."

Self-consciously, I scratch at the facial hair I've trimmed to a neat length but haven't been able to bring myself to shave off yet.

"And those arms," Joanne adds, fanning herself dramatically. "Avery, you didn't tell us he was a Greek god."

Avery rolls her eyes but smiles. "All right, calm down, cougars. Don't scare him off. Though, come to think of it…you like older ladies, don't you, Henry?" I nearly snort at the memory of Avery's island commentary when I told her I had a crush on Ross's mom. "Maybe this is actually a shopping expedition for your new mate."

"I'm a changed man," I tell her confidently, instead of getting embarrassed and tucking my tail. "These days, I find myself liking them a little younger. Twenty-seven, to be exact."

"Oh, he's not going anywhere," Blanche says with a wink. "This boy's in love. Aren't you, Henry?"

Avery's eyes jump to mine, and I balk only slightly at the three-word expression neither one of us has been bold enough to admit yet. I want to, but I hardly think brunch hour with the Golden Girls is the appropriate time.

"Something like that," I settle for saying instead. "I don't have any plans to be anywhere else, with anyone else, anytime soon."

Avery avoids my eyes and messes with the draping on Darla's sweater, but I know what she's thinking. *She loves me too.* It's the only thing that would stun her enough to keep her quiet.

"So…how did you all meet my Avery?" I ask, trying to keep the conversation going without putting too much attention on the only common denominator in this room—my girlfriend.

"*Your* Avery?" Ethel asks, a big smile on her face and a twinkle in her eyes at my slip of the tongue. "She's our stylist, of course."

I smile. *Avery Banks, stylist to the senior population of Miami.* It's both ridiculous and completely perfect for her all at once. I can't help but think this is the true direction she needs to be going career-wise, and this, though adorably weird, is a great start.

"She's the best," Dottie chimes in. "She's been helping us all look fabulous for months now. If it weren't for Avery, I'd still be wearing last season's Ralph Lauren."

"And we can't have that," Joanne adds with a wink.

I glance at Avery, who's doing her best to look unbothered, but the slight blush creeping up her cheeks gives her away.

"She's a godsend," Blanche adds, gesturing toward the rack of clothes. "Just look at all this. Her eye for fashion is unmatched."

"Is that so?" I say, grinning as I turn to Avery, but she just flashes me a knowing look, a silent, *don't you dare say anything right now.*

I give her a grin that says, *I won't embarrass you now, but we'll talk later.*

Avery hands Darla a fancy cardigan and guides her toward the mirror. "Try this on, Darla. See how it pairs with the pants? They're perfect for accentuating your hips. Which, come on, girl, you have to know you have great hips. Don't be afraid to show them off."

Darla blushes but follows Avery's instructions, and I take a moment to glance around the room.

A fancy tea set and an array of finger foods sit on the coffee table in the middle of the makeup, and the rest of the women are sipping tea like this is a weekly occurrence. Which, fuck, *maybe it is?* At this point, nothing would surprise me when it comes to Avery.

"You're really good at this," I say to Avery as the women all stand and move to try on more clothes in the back room.

She shrugs, brushing off the compliment. "It's just a little something I do for fun."

"Fun? Avery, you're basically running a boutique out of someone's condo. This could be your *job* if you wanted it to be."

"Oh no." She groans. "You're not going to start all that crap about never working a day in your life if you do what you love again, are you?"

I laugh because she's funny, but the idea of her being a stylist isn't funny at all. "I'm serious, Ave. Look at the way they light up when you help them. You have a real gift, and from what I can tell, you seem to enjoy it."

"Sure, I like it, but it's not a job. I don't even charge them." Just as she says this, the women file back into the room, now dressed to the nines in the outfits Avery picked for them. Their confidence radiates, and I can't help but feel proud of her.

"Ladies," I say, addressing the group, "if you don't mind my asking, how much are you paying my very talented stylist girlfriend for her services?"

"She never lets us pay," Ethel answers immediately, her eyes narrowing on Avery. "We've tried to several times. Between the group of us, we've talked about anywhere from five hundred to a thousand an hour."

I glance at Avery, who just shrugs again, clearly unimpressed by my line of questioning and the answers it's producing.

Sarabeth agrees. "We'd pay top dollar for Avery's expertise."

"She's worth every penny," Blanche says, nodding.

"I'd sell my husband's golf clubs if it meant keeping her around," Joanne adds with a sly grin.

Avery rolls her eyes but doesn't hide the secret smile that creeps onto her lips. In that moment, I know in so many ways that this is so much more than lunch booty calls and spicy texts and two weeks on an island. A lot of people would think Avery is superficial, but I know better.

I know what lies beneath the surface, I know her heart, and I know the humor she uses to hide it all. I know all of it.

I know all of her.

And one day, she's going to be officially, publicly, one hundred percent mine.

Chapter 39

THE HUM OF LAUGHTER AND THE BUZZ OF CONVERSATION fill my parents' backyard. Fairy lights drape from tree to tree, twinkling in the fading sunlight. It's one of those perfect Miami evenings where the heat isn't oppressive, just warm enough to keep you outside without complaint, and I don't know that I've ever enjoyed it as much as I am tonight.

The gender reveal party for Beau and June's second spawn is in full swing. Of course, I already know what they're having—so do Beau and Henry and my parents and even little Addy—but June is giving her best impression of oblivious, pregnant woman.

Frankly, it's quite the sight, and I silently wonder if she should've considered an acting job in Hollywood with how dedicated she is to this insanity.

Also, it should be noted, she threatened a certain death if any of us even mentioned the word boy before the official gender reveal today.

I'm standing away from the fray of the celebration, taking it all in, a subtle contentment over the last month I've spent in secret with Henry making a smile rest permanently on my lips. It's not like me to stay out of the center of the action and subsequent attention, but for some reason, I'm not feeling like I need it as much these days.

I glance across the pink-and-blue anointed outdoor space at Henry, who stands with Ronnie and Mav about ten feet away shooting the shit, and hide the growing curl of my smile behind my glass of champagne.

My parents have gone all out, as usual, and as a result, it looks like a stork landed here and promptly threw up. A massive balloon arch is set up over the dessert table, and I'm pretty sure my mom ordered enough cupcakes to feed all of Miami.

Family and friends are scattered around. My two sets of grandparents sit on well-cushioned patio chairs, smiling and chatting together. Chef Stone, my parents' chef, is manning the grill, flipping burgers and kebabs, while my mom runs around making sure everyone has a drink in their hand and a cupcake on their plate. Typical Diane Banks behavior.

"Auntie!" Addy's little voice breaks through the noise, and I turn to see my niece darting across the lawn like a petite pink tornado.

But she doesn't run to me, her eyes darting over my shoulder just before she jukes me out. She runs right past me and straight into Henry's arms.

My heart does a stupid little flip as I watch him crouch down and scoop her up with ease. He's smiling that easy, crooked smile of his, and Addy giggles as she wraps her tiny arms around his neck.

"Henny, Henny! Guess whats?" she squeals.

"What?" he asks, tilting his head with mock seriousness.

"I'm gonna has a boy!"

Henry's eyes go wide, and he quickly distracts Addy by pointing to a random spot in the yard. "Oh my gosh, Addy! I think I just saw a butterfly!"

"Wheres?"

"Over there!" He points again, and she follows with her eyes. Clearly, there's no butterfly, only fear that June will pop out of the bushes and pull out a shiv from between her tits. "Oh no, I think it flew away."

Addy pouts. "What color?"

"It was yellow."

"Wellow!" she whines. "I's love wellows!"

"Don't worry, Addy. I'll keep watching for it, okay?"

She nods. "You see and yous tells me, 'kay?"

Henry nods and presses his forehead gently against hers. "You got it."

Addy smiles really big, tapping his cheek with her toddler hand, and then leans in close to whisper something in his ear. Of course, she's almost two, so whispering isn't something she has completely mastered yet, and I can hear her despite the distance. "You plays tea party."

Henry's face lights up with mock seriousness. "Tea party, huh? I don't know, Addy. Do you think I'm fancy enough for a tea party?"

Addy pulls back, studying him intently, then nods. "You needs a hat."

Henry grins. "A hat? Well, if you've got a hat for me, then I'm in."

Addy giggles, and I can't take my eyes off the scene. He's so good with her, so natural. My chest feels tight as I watch him spin her around once, making her laugh even harder before setting her back on her feet.

I don't even realize I've been staring until June sidles up next to me, her pregnant belly brushing against my arm. "He's always so good with her, huh?" she says, nodding toward Henry.

I shrug, trying to play it cool. "Henry's always been good with kids."

June gives me a knowing look, and for a moment, my stomach twists. *Does she know about me and Henry?* The thought makes me feel a little on edge, but before I can overthink it, she smiles and says, "It's just nice to see him so relaxed. He's had a tough year, and it feels like, I don't know, he's finally Henry again, you know?"

Her words brush away my panic, but only slightly. I nod, trying to seem nonchalant. "Yeah."

Henry is standing near the grill now, chatting with my dad and Beau. I catch bits and pieces of their conversation—something about the Miami Dolphins and how their draft picks are looking this year. My dad claps Henry on the shoulder, laughing at something he said, and Beau nods along, smiling.

They love him. My whole family loves him. Hell, they've known him since we were kids. He's practically part of the family already, even though no one knows about us. No one knows that most nights, I'm at his place, curled up in his bed, stealing kisses in the dark and touching like we can't get enough of each other.

I feel June watching me, and I force myself to look away from Henry. "What?" I ask, raising an eyebrow at her.

"Nothing," she says, smirking, but before she can say anything else, my dad's booming voice cuts through the air.

"Who wants more burgers?"

I rub at her belly and turn the attention on her for just a second as the crowd shifts their focus away from us. From a couple of prepubescent girls to this, our friendship has been through it all. I may have thrown a little hissy fit when she and my brother got together, but I'm so thankful for it now.

"I love you, Juni. Even when you're whacked out with hormones or letting my brother get away with entirely too much or stalking my every move. You're the best friend a girl could ever ask for, and I just want you to know…"

"Yeah?"

"I'm so glad it's your vagina about to get ripped open and not mine."

June goes through all the emotions, transitioning quickly from tears to laughter as I flip the script on her, shoving me in the shoulder.

"Oh my God. You just wait, Avery Banks! One day, it's going to happen to you, and if it doesn't, I'm going to spend the rest of our meals together wishing you wrinkles!"

"Ah!" I gasp.

"That's right," she says, doubling down. "If you're celebrating the downfall of my vagina, I'm wishing you crow's-feet. Starting to-morrow at our lunch at the diner."

I shake my head and wave taunting fingers at her as she wad-dles away to mingle with the rest of the crowd, and I do the same. *Oh, June. You don't know what you're starting.*

The evening continues in a blur of laughter and conversation. I move from group to group, chatting with cousins and old family friends, but my eyes always find their way back to Henry. Watching him joke with Ronnie and Maverick. Watching him grab another beer for my dad. Watching him laugh at something my mom says.

He looks so relaxed, so comfortable, so completely at ease. And I realize how much he fits here. *How much he fits with me.*

The thought makes my stomach twist in the best and worst ways because the truth is so obvious it hurts.

I'm in love with Henry.

I've *been* in love with Henry, and leaving that stupid island be-fore I did something impetuous like tell him doesn't change it one bit. I brought the love home with me, and every day since, it's grown.

I've never been in love before, not really. Technically, I don't even know what it's supposed to feel like. All I know is that when I look at him, I feel something *big*. Something overwhelming. Something terrifying and calming all at once.

Addy runs past me again, laughing as my dad chases her, and I glance back at Henry. He's still by the grill, talking with Beau. He's smiling, his whole face lit up in a way that makes my chest ache.

I'm down bad. And there's no helicopter coming to save me this time.

Chapter 40

Henry

THE BACKYARD IS ALIVE WITH CHEERS AND EXCITEMENT. Everyone gathers around Beau and June as they stand in front of a giant black balloon, ready to pop it. Considering that a lot of us already know that they're having a boy, the suspense is almost comical. Kids are squealing, adults are laughing, and Avery and Beau's mom is holding a hand to her chest like the reveal might just be too much for her heart to take.

Everyone is acting their part in June's superstitious game.

I'm standing off to the side, watching it all unfold. My arms are crossed, but my attention keeps flickering to Avery. She's standing next to June, her hand on her best friend's arm, and like always, I can't take my eyes off her.

Beau raises a pin, and the crowd collectively holds its breath. With one quick motion, he pops the balloon, and an explosion of blue confetti rains down. Cheers erupt, and June covers her mouth with her hands, tears spilling down her cheeks as Beau wraps his arms around her.

Their reaction is fucking adorable, but Avery's reaction hits me like a sucker punch to the chest. Her eyes fill with tears as she steps forward to hug them both. A lot of people might see Avery as abrasive and too direct, but I know how soft and gooey she really is on the inside. How she's the kind of loyal and loving and supportive that makes you lucky when you're someone she cares about.

She's gentle with June, whispering something in her ear, and I watch with awe as Juniper's face shifts, a laugh mixing in with her tears as Avery gives her the exact thing she needs in that moment effortlessly. She moves to her brother then, pulling him into a hug that lights up her face as bright as the decorations her mom has dotting the yard, and I watch, transfixed.

God, I love her.

That thought's been simmering in the back of my mind for weeks now, but seeing her here, surrounded by her family, her joy spilling out in every direction…it solidifies my feelings beyond reasonable doubt.

I'm in love with her. Completely, irreversibly in love with Avery Banks.

My chest tightens as I watch her crouch down to scoop up Addy, twirling her around in the grass.

Addy's giggling, her little arms wrapped tightly around Avery's neck, and Avery's laughing right along with her. She's so good with her niece, so sweet and natural, and it's like everything in the world makes sense when she smiles like that.

She's it for me.

For years now, there's been something between us—something bigger than friendship, something more than casual flirtation. We've always been more to each other, and I'm done pretending otherwise. I'm done sneaking around and keeping this thing between us a secret. I want her, and I want everyone to know she's mine.

Avery hands Addy off to her mom and heads toward the house. I watch her go, my heart hammering in my chest. She disappears through the sliding glass door, and without thinking, I follow her.

She heads down the hallway, turning into the bathroom. And I only hesitate for a split second before making my move. Stepping quietly, I push the bathroom door open and slip inside, closing it softly behind me.

She startles, her eyes wide as she spins around to face me. "Henry! What the hell?"

I grin. "Couldn't help myself."

She rolls her eyes but can't hide the small smile tugging at her lips. "You're insane."

"It's all your fault," I say, stepping closer. "You make me this way."

She shakes her head, laughing softly. "This isn't very secret, you know."

"Feels pretty secret to me," I counter, leaning down so my face is inches from hers. "Everyone's out there, and we're in here."

Her laughter dies in her throat as I press my lips to hers. It's not hurried or heated, just soft and lingering, the kind of kiss that makes time stop. She melts into me, sliding her hands up my chest, and for a moment, nothing else exists.

I pull back just enough to look into her eyes. "I couldn't go another minute without doing that."

She smiles up at me, her cheeks flushed. "You're ridiculous."

"Maybe," I admit, brushing a strand of hair behind her ear. "But you like it."

She doesn't deny it, just rolls her eyes again in that way that makes me want to kiss her all over. But I hold back. For now. I have something else up my sleeve. Something way more important.

"Don't make any plans tomorrow night."

Her brow furrows. "Why?"

"Because I have plans. For us."

"What kinds of plans?"

I grin. "I guess you'll just have to wait and see, huh?"

She narrows her eyes at me, but there's no hiding the curiosity in them. "You're infuriating."

"You'll survive," I tease, pressing another quick kiss to her lips. I pause just as I'm about to leave, turning back to her with a grin. "By the way, you're sleeping at my place tonight."

She quirks an eyebrow, crossing her arms. "Oh, am I? You really like taking up all my time, don't you?"

"Guilty as charged," I say, stepping closer to press one last kiss to her lips. "And don't pretend you don't love it."

She shakes her head, but the smile on her face gives her away. "Fine."

"Good," I say, my voice low and filled with promise. "See you out there."

And with that, I slip out of the bathroom, leaving her behind with a smile on her face and my heart pounding in my chest.

I'm in love with her, and I've got a to-do list of related items I can't wait to mark off.

1. Tell Avery.
2. Tell everyone else.
3. Make her mine forever.

With the way we've been for years, all three are a long time coming. When my father died, I thought I'd lost all my family for good.

But Avery was there to remind me I get a chance at a new one. *How fitting that I want to start it with her.*

Chapter 41

The Past

Six months ago

Henry

MY FATHER'S HOUSE IS PACKED TO THE GILLS, EVERY corner, every hallway, every room filled with people who knew him. Some of them are his old friends from past jobs and such, men with strong handshakes and sad smiles who tell me how proud my father always was of me. Others are neighbors, folks who would wave at him every morning as he drank his coffee on the porch. And then there are the ones I don't recognize at all. Faces blurred together in a haze of handshakes, murmured condolences, and too-tight hugs.

It's so strange to be in his house with all these people and he's not here.

I keep waiting to see him walk through the door, but I know it'll never happen because we're all gathered here for his wake.

All I have left of my father are memories and photos and his house and the belongings inside it that I'm not quite ready to pack up.

I know I'm standing in the middle of it all, but I feel like I'm watching it from outside my body. I am a shell of myself, nodding along and murmuring "thank you" over and over like it's on a loop that starts and ends in the same place—with a dead dad.

"Henry, I'm so sorry for your loss," someone says, and I turn to face them. It's an older woman, one of my dad's old coworkers, maybe. Her eyes are kind, but I can't even remember her name. I mumble a quick thanks before someone else steps up to offer their condolences.

Another handshake. Another sad smile.

The weight of it all presses down on my chest, and I feel like I can't breathe. My dad—the one person who's always been there, who's raised me, taught me everything I know, been my rock—is gone. And all these people, with their kind words and pats on the back, can't fill the void he's left behind.

I'm drowning in it.

I scan the room, desperate to find a lifeline that'll keep my head above water just enough to breathe and find it unexpectedly in the soft eyes of Beau's sister, Avery. Standing in the doorway to the living room, she has her gaze locked on me, and like a miracle, when our eyes meet, I feel light enough to keep from sinking to the bottom. She's wearing a simple but surely expensive black dress, her dark hair swept back, and for a moment, it feels like the world pauses.

She doesn't smile or say anything as she walks toward me, but her eyes don't let go of mine and her purpose is clear. When she gets close enough, she doesn't reach out for a handshake or a polite hug like everyone else—she grabs my hand and tugs me out of the room.

"Avery, what are you—" I start to say, but she cuts me off with a look. The kind of look that says, *Don't argue with me.*

She leads me down the hallway, past the kitchen where more people are gathered, and into my dad's study. It's quieter here, the noise of the wake muffled by the walls and the closed door. She lets go of my hand and turns to face me, her expression softening.

"This is total shit, Henry," she says, her voice firm but gentle. "I can't believe your dad died. I'm so sorry."

Her words hit me like a punch to the gut, but in a strange way, they're exactly what I need to hear. No sugarcoating, no platitudes. Just the raw, honest truth.

"Yeah," I say, my voice cracking. "It is."

She steps closer, wrapping her arms around me, and I don't hesitate to pull her in. She's smaller than me, but the way she holds me feels like she's trying to take some of the weight off my shoulders. Like she's trying to carry it with me.

"It's not fair," she says, her cheek pressed against my chest. "Your dad was one of the best people I've ever met. He didn't deserve this. You didn't deserve this."

I swallow hard, my throat tight. "I don't know what I'm supposed to do now, Ave. He was my only family."

She pulls back just enough to look up at me, her hazel eyes filled with a mix of sadness and determination. "You're supposed to keep going. You're supposed to live your life the way he would've wanted you to. And when it gets too hard, you're supposed to lean on the people who care about you. Like me."

Her words knock something loose inside me, and before I can stop myself, I'm letting it all out. The grief, the anger, the overwhelming sense of loss.

Avery holds me through it, her arms wrapped tightly around me, her presence steady and grounding.

When I finally pull back, wiping at my eyes, she gives me a small smile. "Feel a little better?"

I let out a shaky laugh. "A little."

"Good." She reaches up to smooth out the lapel of my suit jacket, her touch gentle. "Now, let's get back out there and try to get through this thing together. Though, I can't promise I'm keeping these heels on. I don't know what the hell Prada put in these, but I'm pretty sure it's knives."

I quirk an amused brow at her. "Is this your way of trying to get my condolences for your feet?"

She shrugs. "I mean, it'd be nice."

Fuck me, she's a character.

"I'm sorry to hear your feet are hurting you at my father's wake, Avery."

"Thanks, Henry," she says, patting my shoulder before taking my hand again. She gives it a reassuring squeeze. "Now, let's do the damn thing."

Avery isn't just my best friend's sister right now. She's the exact thing I needed.

We step into the noise and the crowd, and for the first time today, I feel a little less alone.

Chapter 42

Avery

THE DINER IS EXACTLY THE KIND OF PLACE YOU'D EXPECT June to love. Kitschy, borderline tacky, with retro vinyl booths and a jukebox in the corner that looks like it hasn't worked in decades. The walls are plastered with black-and-white photos of old Miami, the kind of thing that screams "vintage" but is probably more thrift-store find than authentic.

It's Sunday, and the place is packed—waitstaff buzzing around with plates piled high with pancakes and greasy burgers. The smell of syrup and coffee lingers in the air, and the low hum of conversation fills the space.

June sits across from me, glowing in that way only pregnant women can. Her little belly is getting bigger, and she rests her hands on it like she's cradling the life growing inside her.

She's adorable and so genuinely happy it's almost infectious.

"You look so cute," I tell her, reaching across the table to touch her belly. "Seriously, you're like one of those pregnancy Pinterest boards come to life."

June laughs, her smile widening. "I feel like a whale."

"Well, you're the cutest whale I've ever seen."

"Shut up." She rolls her eyes but doesn't stop smiling. Just then, I feel it. A little flutter beneath my hand.

My eyes widen as I look at June. "Was that…did he just kick?"

"He did!" she says, beaming.

My throat tightens, and I feel an unexpected wave of emotion. I blink quickly, trying to fight back the tears threatening to spill. But June notices anyway.

"Avery, are you…crying? Oh my God, are you okay?" she asks, bordering on frantic. I don't blame her. This isn't like me.

I snort, trying to shake it off. "I'm fine. I think your pregnancy hormones are doing some kind of osmosis shit and seeping into my brain."

She laughs, and the sound is enough to ground me. But deep down, I can't ignore the strange feeling in my chest. A desire I've never really felt before. *Kids? Me?* The thought is enough to make my head spin.

My phone buzzes on the table, and I glance at the screen. It's Henry. A slow smile spreads across my face as I read his text.

Henry: Don't forget about tonight.

And I can't stop myself from responding.

Me: What's tonight?

Henry: You know what tonight is.

Me: Actually, I don't. So, why don't you tell me?

Henry: Nice try, honey. My lips are sealed. Think back to your parents' bathroom if you need a frame of reference. You, me. Plans. That's all you're going to get.

I bite my lip to keep from grinning like an idiot. I can still feel the warmth of his hands on my body from this morning. I already tried to get him to tell me about whatever he has planned for tonight, but it ended with me bent over the balcony railing with Henry's cock inside me while he fucked me so good I forgot my own name.

Does that make me an exhibitionist? It's certainly an interesting question to consider…

"So, what's new in your life?" June's voice pulls me out of my reverie, and I quickly lock my phone, sliding it facedown on the table.

"What do you mean?"

"I feel like we haven't really had a chance to catch up. You're always so busy. We haven't really gotten any best-friend time since…" June trails off and starts to get tears in her eyes. Clearly, thinking about the thirteen days Henry and I were missing.

"Don't you dare start with that," I quickly chime in, pointing an index finger toward her. "Do not start breaking down before we even get our food."

"I'm sorry!" June sniffles. "It's a little hard to just get over the two weeks you thought your best friend died, Avery. I have a heart, you know. I'm not soulless." She dabs a napkin at her eyes, sniffling a little more. "Also, I really think you're losing sight of our agreement."

"What agreement?"

"You keeping me updated about where you are," she expands, and her brow furrows in determination. "Honestly, I think you just need to share your location with me. That would make things way easier than me having to constantly call and text you."

"You want to *track* me?" I ask, horrified.

"Yeah." June nods like it makes complete sense. Like it's not at all an insane request. "I track Beau."

A laugh jumps from my lungs. "He's your husband, Juni."

"And you're my best friend," she retorts like her argument holds weight.

"Yeah, no. I have boundaries."

June stares at me like boundaries isn't even a word. Immediately, my mind is reeling over the consequences of sharing my phone location with June. Surely she'd get real damn suspicious if she started to see me at Henry's apartment every single night of the week.

Luckily, the server arrives at our table, setting down our plates and distracting my stalker best friend from her insane request.

June's cheeseburger looks juicy and perfectly messy, while my chicken Caesar salad is topped with crisp romaine and grilled chicken. We're actively eating when my phone buzzes again, but I quickly glance at the screen—it's only Ethel—and place it back on the table to avoid June's prying eyes. Goodness knows, if she got ahold of the messages between Henry and me, she'd reach another level of hormonal.

Instantly, guilt sets up shop in my stomach. The mere idea of keeping something like this from my best friend is…hard. I don't like keeping things from June, and if I'm honest with myself, it's bordering on hypocritical, considering how upset I got with her when I found out she was in a relationship with my brother.

"June…" I say, my voice quieter than normal as I stare down at my chicken Caesar salad.

"Yeah?" she asks around a mouthful of burger.

My stomach churns as I try to find the right words to express everything I'm feeling, everything I've been up to, and all the questions I have about the future. She's my best friend, and her input is invaluable in everything happy and sad and in between, and keeping the news of Henry from her is only hurting us both.

But God. It's big.

And juicy.

And so, so uncharted in the territory department.

Not to mention, her hormones are a wreck, and I don't want to be responsible for a pregnant woman's public breakdown.

I take another deep breath to ready myself, but instead of steadying, my stomach pitches, the smell of Caesar dressing and chicken hitting me straight in the face in a way I don't expect.

A wave of nausea crashes over me, and I swallow hard, reaching for my water.

June pauses mid-bite of her cheeseburger, her eyes narrowing as she watches me. "You okay?"

"Yeah," I say, forcing a smile. But when I take a bite of my salad, the nausea intensifies, and before I know it, I'm bolting for the bathroom, my feet scrambling on the black-and-white diamond tile the whole way.

When an older woman in an electric-blue sweater gets in the way of the bathroom door just as my vomit threatens, I have to shove her out of the way with way less gentleness than both she and I would like.

I want to apologize, but if I open my mouth, even for a single word, I'm going to spray chunks.

Shoving through the door and screeching into a stall, I lean over the toilet bowl and let it all go in ugly, retching waves.

When it's over, I lean against the wall of the stall, catching my breath. The nausea is gone, replaced by a weird sense of relief, but the disgust is alive and well.

Ugh. I hate throwing up so much, and the *last* thing I need right now is a stomach virus while I'm trying to gain back a little bit of the weight the island took.

Normally, I'd take life's blessings for what they are on the diet front—like the time I got a stomach virus two weeks before senior prom and my body ended up looking banging in my dress—but of all the times I've needed it, this isn't one of them.

I take a quick glance at myself in the mirror, thankful I didn't manage to get particles of vomit on my new short-sleeve knit Chloé sweater I bought the other day at Saks when I was shopping for Blanche and Darla. After a quick fluff of my hair, I wash my hands and head back out into the diner.

When I return to the table, June looks concerned. "Are you okay?"

"Yeah. Just had to puke. But I'm feeling better now."

"You *puked*?" Her eyes widen. "Oh my God, Avery."

"It's no big deal."

"Holy hell," June mutters through a soft laugh. "Maybe my pregnancy hormones really are getting to you..." She pauses, but then her face morphs from carefree and smiling to eyes narrowed and analyzing my face. "Wait…you don't think you're—" she drops her voice "—*pregnant*, do you?"

Now, it's my turn to laugh. "Get real, Juni. You have to have sex to get pregnant."

But you are having sex, my mind reminds me. *A lot of it.*

Holy hell. That's right. I'm *not* a virgin anymore. Not by a long shot.

"Finally, a life update!" June says through a snort. "So, I guess my best friend doesn't have any man in her life at the moment."

Her words are another punch to my already tenuous gut. It wasn't my intention, but I've been keeping *a lot* of shit from my best friend.

Not only does she not know about my pre-Henry virginal status, but she doesn't know about my post-virginal status with Henry either—my brother's best friend whom I've been fucking every chance I get for the past several weeks.

June starts talking about something adorable Addy did the other day, but I'm mentally spiraling.

Henry and I have sex without protection—lots. Sure, he pulled out on the island and I've been on birth control since we got back, but *nothing* is foolproof. If that *Friends* episode with Ross and the condom company is anything to go by, there's literally nothing when you're fucking that is one hundred percent safe.

Immediately, my stomach tightens—and it's not from the nausea.

"Avery? Are you even listening?" June asks.

"I gotta go," I blurt out. "I have a…" I pause, my mind moving ninety miles per hour as I try to pull a random excuse out of my ass. "A Botox appointment. Yeah. Totally forgot about it."

"Botox?" June repeats, confused. "On a Sunday?"

"It was the only time Fredrick could fit me in. And he'll be so pissed if I'm a no-show," I say, grabbing my purse before tossing one of my credit cards down onto the table. "Lunch is on me. Love you!" I call over my shoulder as I head straight for the door.

I should feel like the world's worst best friend, but fuck, I can't focus on anything but the giant pregnant elephant in the room.

As I step outside, the Miami sun feels too bright, too hot, and my mind is racing.

I've got a bad feeling all that vagina-taunting to June is about to bite me right in the center of my own cooch.

Pregnant?

Shit. *Talk about committing, Avery.*

Chapter 43

Avery

I'M IN FULL-ON PANIC MODE, AND EVERY POSSIBLE WORST-CASE scenario is playing out like a bad Lifetime movie marathon, and as luck would have it, that's when I'm my very most efficient.

Rules? Don't know them.

Laws? For breaking.

Waiting my turn? Who's she?

I need some answers, and I'll be damned if I'm not going to get them—conscious decision-making or not.

I don't even remember deciding to go to an OB-GYN, but next thing I know, I'm standing in front of the receptionist at Miami's most expensive OB practice. The sign on the door says this place is run by Dr. Sofia Moretti—the same Dr. Sofia Moretti who's been quoted in magazines as being the go-to OB for celebrities. She's also one of very few doctors in the city who takes Sunday appointments—though, you are supposed to *schedule* said appointment rather than show up unannounced—and apparently, she delivered Stella St. Clair's twins last year—yes, *the* Stella St. Clair, international pop icon and TikTok sensation.

Surely if this doctor can deliver Stella St. Clair's twins and keep it from the press for two WHOLE months, she can handle my currently fucked-up situation.

I push open the door, and it bangs against the wall with a

thud. The waiting room is filled with women—expectant moms with bellies in all shapes and sizes—and the receptionist looks up at me with a raised brow. She's in her late forties with glasses that rest low on her nose and the permanent air of someone who's seen too much nonsense to have patience for it.

"Excuse me, can I help you?" she asks, her voice imbued with annoyance.

"I need to see the doctor," I say in a rush, speed walking over to her desk. "Right now."

"Do you have an appointment?" she asks, her tone making it clear she already knows the answer.

"No," I reply, trying to sound calm and collected when, in reality, I'm seconds away from throwing myself across her desk. "But this is an emergency. One of those circumstances where you have to make an exception to the appointment rule."

She blinks. "An emergency?"

"Yes," I say, nodding furiously. "Like, a…possible baby emergency. Hence, the reason I'm here. At an OB-GYN."

"We don't usually do walk-ins," she says, her fingers hovering over the keyboard. "But I can look at the schedule and see if Dr. Moretti has any openings this week."

"This week?" I question, my voice rising in panic. "No, that won't work." I lean in, lowering my voice like I'm about to spill state secrets. "Listen. I need an appointment *now*. I might be pregnant. And I'm not supposed to be pregnant. Like, me being pregnant right now is absolute insanity and I need to figure out what in the hell is happening and I can't just go to some rando clinic because do I look like the kind of girl who goes to rando clinics? Um, *no*. I need to see Dr. Moretti." I pull a credit card out of my wallet and slam it down on the desk. "Charge me whatever, but I need to see the doctor."

Her lips twitch and I think she's about to smile, but she just shakes her head. "One moment."

She picks up the phone and proceeds to have a quiet

conversation that I can't hear before she hangs up. "We don't usually do this, but I recognize you from the news… You're one of the island survivors, aren't you?"

Panic floods my veins and makes my eyeballs widen comically. She shakes her head. "Don't worry, I won't say anything. I imagine you've been through enough." Then she looks both ways before handing me a clipboard with a stack of papers on it. "Fill out this new patient registration form and take a seat. Dr. Moretti will fit you in."

Quickly, I scratch down all my info on the sheet without even moving from the window, courtesy be damned, and hand it back to her.

"Thank you," I say, and she nods then jerks her chin at the waiting room chairs. I comply, pulling a silk scarf out of my bag and wrapping it around my head. Now that she mentioned knowing me, I'm a little afraid everyone else will too. Luckily, the place is ridiculously fancy, with chandeliers, a coffee bar, framed photos of smiling babies on every wall, and a huge spread-out waiting room. It's more spa than medical office, and I find a quiet corner away from all the other patients.

I don't know how long I stare at the wall before a nurse calls my name, but I don't think it matters. Time is a chasm, reality is warped, and I might be motherfucking pregnant. This isn't exactly something I had on my schedule, and it takes as long as it takes. The nurse is young, with a bright smile and a clipboard that she clutches like it's her lifeline when I get her in sight, waiting at the wooden door next to the sign-in desk.

"Ms. Banks?" she says, and I'm thankful they had the forethought not to say my first name, given the circumstances.

As I approach her, I smooth my hands nervously down my Prada jeans. "That's me."

"Right this way," she says, leading me down a hallway lined with more baby photos. "So, you think you're pregnant?"

"I don't know," I say, my voice tight. "But I need to know for sure. Like, immediately."

She nods, her smile never faltering. "We'll start with a pregnancy test, and Dr. Moretti will see you after that."

I follow her into an exam room, where she hands me a cup. "You know the drill, right? Pee in this, bring it back to me, and we'll dip a strip. Easy as that," she says with a wink when my whole body locks up.

I trudge through the motions of pissing in a little cup via an unruly tool with which you can't control the spray—kind of like putting your thumb over a garden hose—and blow out a breath when I manage to fill it halfway.

I seal it, wash my hands, hand it off to the nurse outside the door, and return to the room, jumping up onto the paper-covered table and sinking my head into my hands.

My God, how times have changed.

Five minutes of staring at the door like it's about to burst into flames later, the nurse returns, looking entirely too calm for someone holding my future in her hands.

"Congratulations," she says, her smile tenuously bright. "You're pregnant."

My stomach pitches to the side, and my ears start to ring. "What?"

"The test is positive," she repeats. "Your feeling was correct, and you are, in fact, pregnant."

"No," I say, shaking my head. "That's wrong. It has to be wrong. I think you need to do the thing where you put goo all over my belly and see inside my uterus. They do it on *Grey's Anatomy* all the time."

"An ultrasound?"

"Yes, that." I nod manically. "Do that. Because I think your tests are expired or something."

"That's not how that usually works," she says. "Our tests aren't like home tests, and they are very effective. But I'll let the doctor know your request if you feel really strongly—"

"I feel strongly. Very, very strongly. I'm the freaking Hulk over here, okay? World's Strongest Man Winner. Omnipotent and omnipowerful like God Almighty, for the purposes of this moment, you know?"

She smiles. "I'll try my best."

She leaves, and I reassume the fetal position, tucking my knees to my chest and rocking myself.

A few minutes later, there's a knock on the door, and the nurse holds it open for a beautiful redhead in a lab coat with an air of authority about her as she enters. "Hi, I'm Dr. Moretti," she introduces herself. "And you must be Avery."

I nod.

"I hear you just got some big news."

I shake my head. "No, no. No news. Because your tests are wrong. They have to be."

Dr. Moretti smiles. "I don't think there's anything wrong with our tests, Avery, but I do understand the shock that comes with finding out you're pregnant, if it's not something you've been planning for."

"With all due respect, there's no way I'm pregnant, okay? It's…impossible. Immaculata, you know?"

"Immaculate?"

"Yes! That!"

"Are you saying you haven't had sex, Avery?" Dr. Moretti asks, her beautifully shaped brows drawing together.

"Ye—well. Technically, no. But, like, I *just* started. Twenty-seven years of no boom-boom in the hoom-hoom, and I finally do it, and you're telling me it made a baby?" I shake my head. "No way."

Dr. Moretti smiles, glancing back at the nurse and nodding. "Okay. Let's do an ultrasound, just to get a look for sure if it'll make you feel better."

"Yes!" I nod. "Please. I need to feel better."

Her smile is conciliatory in a way I don't like, so instead of focusing on her, I ignore it.

"So, let's do it. Whip that thing out," I say, pulling up my shirt.

Dr. Moretti's smile lifts to her eyes. "Because of the suspected early progression of the pregnancy, we'll need to do the ultrasound transvaginally. Nurse Higgins and I will step out. You'll remove your clothes and then put on this paper gown with the opening in the front, okay? We'll come back with the machine when you're ready."

I nod woodenly, despite not liking the sound of the word "transvaginally" at all.

The nurse hands me a gown before her and Dr. Moretti leave the room. And I do as I'm told, my hands shaking as I remove my Louboutins and jeans and panties, and shortly after my bare ass hits the scratchy-paper-covered table, there are three soft knocks to the door.

"You can come in."

Dr. Moretti and her nurse step back inside, and the nurse turns down the lights.

"Now, since we're not sure how far along you are, we're going to have to start with a vaginal ultrasound," the doctor explains again. "It won't hurt. You'll just feel some pressure. Go ahead and spread your legs for me, and scoot down on the table if you can."

Good grief, the things women have to go through.

I hold my breath, and just like that, things are *started.*

I can feel her moving the wand around inside me, and I close my eyes tightly, refusing to look at the screen.

"Okay, Avery," she says after a moment. "I can confirm that you are pregnant. You look to be about eight weeks along."

My eyes fly open. "Eight weeks?"

"Yes," she says. "I'd say your date of conception is on or around January 10th or so."

January 10th? While we were still on the island.

"Holy fucking shit," I blurt out in a rush. "Did I get pregnant the first time I had sex? What is this, an episode of *The Secret Life of the American Teenager*? Am I Amy Juergens?"

Dr. Moretti raises an eyebrow. "Well, I can assure you that it's not a TV show. But yes, it does happen."

I'm having an out-of-body experience as she turns on the volume, and the sound of a heartbeat fills the room. It's fast, steady, and impossibly real.

"That's your baby's heartbeat," she says softly.

There's a baby. In my uterus. A baby that's half me and half Henry, growing inside me.

For a moment, warmth washes over me. The sound of the heartbeat, the knowledge that this tiny life is mine… It's overwhelming in the best way.

But then fear creeps in. *I'm pregnant. I'm going to be a mom.* And no one in my life even knows I'm in a relationship.

Because it's a secret freaking relationship with the father of my baby, who just so happens to be my brother's best friend.

Dr. Moretti hands me a packet of information and a couple of ultrasound photos. The receptionist schedules my next appointment, but it all feels like a dream. I float through the motions, my mind spinning like an out-of-control top.

When I walk out of the office, I don't know what to do or where to go. So, I just sit there in my car, in the middle of the parking lot, with ultrasound photos of my baby—*oh my God, my baby*—clutched to my chest.

My phone buzzes from my purse—that's apparently still on my shoulder—and I pull it out to find a message that makes tears fill my eyes.

Henry: Can't wait to see you tonight.

A few hours ago, I felt the same. Now, I don't even know my own name.

How the hell am I supposed to tell Henry I'm pregnant when I can hardly believe it myself? Especially when it's all my fault.

The whole reason Henry and I even had sex in the first place is because of me. I'm the one who convinced him on the island, maybe even manipulated him into it.

I seduced him. Not the other way around.

I'm a trapper. A baby trapper. *I trapped Henry!*

My God. Everything's about to change. And he has no freaking clue it's coming.

Chapter 44

THE DRIVE TO BEAU AND JUNE'S HOUSE FEELS LIKE IT TAKES forever, even though it's only twenty minutes from Dr. Moretti's office. My hands grip the steering wheel, knuckles white, my stomach churning. The reality of my doctor's appointment is still sinking in, and the more I try to process it, the less it makes sense.

I'm pregnant. With Henry's baby. *How did this happen?*

I barely remember parking the car, let alone walking up to their front door. When I knock, it feels like an eternity before it opens, and there stands June, Addy perched on her hip. Her little pregnant belly is prominent beneath her soft sweater, her blond hair pulled back in a messy bun. She looks glowing and adorable—as always—and I'm struck by the contrast between her put-togetherness and my barely-holding-it-together mess.

"Avery!" she says, smiling. Then she pauses, her brow furrowing slightly. "You okay?"

"I'm fine," I lie. Because that's what I do.

Addy's tiny voice interrupts us. "Auntie Avie!" she exclaims, squirming to get down. June sets her on her feet, and Addy bolts toward me, wrapping her little arms around my legs. "Pays tea partys?"

"Maybe later, sweet pea," I manage, forcing a smile. "Is…uh… Beau home?" I ask, looking back at June.

"Nope." She shakes her head. "Left to go golf with Neil about an hour ago." She reaches for her purse and pulls out her wallet. "You left your credit card at the diner," June says, handing my Black Amex over to me. "Thanks for lunch, by the way."

Lunch? Oh, right. That's when I freaked out and bolted. It was mere hours ago, but it feels like a lifetime.

"How was your Botox appointment?" June asks casually as she ushers me inside.

I blink at her, completely blanking. "My what?"

"Your Botox appointment?" she repeats, giving me a confused look. "You know, the one you rushed out of lunch for?"

Crap. That's the excuse I gave her. "Oh. Right. That. I didn't actually have a Botox appointment."

"What do you mean?" June's confusion deepens. "Then where did you go?"

Before I can answer, a wave of nausea rolls through me like a freight train. "Excuse me," I mutter, bolting toward the bathroom. I barely make it to the toilet before I'm heaving.

"Avery?" June's voice is behind me, soft with concern. She's there, gently patting my back as I retch. Addy's little voice comes from the doorway.

"Auntie Avie sick?"

"Auntie's just feeling a little under the weather, Addy," June says, standing up to lead Addy away. "Go watch your show, sweetie. Mommy will be right there."

By the time June comes back, I'm sitting on the bathroom floor, clutching a hand towel and dabbing at my sweat-dampened face. She crouches down beside me, her eyes filled with worry.

"Avery, what's going on?" she asks softly.

And just like that, the dam breaks. It's an overload of information, and I start spilling it, haphazardly as it may be. "I was a virgin," I blurt out, my voice cracking.

June's eyes go wide. "Excuse me?"

"I was a virgin," I repeat, more firmly this time. "Before the island. Before Henry. I know you probably thought I was banging all those dudes, but I was a virgin until the island."

June sits back on her heels, her jaw practically on the floor. "Wait. You mean…"

"I had sex with Henry," I say, the words tumbling out in a rush. "I seduced him. And ever since we got back, we've been secretly fucking all over the city."

I hold my breath, waiting for her reaction to the news I've dropped so far. Clearly, I haven't dropped *all* the bombs, saving the most earth-shattering for last, but I honestly don't know how my best friend is going to react to me keeping shit from her.

June's eyes somehow get even wider. Her lips part, but no words come out. Then, finally, she grins. "Oh my God."

I blink. "Why are you smiling?"

"Because!" she says, laughing now. "I had a feeling something was going on between you two. Honestly, I've been wondering for a while. Even before the island."

"What? Why?"

She shrugs. "Because you guys have always had a little…something-something. Some kind of undeniable chemistry."

"Oh, we have undeniable chemistry, all right," I mutter. "It's literally growing inside me right now."

June freezes, her gaze dropping to where my hand is resting on my belly. "You're pregnant?" she whispers, her voice full of awe.

"Yes, I'm pregnant," I snap. "With Henry's baby. And he doesn't know. But that shouldn't be a surprise, because he doesn't know I'm in love with him either."

"Oh my God, Avery!" June exclaims, pulling me into a tight hug. "You're pregnant!"

"Yes, June," I say, exasperated. "I'm pregnant. This is going to change my life forever. I don't know how to be a teen mom!"

"Teen mom?" June repeats, laughing. "Avery, you're twenty-seven. Like me."

"Don't make this about you!" I wail.

"You're pregnant," June whispers again, tears in her eyes. "Avery, there's a little baby growing inside your belly." She hugs me again. "And you and I, we're pregnant together. Our babies are going to be the same age." She leans back, brushing my hair out of my face. "I know this is a lot to process, Avery, but this is a good thing. This is a great thing. This is the best thing, actually."

"The best thing?" I repeat, incredulous. "June, I didn't get Louboutins for half off. I'm pregnant. With child."

"Yeah," June says, smiling even bigger. "You are."

I search her face, and she hugs me again. "It's going to be okay, Avery. I promise. I think you just need to talk to Henry."

Oh, Henry. Just the thought of telling him makes my stomach churn all over again.

"I don't know, June."

"I do," she says firmly. "Henry is a good guy. And sure, I don't know everything that's gone down between you two—*clearly, because you were keeping sneaky secrets from your best friend.*" She eyes me knowingly. "But I know the way he looks at you. I know the way he's looked at you for years."

"And how does he look at me, June?"

"Like his whole heart is in his eyes."

God, I hope she's right.

"Just tell him, Ave. Just go to him and tell him."

"I..." I pause, trying to find the words. "I think I need a moment, you know? I need to wrap my mind around all of this."

"I know you're scared, but now isn't the time to run. Now is the time to face everything head on."

I nod, but deep down, I'm not so sure. I feel a lot like running—straight back to my condo and burrowing under my comforter for the next nine months. Surely my baby and I can survive on DoorDash takeout. Hell, maybe Dr. Moretti can make house calls for all my OB appointments.

"You're strong, Avery," June says, holding both of my hands.

"One of the strongest people I know. You've got this. And you know that I'm here for you. I'm always here for you."

Right now, I don't feel very strong at all. But with the way June is looking at me, the love and care that sit in her eyes, all I can do is hug her tightly.

"Thanks, Juni," I whisper into her ear. "I love you."

"I love you too. Even though you were keeping all these secrets from me."

"I'm sorry," I whisper.

"It's okay."

I think about how amazing June is. How amazing she's always been. She never judges and she doesn't hold a grudge, and she hasn't even brought up the fact that I wasn't quite so demure when she was keeping secrets from me. She's the best best friend anyone could ever have.

"So…" June pauses. "How are you going to tell Beau?"

"How am I going to tell, Beau?" I scoff. "He's *your* husband. Pretty sure that's your job, babe."

"*Avery.*"

"What?" I say, feigning innocence. "He got signed over to you when you said 'I do.'"

"Oh my God, Avery."

I hug her again and start to head for the door.

"Where are you going?"

"I don't know." I grab my purse, but before I can leave, June takes my phone.

"What are you doing?"

"Nothing."

When she hands it back, I realize she's set it up so she can track my location. "You're fucking with me, right?"

"No. I'm not. And don't you dare turn it off," she demands with an index finger pointed directly in my face.

"You're a psycho."

"No, I'm not. I just love you, and trust me, now that you're about to be a *mom*…"

I screech.

"You'll understand there's a difference."

I roll my eyes, and June hugs me one more time.

"Tell him," she whispers.

I nod, even though my mind is screaming at me to run. Right now, telling Henry I'm pregnant feels impossible.

You've done it before. You thought surviving the island was impossible too, my mind encourages, but I shake my head to clear it.

What do you know, ya dumb bitch? You're the one who got me pregnant.

Chapter 45

Henry

I CHECK MY WATCH AND SEE IT'S 7:59 P.M. MY BODY IS FILLED with nerves and anticipation, and I can't stop myself from pacing in front of the floor-to-ceiling windows of my apartment. The city lights below glimmer, but my mind is somewhere else entirely. *Avery.* Tonight is the night. The night I'm finally going to tell her how I feel, how much she means to me, and how I don't want to keep sneaking around anymore.

I want to be together. For real.

I glance at the clock above my television, 8:00 p.m. I know Avery well enough not to expect her on time, so I'm not worried. I mean, if anyone makes a point of being fashionably late, it's my girl.

The restaurant is ready, the rooftop set to perfection. Soft lighting, a private chef, and a table for two overlooking Miami. It cost a fortune, but I don't care. Avery is worth it. She's worth everything fancy she begs the world for.

I check my phone. No text. No call.

At 8:20 p.m., when there's still nothing, I fire off a quick text.

Me: You on your way?

I stare at the screen, willing the dots to appear. Nothing.

8:30 p.m.

I try calling her. It rings and rings and rings. Then her voice mail picks up. Her voice, sweet and teasing, fills my ear, *"You've reached Avery Banks. I'm busy doing something you wish you were doing, so leave a message."*

I hang up without leaving one and grip the edge of the counter. This isn't like her. Sure, she's chaotic and unpredictable, but she'd never just ghost me.

8:40 p.m.

Panic starts creeping in, and my mind races through worst-case scenarios. *Did something happen to her? Is she okay?* She was fine this morning. We texted a bit, and everything seemed normal. But now? Radio silence.

I grab my phone again and text her.

> **Me: You okay, babe? I'm starting to get a little worried.**

Still, no response. I try calling again. But I get her voice mail— again. My chest feels tight, and I'm pacing the apartment like a caged animal. *What the hell is going on?*

By 9:00 p.m., I'm fully panicking. I've called and texted her two more times, each message more frantic than the last.

> **Me: Avery, seriously. Just let me know you're okay.**

> **Me: If I don't hear from you soon, I'm coming to your place.**

The last time I felt this kind of fear was when I was diving out of the plane with Avery secured against me and praying to God that I was going to keep her alive. And my mind keeps jumping to the worst conclusions. *What if she's hurt? What if she's…* No. I can't think like that. But the worry is gnawing at me, and I can't shake it.

I grab my jacket and keys, ready to head to her place, when my phone buzzes. My heart leaps, and I snatch it off the counter, praying it's her.

But it's not.

Maverick: YOOOOOOO. Come to Allure, you asshole!

I don't even have the energy to reply. Not right now when I'm this fucking terrified something has happened to Avery. A pang of guilt over leaving her that morning on the island only intensifies the burn in my stomach, and just like that, I'm done waiting.

As I drive through the city, my mind replays every interaction we've had over the past month. The way she laughs, the way she looks at me when she thinks I'm not paying attention, the way she feels in my arms. She's everything I never knew I needed, and the thought of something being wrong… It's unbearable.

Fuck.

By the time I reach Avery's condo building, my body feels like a live wire, stress and worry and anxiety damn near choking the life out of me. I don't waste any time parking and heading in the lobby doors. And once I'm in the elevator, the ride up to Avery's floor feels like it takes decades.

The elevator dings, and I step out, striding straight for her door. My pulse pounds harder with every step. And when I reach her condo, I knock. Firm, but not aggressive.

No answer.

I knock again, louder this time. Still nothing.

Fuck. I'm ten seconds away from ripping this fucking door off the hinges with my bare hands.

Pulling out my phone, I hit her name and press call. The phone rings, and I hear it—through the door. She's inside. I know she is. The faint sound of her ringtone filters through, and then the sound of footsteps fills my ears before the ringtone cuts off abruptly. Like she's grabbed it to silence it.

My anxiety wanes, but my jaw tightens.

I swear, I'm going to spank her pretty little ass so hard if she's put me through all this just because she's avoiding me.

"Avery, it's me, babe. Open up," I say, my voice steady but demanding.

Silence.

I lean my head against the door for a moment, closing my eyes and testing my well of patience. "Avery," I call again, knocking one more time. "What's wrong? I'm worried about you. Why didn't you show up tonight?"

There's a pause, and then, finally, her voice comes through, muffled by the door. "Trust me, Henry. You don't want to know."

I roll my eyes.

"You're wrong," I say, stepping closer to the door. "I do want to know. Talk to me."

"Not this," she says, her voice breaking and softening me entirely. She's not just throwing a tantrum—she's genuinely upset. "You don't want to know this."

"Avery," I say softly, pressing my palm flat against the door. "Please, just open the door so we can talk. Whatever it is, I'm here. I'm not going anywhere."

For a moment, there's only silence. Then I hear movement. Her footsteps, I think. My breath catches in my lungs. The sound of the lock clicking echoes in the hallway, and finally, the door opens just a crack. Enough for me to see her face.

Her eyes are red, her cheeks streaked with tears. She looks like she's been crying for hours, and the sight of her like this nearly breaks me.

"Avery," I breathe, stepping closer.

She doesn't say anything. She just stands there, her hand on the edge of the door, staring at me with an expression that's a mix of heartbreak and fear.

I take another step forward, my voice gentle. "Talk to me, Ave. Please."

Her lips part like she wants to say something, but then she presses them together tightly and shakes her head.

I reach out, brushing my hand lightly against the edge of the door. "Whatever it is, we'll handle it. Together."

She looks down, her shoulders trembling, and after what feels like an eternity, she steps back, opening the door wider to let me in.

Step one accomplished. Step two, though? *Seems like it might be harder.*

Chapter 46

Avery

Henry steps into my condo, and I close the door behind him, my hand trembling as I turn the lock. His beard is neat, his tan evening out beautifully, and his sweet blue eyes are bright with worry, looking every bit like the man who has completely consumed my thoughts for weeks now. His hands fist at his sides as he works to be calm for me, his hair just a little bit tousled from the frantic state I no doubt left him in by not showing up at his apartment at the agreed-upon time, and God…it's all too much.

I feel like I'm going to break apart.

"Avery," he says tenderly, taking a step toward me. His voice is gentle and soothing, but his unwavering patience only makes my heart race faster. I did this to him, and it all started the night I wouldn't take no for an answer. "What's going on? Talk to me."

I shake my head, stepping back, wrapping my arms around my body as if I can hold myself together if I squeeze tight enough. But bone and flesh don't shatter like glass, and my arms aren't glue. This problem is much bigger than that.

"You shouldn't be here," I whisper. My voice cracks, and I hate it. It's the opposite of everything I've prided myself on being for my entire life and unsurprisingly uncomfortable. Wearing someone else's shoes is always tough when they aren't the size you're used to. "I…I can't do this right now."

"Can't do what?" He takes another step forward, his hands reaching for me but stopping short when I jump startle, like he's afraid I'll bolt. "Avery, please. It's me. Remember? The one person in the world who's seen you at your most vulnerable and you the same for me. You can tell me anything, and not only that, if it's got you this worried, you should. How else am I going to help?"

Tears blur my vision, and I press my hands to my face, trying to stop them, but it's useless. The weight of everything is crashing down on me.

I'm pregnant.

I'm in love with him.

And I'm terrified that telling him the truth will ruin everything.

"Avery," he says again, his voice firmer now. He closes the space between us, his hands gently pulling mine away from my face. "Look at me. Please, just look at me."

I do, and the concern etched into his features is my undoing. My breath hitches, and a sob escapes before I can stop it. I am raw and unfolded in front of him, just like I've been several times before.

I am fighting for my life, but this time, in an entirely different way. Whereas the island felt like the two of us against the world, this feels like the world and me against Henry.

"Hey, hey," he murmurs, pulling me into his arms. "It's okay. Whatever it is, we'll figure it out. I'm here. I'm not going anywhere."

His words only make me cry harder because they're both exactly what I need to hear and exactly what I'm afraid I don't deserve.

He strokes my hair, his voice steady and calm. "Ave, focus. I need you to focus for the next ninety seconds, just like you did for me before we hit the water. Tell me whatever it is, and then tread as fast and hard as you need to to stay afloat while I do the rest. I've got you. Don't you know I've got you?"

I pull back slightly, just enough to look up at him. His hands stay on my arms, grounding me, and I take a shaky breath. "Henry, I...I don't even know where to start."

"Start anywhere," he says softly. "Just start."

I look into his eyes, and the love I see there makes my chest ache.

He loves me. I know he does. And he deserves someone who isn't afraid to shoot it fucking straight. He deserves to have the chance to freak out himself, and there isn't a snowball's chance in hell he'll do that if I'm still backsliding down Menty B Mountain.

I look into his eyes and steady my breathing, but he dives in before I can. *Sweet Henry, always taking care of me.*

"I love you," he says. "I want to be with you. That's what tonight was all about—me telling you what I should've said before we left the fucking island. There isn't one thing you could say to me right now to change my mind either."

The words hit me like a tidal wave, and my breath catches in my throat. He steps closer, his hands moving to cup my face, his thumbs brushing away the tears on my cheeks.

"Henry…" A sob escapes my lips, and I shake my head, tears streaming freely now. "I love you too, so much. More than I've ever loved anyone or anything, my designer collection included." I admit my truth through shaky breaths. "But that's the whole freaking problem. Because for as much as I love you, I'm about to have to love something more. And if you're not ready or not—" I shake my head, cutting off my ramble. "I'll understand, okay?"

He searches my face, his lips parting in preparation to console me again, but I don't torture him with more blind placations.

Instead, I tell him the truth, and I do it with a steel rod in my spine. In this moment, I am strong, just in case he can't be.

"I'm pregnant."

Chapter 47

Henry

AVERY'S WORDS HANG IN THE AIR LIKE A FRAGILE THREAD, the fear in her eyes presenting as misty, unshed tears. She's afraid how I'll react, obviously, but I'm not scared of anything.

Not as of one second ago. Not anymore.

"You're pregnant?" I ask, my voice catching on the emotion welling up in my chest.

She nods, her fingers white from their pressured twist among themselves.

"We're pregnant?" I repeat, closing the distance between us. "Me and you, we're having a baby?"

She nods again, her eyes searching mine with a different kind of sheen as hope starts to blossom at my tone, and I don't make her wait to know for sure.

This is divine intervention—a miracle and a blessing and a physical cue from the universe that the life-changing experience of the island wasn't temporary and it wasn't metaphorical. It was guidance.

Toward each other and toward a dream of a fucking life.

Without pause, I pull her into my arms, wrapping her tightly against me. "Avery," I murmur into her hair, my voice filled with awe and rapidly forming tears. "We're having a baby."

"You're not upset?" she asks, her voice trembling as she pulls back to look at me.

I cup her face gently, my thumbs brushing away the tears on her cheeks. "Why would I be upset? The woman I love more than anything in this world is having *my baby.*"

For so long, I've felt so alone in this world. As a kid, when my mom left. And not that long ago, again, when my father took his last breath.

But now, I have Avery and our soon-to-be son or daughter and a future filled with memories I'm determined to make good.

"You're my family, Avery," I say soundly, the only break in my voice a catch of unbridled happiness. "Me, you, and that little baby inside your belly. We're a *family.*"

"We're a family," she repeats, and her lip trembles. As her tears return, their sentiment changes, a burst of happiness pushing her onto her toes to get closer. She wraps her arms around my neck and kisses me, hard and fierce, pouring everything she's feeling into our connection.

I kiss her back with everything I have, moving my hands to cradle the back of her head as I press her closer. "I love you, Avery," I whisper against her lips. "I love you so damn much."

She pulls back just enough to look at me, her eyes shining with tears. "I love you too, Henry. So, so, so much."

I lean my forehead against hers, catching my breath as I drift my hand down to her belly. Gently, I press my palm against it, my heart swelling at the thought of what's growing inside her. "There's a baby in there," I say, my voice filled with wonder. "Our baby."

She places her hand over mine, and her smile is so radiant it feels like the sun has come out just for us. "Our baby," she echoes softly.

I kiss her again, this time slower, savoring the feel of her lips against mine. "I love you," I whisper again, because I can't say it enough.

The kiss deepens, and I feel her hands move to my shoulders, holding on to me like she doesn't want to let go. I don't want her to either. I don't ever want to let her go.

And I won't.

I slide my hands to her waist, then to her hips, and I lift her into my arms. She lets out a soft laugh against my mouth, and I can't help but grin as I carry her toward her bedroom.

When we reach the bed, I lay her down gently, like she's the most precious thing in the world. Because she is. She's my world. My everything.

I climb into bed beside her, trailing my hands over her body as our kisses grow more heated. But it's not just about the heat. It's about the love—the overwhelming, all-consuming love I feel for this woman.

"I love you," I tell her again, my voice rough with emotion.

Her eyes shine as she looks up at me, sliding her hands into my hair. "I love you too, Henry."

And then I'm lost in her. In us. In the love we've always shared but are finally ready to embrace completely.

I make love to her with everything I have, and for the first time in my life, I feel like I'm exactly where I'm meant to be.

Chapter 48

"I CAN'T BELIEVE OUR BABY IS IN THERE," HENRY SAYS, HIS hand resting gently on my belly. We're completely naked, cuddled up together in my bed, and I don't think I've ever felt more at peace than I do now. "*Our baby*," he says again, his voice all soft and dreamy. "How lucky are we."

"I'm really lucky, but you're, like, the luckiest person in the world, you know?" I tease, smiling down at him. "I mean, not only do you have me, but I'm having your baby."

"You're wrong, actually," he disagrees with a wink. "I'm damn lucky, but your dad might be even luckier."

"What do you mean?"

"He just took three years off his contract to support you."

"What?"

"That's my job now."

His hand moves in slow circles over my belly, his fingers tracing a path that's as tender as it is mesmerizing. There's a warmth in his touch, one that seeps straight into my heart and almost brings tears to my eyes. Almost, because if I let them fall, Henry would catch them, kiss them away, and call me out for being a softy. And that's June's MO, not mine.

I can't help but think about how far we've come. All the years I've known him flash through my mind like a movie reel. Teenage

Avery with a secret crush on her brother's best friend. Seeing him at clubs as an adult, his easy smirk making my stomach flip every time. That time we kissed at Allure—hot and fleeting, like a spark that didn't have the chance to catch fire. Then, the Halloween party at my parents' house. Another kiss, but one that felt like an all-consuming shock to my nervous system.

And then, the island... The island changed everything.

Henry was my anchor on that island. My protector. If it weren't for him, I don't know if I would've made it. I don't know if I'd have even gotten out of the plane after the pilot died mid-flight. But Henry... Henry made sure I did. He made sure I survived. And not just physically. He gave me something to hold on to, something to fight for.

He's not just my guy. He's my man. My baby daddy. My everything.

My eyes drift to his face as he presses another kiss to my bare belly. "Are you sure you can handle it? I can get a job if I need to."

When he smiles, I roll my eyes.

"A real job, I mean. Where I make money."

He laughs. "I can handle it, but more than that, I want to. If you want to work, I think you should—for yourself, for the passion, for...fashion. Because let's be honest, that's where you belong. But that money is yours. I don't want it and I don't need it and I promise I'll never push you not to spend it. That guy who talked to you in the airport hangar like he knew something was a fool, Ave. You're a brilliant, capable woman, and you deserve every bit of financial independence you want. My job is to be smart enough, quick enough, and savvy enough to keep up."

"All right." I let out a dreamy sigh and pretend my eyes roll back in my head. "You've done it. I think I just came."

He laughs, his deep chuckle vibrating against my skin, and I can't help but grin. But then his laughter fades, replaced by a look in his eyes so hot it feels like I'm standing on vigorously shifting tectonic plates. Before I can say another word, he moves back up the bed, pulling my body over his until we're nose to nose, chest to chest.

"I want to marry you," he says, his voice soft but sturdy.

I blink, my heart stuttering in my chest. "Are you asking me or telling me?"

"Avery," he begins, his voice tinged with that playful yet serious tone he gets when he's about to say something that'll change everything. "You're the person I want to wake up next to, the person I want to argue over throw pillows with, and the only person who could make me consider tossing out my favorite couch because 'it doesn't match the vibe.'"

His gaze locks on mine, and I drown in the intensity of it. "You've turned my world upside down in the most beautiful way, and honestly, I can't imagine my life without your sass, your fire, and the way you somehow make me believe I'm better than I am."

He presses a kiss to my lips, soft and lingering, before pulling back just enough to look into my eyes again. "You're it for me—my past, my present, my forever. So yes, I'm asking you to marry me. Begging you, actually. Not because life will be perfect—it won't be—but because I'll make damn sure it's one hell of a ride. And there's no one else I'd rather have by my side, rolling their eyes and giving me attitude and constantly surprising me the whole way."

Tears fill my eyes before I can stop them, and I nod, my forehead brushing against his. "Yes," I whisper, my voice trembling. "Yes."

He kisses me again, this time deeper, and I feel everything in that kiss—his love, his promise, his unwavering commitment to us. My heart feels like it's going to burst, and for the first time in what feels like my entire life, I'm not uncertain of what's next. I know. I'm ready.

But then a thought pops into my head, one that makes me pull back and look at him with a determined gleam in my eye. "But I don't want to wait."

He looks at me, his brow furrowing slightly. "What do you mean?"

"I mean," I say, tracing a finger along his jawline, "I want to get married now."

"As in, right now?"

"As in, however quick you can get us a flight to Vegas," I clarify, grinning. "But, like, a private flight. No commercial bullshit, Henny."

His laughter rumbles through his chest, and he pulls me closer, his eyes shining with amusement and love. "What'd I say?" He kisses me again, his smile pressed against my lips. "I've got to be ready to keep up, and I promise I'm up for the challenge. Vegas it is, baby. Let's do it."

Chapter 49

February 24th

Henry

THE PRIVATE AIRPORT IN MIAMI IS SLEEK AND MODERN, with floor-to-ceiling windows that let the bright Florida sun pour in. Planes of every size sit on the tarmac, their polished exteriors gleaming like mirrors. Avery stands next to me, looking effortlessly beautiful as always, with her single suitcase parked neatly by her feet.

"I'm impressed," I say, nodding toward the suitcase. "One bag? Really? Who are you, and what have you done with Avery Banks?"

She smirks, flipping her hair over her shoulder. "What can I say? Surviving on whatever I could fit into a fanny pack for two weeks changes your perspective."

I narrow my eyes. "You're so full of shit, baby. I know your ass is already planning on doing some shopping the moment we land."

"Well, *duh*. I didn't exactly have time to find a wedding dress."

I laugh, but the sound fades as we walk toward the plane. The shiny jet sits waiting for us, its engines humming softly. For a moment, the reality of boarding another plane hits both of us at once. I see it in the way her hand tightens around my arm, her teeth sinking into her bottom lip as she fidgets slightly. My own chest feels heavier, memories of that flight that led us to the island flashing through my mind.

Before we reach the steps, I stop us and pull her into my arms. "We're going to be safe," I whisper, brushing a kiss against her temple. "I won't let anything happen to you or our baby."

She looks up at me, her eyes soft and full of trust. "I know." She presses a kiss to my lips. "It's not in your vocabulary to let me down. Now, let's go get hitched."

I chuckle, but as she starts up the steps, a thought grips me.

Something I need to do before we take off.

"Hey, I'll be right there," I call after her. "I need to make a quick call."

She glances back, curious but not pressing. "Okay."

Turning to the flight attendant, she switches gears instantly. "How many pilots are on this flight?" I hear her ask. "And are any of you trained in emergency medical situations?"

The seriousness in her tone is so perfectly Avery, I can't help but smile.

Shaking my head, I pull out my phone and hit dial.

"I've been waiting for this call." Beau's voice—sharp but laced with humor—greets me by the second ring.

"Oh yeah?"

"Oh yeah," he says. "I mean, my best friend is apparently in a secret relationship with my sister, but funny thing is, I didn't hear this news from him. I heard it from my wife."

Oh shit…

"Be nice, Beau!" I hear June yell in the background.

"So, about that," I begin, a cringe taking shape on my face. "I've been meaning to tell you."

"Meaning to, but just haven't gotten around to it?" Beau asks.

"Things have been a little busy."

"Too busy to call your best friend and tell him you're not just in a relationship with his sister but also having a baby with her?"

Well, *fuck.* "So, it seems like June really cleared it all up for me, huh?"

"She told me, sure. Wouldn't say she cleared it up. Pretty sure that's your job."

"I'm sorry, Beau," I apologize immediately. "It wasn't my intention to keep this from you. You're my best friend, man. That's the last thing I wanted to do. Things just… Being on that island with Avery, it changed everything."

The line goes quiet for a moment before Beau speaks again. "Do you love her?"

"More than anything," I say without hesitation. "I love Avery more than I've ever loved anyone or anything. And I swear, Beau, I'm going to take care of her. Take care of her and our baby. Protect them. Make sure they know every day how much I love them."

"You know what's wild?" Beau questions after another long and excruciating pause. "I actually know all that to be true. You took care of Avery on that island, and fucking hell, it couldn't have been an easy feat being stranded with her." He laughs softly. "But I know you'll take care of her, Hen. Damn, though. My best friend and my sister. Who would've thought?"

"So, you're not mad?"

"Let's just say I'm adjusting to the idea. Might need a little time to fully wrap my head around it."

Avery appears at the top of the plane stairs, gesturing for me to hurry up.

"How much time are we talking?" I ask. "Think you can wrap your head around it in, say…five hours?"

"Five hours?"

"Yeah, five hours. That's when we'll land. In Vegas."

"Vegas? What the fuck are you talking about, Hen?"

"So, there's another thing I've been meaning to tell you," I say and shut my eyes for a brief moment, clutching the back of my neck with my hand. "Your sister and I are getting married. Today."

"You've got to be fucking kidding me," Beau mutters, but then he starts laughing. "You're such a bastard, you know that?"

"I do. But just remember, I'm a bastard who loves your sister more than anything in this world," I say, grinning. "Now, I gotta go. See you on the other side, *bro-in-law*."

"You're such a dick," Beau laughs before the line goes dead.

Sliding my phone into my pocket, I head toward the plane, but I get a series of texts as I climb the stairs.

> Beau: You're a total asshole.
>
> Beau: But I love you so much, Henry!
>
> Beau: You're a total dick.
>
> Beau: But I'm so, so, so happy for you!
>
> Me: Why do I get the sense this is both Beau and June texting me?
>
> Beau: Probably because it is. I'm on my phone, and my nosy wife is texting from my iPad.
>
> Beau: Nosy wife? Excuse me?
>
> Beau: BEAUTIFUL wife, I mean.
>
> Beau: That's what I thought.

Shaking my head, I step inside the plane and find Avery already seated comfortably in one of the leather chairs, her legs crossed. I sit across from her, immediately pulling her feet into my lap. I remove her heels and start massaging her feet.

She smiles at me. "If you keep doing shit like this for the rest of our lives, married life is going to be grand."

"I rub your feet, you rub my cock kind of thing?"

Avery laughs and rolls her eyes, and I just grin back at her, tickling her toes. She giggles, her laughter filling the cabin and settling something deep inside me.

This is it. This is us. And in just a few hours, she'll be my wife.

The lights of the Vegas Strip twinkle outside the chapel's stained-glass windows, neon blending with soft candlelight. It's almost surreal, standing here in a black suit Avery picked out for me, feeling more nervous than I ever have in my life. And I've jumped out of planes and bungee-jumped off fucking mountains.

But nothing compares to this. This moment right here is the most important of my life.

I turn my head slightly, and there she is.

My Avery.

She's standing at the other end of the aisle in a white dress that clings to her in all the right places, with lace sleeves and a neckline that's sweet and sexy all at once. Her brown hair is swept up, but a few loose curls frame her face.

She looks…perfect. Ethereal. *Mine.*

"You're so fucking beautiful, baby!" I call toward her, loud enough that everyone in the room can hear me. Not that there's a huge crowd. Just a couple of the chapel staff and the Elvis impersonator standing by the door. But still, Avery blushes, and it's my new favorite sight.

She reaches the front of the room, and when I take her hands in mine, they're warm and steady. Unlike mine. *Damn, how is she this calm?*

"You good?" she asks, her hazel eyes twinkling as she whispers just to me.

I nod. "Better than good. You?"

"I'm marrying you, Henny," she says with a grin. "Of course I'm good."

The officiant clears his throat, clearly used to wrangling couples who can't keep their hands or eyes off each other. "Shall we begin?"

Avery nods, squeezing my hands once. "Let's do it."

As the officiant starts talking, saying the usual stuff about love and commitment, I'm not really listening. I'm just watching Avery, marveling at how she's moments away from being my wife. Being mine forever. Her lips curve into a soft smile, and I'm hit with a wave of gratitude so strong it's hard to breathe.

The officiant goes through his whole spiel, and the entire time, I can't take my eyes off her. *Fuck, I love this woman.*

Truthfully, I'm not even sure what he's saying for the most part, but I do know when I need to start paying attention.

"Do you, Henry Callahan, take Avery Banks to be your lawfully wedded wife?"

"I do," I say without hesitation.

"And do you, Avery Banks, take Henry Callahan to be your lawfully wedded husband?"

"Hell yes," she answers, making the officiant grin.

"By the power vested in me by the state of Nevada, I now pronounce you husband and wife. You may kiss your bride."

I don't waste a second. I pull her close, cradling her face in my hands, and kiss her like my life depends on it. She wraps her arms around my neck, and she melts into me, her lips soft and warm and perfect.

The room erupts in cheers—probably thanks to Elvis—but I barely notice. All I can focus on is Avery. My wife.

When we finally pull apart, her cheeks are flushed, her eyes shining with happiness.

"We did it," she whispers.

"Damn right, we did."

And then I kiss her again, because I can. Because as of today, she's officially *mine.*

Chapter 50

Avery

HENRY AND I PULL UP TO MY PARENTS' HOUSE, MY ASS IN his Range Rover and my heart in my throat. Their mansion looms large and elegant in the warm Miami evening, its lights spilling out like an inviting beacon. The only thing not inviting is the fact that we're about to walk into a dinner where my mom and dad have no idea we got married. Or that I'm pregnant.

Henry cuts the engine and turns to me, his hand resting on my knee. "Are you still regretting not calling them before we headed to Vegas and got hitched forty-eight hours ago?"

I sigh and tilt my head toward the seat. "No… Yes… I don't know."

He chuckles, brushing his thumb lightly against my skin. "You don't know?"

"Relax," I say, rolling my eyes to mask my nerves. "I'll find a good way to tell them we're married."

"And pregnant."

"That's in the fine print. Let's start with the main contract first." I wave him off. "Just like I trusted you to keep us alive on that island, you're going to have to trust me to handle what I handle best. Henny, you know I have a way of telling people what they might not want to hear and still getting them to love me in the process. It's my charm."

Henry grins, but his eyes are tender, like he knows how much I need his quiet reassurance. He leans over and presses a kiss to my temple. "You're definitely something, babe."

I glance toward the house and take a steadying breath.

Here goes nothing.

When we walk inside, my mom is there to greet us at the door, her usual polished self in a cream blouse and gold jewelry. She smiles warmly, pulling me into a hug first, then Henry.

"It's so nice to see you two," she says, oblivious to the whirlwind of news we're carrying or the fact that Henry and I arrived together—like a couple.

We head toward the kitchen, where the rest of the family is gathered. Beau and June are sitting at the island, with little Addy on Beau's lap, stealing bites of fresh bread from the charcuterie board Chef Stone must've just set out. My dad is standing by the counter, sipping on a glass of wine.

But as we step fully into the room, my mom pulls something out from behind her back and plops it down on the counter in front of us. A tabloid magazine. Right there on the cover is a picture of Henry and me outside the Vegas chapel, the headline blaring, **Island Survivors Tie the Knot!**

"Got any news to share?" my mom asks, arching a perfectly shaped brow.

Henry freezes next to me, his eyes wide with panic. And Beau bursts into laughter so loud it makes Addy jump.

I stare at the magazine for a beat, my mind spinning. Then, in true Avery Banks fashion, I recover. Cool as a cucumber, I flash them all a breezy smile. "Oh yeah, Henry and I got married."

"Yeah, that's exactly what this tabloid told us," my dad says, tapping his finger against the headline. "Which is wild because I thought this was news I'd hear from my daughter and…new son-in-law."

Henry grimaces. "I'm sorry, Neil. Everything happened kind of fast."

"And I'm pregnant too," I chime in, because *why not drop all the bombs at once?* Henry's head whips toward me like I just said aliens landed in the backyard.

Both of my parents' jaws drop.

"But that's not why we got married," I add quickly. "We got married because Henry is madly in love with me and couldn't imagine spending another day without me as his wife."

Henry, to his credit, chuckles and wraps an arm around me, kissing my forehead. "She's not wrong."

"See? He loves me." I grin up at him. "And I love him too."

For a moment, it's as if everyone else in the room disappears. We're lost in each other's eyes, and I'm hit with this overwhelming wave of love for the man standing beside me.

Then my dad clears his throat. "I mean, I was a little hurt," he says, rubbing the back of his neck. "But then I thought about how much money I'm going to save."

"Money you're going to save?" I ask, confusion probably making those horrid eleven lines want to pop out on my forehead.

"No wedding," he says with a smug grin.

"Oh, Daddy, you're so funny." I pat his arm, giving him a sweet smile. "Of course I'm having a wedding. A *big* wedding. I mean, obviously, we're looking at the Biltmore or Vizcaya Museum for the reception—somewhere with *grandeur*, you know? Chandeliers and maybe peacocks roaming the gardens for dramatic flair. And then there's the dress—I'm thinking something custom from Oscar de la Renta or maybe Monique Lhuillier. And, of course, Louboutins for the shoes because what kind of bride *doesn't* wear red bottoms? Oh, and we'll need to book a live band—like one of those insane ten-piece jazz orchestras. Maybe we'll fly them in from New Orleans or Memphis or New York or something. And, of course, the catering will have to be Michelin-star quality. You wouldn't want me serving the guests just *anything*, right?"

I rattle it all off like it's no big deal, while my dad just stands there blinking at me, probably calculating how much this is all going to cost in his head.

"But," I add with a sweet smile, "don't worry. You have at least a year to save for it. No way I'm going to be one of those pregnant brides."

My dad sighs heavily, rubbing his face, but then he laughs, shaking his head. "God help me."

"Actually," my mom speaks up. "We have some news. Something we want to show you two." She leads us toward the terrace doors, which are covered with blackout curtains. With a little flair, she pulls the curtains back to reveal the terrace, and my jaw drops.

The terrace is covered in twinkle lights, with flowers and balloons everywhere. A lit-up sign reads, **Congratulations, Henry and Avery!** And out there waiting for us is everyone we love—Ronnie, Maverick, my grandparents, Henry's employees from Adrenaline Junkie, my old lady gal pals from The Pines. The works.

"You planned a party for us?" Henry asks, his voice laced with surprise.

"Beau and June might've given us a heads-up before the tabloids did," my mom says with a soft smile on her lips. "And there was no way we weren't going to celebrate."

"Oh my God!" I exclaim, practically bouncing on my toes. "You guys love me so much!"

Henry laughs, pulling me into his arms. "Ready to celebrate with me, Mrs. Callahan?"

I smile up at him, my heart so full it could burst. "Let's do it, Mr. Callahan."

As the terrace doors open and everyone yells "Congratulations!" I can't help but think about how lucky I am. Not because of the party, not because of the lights or the flowers, but because of the man standing beside me.

My Henry. My husband. My forever.

Epilogue

Part One

14 weeks later…

Henry

AVERY'S FACE LIGHTS UP AS SOON AS I UNCOVER HER EYES, the bright luxury of Hermès Paris bathing us in gentle light. The streets are fairly quiet this evening, and the glass storefront beckons almost as if it's here only for us.

Avery turns and hits me in the stomach, her excitement at my surprise obvious. "Oh my God, Hen! Hermès!" She rolls up on her toes and pushes her lips to my mouth before pulling back, beaming. "Okay, okay, forget everything I said in the hotel earlier. You're allowed to plan surprises. Definitely. A lot of them. As many as you want."

I chuckle. "Yeah, yeah. I had a feeling you'd change your tune."

"What are we doing here? Do you have an appointment? Wait…do you even know that you need an appointment to come to Hermès? Oh God, Henry."

I laugh again, this time a little harder. "Yes. I know you need an appointment. I made one and have even chatted with the sales team about what I was wanting to do, and they're all on board. Dr. Moretti's office sent over the results, and they're all ready. Just waiting for us."

"Dr. Moretti? Sent the results? What are you talking about?" She puts a hand to my forehead. "Are you feeling okay? You know this is a store, right?"

My smile is so big my face feels tight. My God, surprising her with this makes me feel like a superhero.

"Yes. I'm very aware that this is a store—and even more aware of the usual price tag. But this is a special occasion, and I wanted the venue to be appropriately Avery-themed."

"Hermès is a good choice," she admits, humming, and I laugh. "Good."

"So, what's happening?" she begs again, shaking me. "What's happening?"

"Let's go inside and find out," I suggest, putting a hand to the small of her back and pushing her gently toward the door. She goes willingly, if inquisitively, and when we step inside to a ready and waiting staff, her eyes light up all over again.

"Henry Callahan, you are so close to getting so damn lucky tonight."

The salesman in front of us looks down to avert his eyes, a small grin lifting his lips, and I outright laugh. "Good. I have a feeling it's going to get even closer very soon."

"Mrs. Callahan?" the salesman says, clearing his throat when I turn to face him. "Would you like to know the gender of your baby?"

"Oh my God," Avery whispers harshly, her hands flying to her mouth and her gaze locking with mine.

"You didn't."

"I did. In the box in front of him is a mini Kelly. Depending on the gender of our baby, enclosed in the results sent over by Dr. Moretti, is a blue or pink bag, waiting to be loved by you."

"I love you," she says, her eyes locked on mine despite how desperate I know she is to see the damn bag.

"I love you too. More than anything." I wink at her. "Now, get over there so he can open the box, and we can find out."

Part Two

17 weeks later…

Avery

The fifth floor of Luxe is alive with energy, gowns shimmering under the soft lighting, and the ladies from The Pines flit between racks of couture like kids in a candy store. It's exactly how I imagined it when Henry convinced me to finally go all in and create my own styling company. It feels like a lifetime ago that I admitted to Henry how I've always felt about Beau being the only Banks child with expectations of great things. That I'm supposed to be the fun, wild, completely unserious Banks sibling. Clearly, I'm still the most fun anyone could ever have, but I'm also more. I'm smart and capable and I can do great things too.

Henry—my handsome, wild, also-happens-to-have-a-perfect-cock-that-knocked-me-up husband—helped me realize that.

And Luxe isn't just a dream anymore; it's a powerhouse. And today, it's buzzing as usual, with my beloved troublemakers—Ethel, Blanche, Dottie, Joanne, and Sarabeth—trying on gowns for their charity dinner.

The space is perfect: polished marble floors, velvet furniture in shades of blush and champagne, and mirrors that make you feel like you belong in the pages of *Vogue*. It's modeled after Hermès' private shopping floor in New York—because every client deserves to feel like a star.

But right now, I'm a very pregnant star whose uterus is doing that stupid practice contraction thing. Braxton-Hicks, I think they're called. It's like my uterus thinks it needs to prepare for the Olympics or something. *Relax, sheesh. The baby isn't due for another week.*

I adjust the strap on my stilettos—yes, I'm still wearing heels at thirty-nine weeks pregnant because who says you can't be glam when you feel like a walking watermelon—and try to focus on Ethel twirling in front of the mirror in a gold gown.

"Darling, what do you think?" she asks, spinning with dramatic flair.

"It's stunning," I say, keeping my voice even as another practice contraction rolls through my belly.

"Are you sure, honey?" Blanche chimes in. "You're sweating like a man at a summer barbecue."

"I'm fine," I say, brushing a strand of hair out of my face and plastering on a smile.

"You're not fine," Ethel says, narrowing her eyes. "I think you're in labor."

"I'm not in labor!" I snap, laughing it off. "My due date isn't for another week. These are just those fake contractions. Braxton-Hicks or whatever."

The next contraction, though, makes me clutch the edge of a nearby chair.

Blanche crosses her arms. "Avery, honey, you're in labor."

"I'm not."

"You're hunched over like a shrimp cocktail," Dottie says. "I'd say that's a sign."

"Relax, everyone. I'm fine." I wave them off. "Try on more dresses. I'll grab some water and be right back."

They don't look convinced, but I make my escape, my heels clicking against the marble as I head toward the bathroom.

Once inside, I lock the door, lean against the counter, and try to breathe through another contraction.

"Okay, baby," I whisper, pressing my hands to my belly. "Listen, I know you're eager to make your grand debut, but it's not time yet, okay? Mommy isn't ready. Daddy isn't ready. Your nursery isn't even fully organized yet, and I don't even have my hospital bag packed. And plus, I took you to be more of a fashionably late kind of baby. I mean, I am your mother after all."

Another practice contraction hits me again, but it's so sharp and intense I'm starting to wonder how much more practice my uterus can do before it's not practicing anymore.

Surely I'm not having this baby today…*right?*

Part Three
Henry

My phone vibrates against the console as I pull into the parking garage behind Luxe. Another text from Ethel.

> **Ethel: Henry, dear, Avery still hasn't come out of the bathroom. We're getting worried.**

I take the stairs two at a time, my heart racing. Luxe's fifth floor comes into view, and it's chaos. Blanche, Dottie, Joanne, Sarabeth, and Ethel are all pacing near the fitting area, their glittering gowns forgotten. Laura, Avery's assistant, stands stiffly by the bathroom door, her expression a mix of fear and panic.

"Tell me she's not going to have her baby in our bathroom," Laura blurts the moment she sees me.

Fucking hell, I'd prefer not.

"She's fine," I assure her, but my gut twists.

"She's not fine!" Ethel protests, waving her arms. "She's been in there forever, Henry. Forever!"

"Relax, ladies. I've got this."

I knock gently on the bathroom door. "Hey, baby, it's me."

"I'm fine," Avery's voice calls back, but it's strained, and I can hear her breathing through another contraction.

"Of course you're fine, honey," I say lightly. "I just wanted to stop by and say hey. Give you a kiss."

"I'm fine," she says again, her tone sharper now. Classic Avery.

"How about you open the door for me, then? Just for a second?"

There's silence on the other side, and then, finally, the door unlocks and cracks open.

Avery is leaning against the sink, her face damp with sweat, her normally flawless makeup smudged. She looks exhausted, but she's still stunning. Even in fucking labor, this woman takes my breath away.

"Hey, beautiful," I say softly, stepping inside and shutting the door behind me.

"Don't start with the sweet talk, Henry," she snaps, clutching the counter as another contraction hits. "It's fine. Just practice contractions."

"Are you sure, baby?" I question the obvious. "Because those look pretty intense."

"I'm fine, Henry," she snaps. "I can handle this."

"Sure you can, baby," I say, walking over to her. "But you don't have to handle it alone."

"I'm not alone. I have five busybodies and a panicked assistant waiting for me outside." She groans as the contraction eases. "And now you."

"Lucky you," I tease, but my heart aches seeing her like this.

"I swear to God, if you start being all cute and supportive, I will scream."

"Noted," I say, suppressing a smile as I reach out and gently rub her back. "But let me just be a little supportive, okay? I've got you, Avery."

She leans into me, and for a moment, she lets herself melt into my arms. "I'm scared, Henny,"

she whispers, her voice cracking. "I'm really scared."

"I know, baby," I say, pressing a kiss to her temple. "But you don't need to be. I've got you. I'm not going to let anything happen to you or our baby. I promise."

Her wide hazel eyes meet mine, filled with tears. "You promise?"

"I promise," I say firmly, brushing her hair away from her damp forehead.

Another contraction hits, and she grabs a fistful of my shirt, groaning through the pain. "Henry…I need drugs. Get me to a hospital now."

I grin despite myself. "How about we get out of this bathroom first?"

"*Henry.*" Her tone is all Avery—sharp, demanding, and a little bit desperate.

"Okay, okay," I say. "Let's go have a baby somewhere other than a bathroom."

I don't waste time lifting her into my arms. "I'm too heavy for that!" she tries to refute, but I ignore her.

I'll fucking carry this woman all the way to the hospital if I have to.

"I've got you, Avery."

And as I carry her out, past her worried entourage, I feel nothing but pride, love, and the thrill of what's about to come next—*we're about to meet our baby.*

Part Four

Avery

I'm going to be honest; I don't think anyone fully prepares you for what it feels like to push an entire human being out of your body. If it weren't for the epidural, I'm positive I'd be screaming bloody murder right now. Because, really, who wants to feel their vag being ripped to shreds?

Henry is holding one of my legs, and a nurse has the other. His face is lit up with this stupidly handsome grin that has no right being so distracting right now.

"Henry," I manage between pushes. "I really don't think you need to be all up in it, you know?"

He just smiles, leaning down toward me. "I love you. You're beautiful. And I say this with all the love in the world, but shut up,

Avery. I'm going to be all up in watching my beautiful wife bring our baby into this world."

I glare at him, but I'm too focused on the task at hand to argue.

June is standing on one side of me, holding my hand, her other hand resting on her still-slightly-rounded belly. She just had Caleb a few months ago. My little nephew with his fat cheeks, bald head, and the most pinchable smile you've ever seen.

My mom is on the other side, brushing sweaty strands of hair away from my face, whispering, "You're doing so good, sweetie. Just a little more."

Dr. Moretti glances up from the foot of the bed. "Avery, the baby's crowning. On the next contraction, I need you to push."

"Got it," I pant, bracing myself as another contraction tightens my body like it's in a vise grip.

Henry gives my leg a reassuring squeeze. "You've got this, baby. Strongest woman I know."

My heart squeezes at his words. But then, because I'm me, I decide to multitask. "Henry," I start, between breaths, "I think we can both agree that, right now, I'm doing the most out of the two of us."

He narrows his eyes, grinning like he already knows where this is headed.

"I mean, I'm pushing our baby out of my body," I continue, giving him my best doe eyes.

"Uh-huh," he says, laughter in his voice.

"So, I think we can also agree that I should get the final say on the house." We've been house hunting for months now but haven't found anything we've agreed on or loved enough to buy. And while Henry's condo is nice to live in, it's a bachelor pad. Sure, it has a spare bedroom for the baby's nursery, but it's not where I want to raise our baby.

The man actually chuckles. "Okay, Avery. You get the final say."

"Good." I wince as another contraction builds. "Because I already told our Realtor this morning to put a bid in on that house on Maple." By the way, it's a gorgeous two-story home that has five bedrooms and four bathrooms and the most perfect gardens and terrace I've ever seen—aka the ideal place for our family.

His grin falters for half a second. "The one overlooking the water?"

I nod, gripping his hand as the contraction slams into me. "They accepted it, by the way," I say through gritted teeth.

Henry just laughs and presses a kiss to my knee. "Of course they did."

Before I can retort, Dr. Moretti chimes in. "Avery, the baby's head is out. One more big push, okay?"

It's like the room holds its breath as I push with everything I've got. And then, the most beautiful sound fills the air—our baby's first cries.

"It's a girl!" Dr. Moretti announces, and the room erupts with emotion. I already knew—Henry made sure of that with my perfect pink Kelly bag, but hearing it from the doctor's mouth is like an out-of-body experience.

Tears stream down my face as the doctor places our daughter on my chest. She's warm and squishy and perfect. I can't stop crying as I run my hand over her soft head, already covered in a patch of dark, silky hair.

June is crying. My mom is crying. And Henry… Henry has tears in his eyes as he leans down to press a kiss to my forehead.

"I love you," he whispers, his voice thick with emotion.

"I love you too," I whisper back, my heart bursting.

He kisses our daughter's tiny head, his hand brushing her little cheek. "And I love you, Coco Callahan."

I blink up at him, my heart skipping. "We're naming her Coco?"

Henry nods, smiling down at our baby girl. "Yeah. Our little Coco."

Coco was my top pick—a la Chanel—though Henry pretended to be unsure until now. And as I look at our little daughter, at her big eyes and adorable cheeks, I know he's right. She's our Coco.

Tears spill down my cheeks as I cradle her closer. I've never felt so much love in my life.

Henry kisses my forehead again. "I love you, Avery. And I can't wait to raise our little Coco in our new home."

I laugh through my tears, looking up at him. "You're the best, Henny."

He smirks. "I know."

And as I look at him and our beautiful baby girl, I know one thing for sure—I get to spend forever with the two most important people in my life. My very own family.

Sad you've made it to the end of Henry and Avery and missed out on June and Beau's book? Read *Meet Me at Midnight*!

Need more Max Monroe right now?

Make sure you don't miss Avery's brother Beau and her best friend June's love story in *Meet Me at Midnight*.

And if you've already read Meet Me at Midnight, but you're still in the mood for brother's best friend love stories, we have the perfect book for you! See below…

Mabel "Maybe" Willis died a virgin at the very young age of twenty-four. She leaves behind her parents, Betty and Bruce, her brother, Evan, a laptop filled with one too many Jason Momoa memes, and a Kindle library with more books than one human being could ever finish in a lifetime.

Cause of death: a text message.

Okay. So, I didn't die. But I did send my brother's best friend the most embarrassing text message possible.

Deflower me, please? I said.

Yeah. Send help.

Read *My Brother's Billionaire Best Friend* today!

Sign up for our newsletter, and we'll keep you up-to-date
on all the book news, AND a lot of times we share fun
teasers and excerpts!

www.authormaxmonroe.com/newsletter

Plus, our newsletter is hilarious! Laughs guaranteed. If you're already signed up, consider sending us a message to tell us how much you love us. We really like that. ;)

Need EVEN MORE Max Monroe before our next release?

Never fear, we have a list of nearly FIFTY other titles to keep you
busy for as long as your little reading heart desires!
Check out our Suggested Reading Order on our website!

**www.authormaxmonroe.com/max-monroe-suggested-
reading-order**

Follow us online here:

Facebook: www.facebook.com/authormaxmonroe

Reader Group: www.facebook.com/groups/1561640154166388

Twitter: www.twitter.com/authormaxmonroe

Instagram: www.instagram.com/authormaxmonroe

TikTok: vm.tiktok.com/ZMe1jv5kQ

Goodreads: https://goo.gl/8VUIz2

Acknowledgments

First of all, THANK YOU for reading. Thank you for supporting us, for talking about our books, and for just being so unbelievably loving and supportive of our characters. You've made this our MOST favorite adventure thus far.

THANK YOU to each other. Monroe is thanking Max. Max is thanking Monroe. *Blah, blah, blah.* We do this in every book, but we don't care. We are so grateful for each other and this awesome journey that is writing together. Cheers to many more books!

THANK YOU, Lisa, our editor. Our main squeeze. Our number one lady. You're even reading *and* editing this right now, and for that, we are thankful. (Fingers crossed for no typos! LOL!)

THANK YOU, Stacey, for making the insides of our book look so pretty!

THANK YOU, Peter, for rocking our covers. You're the best!

THANK YOU to the people who love us—our family. We couldn't do any of this without them.

As always, all our love.
XOXO,
Max Monroe